NO RESERVATIONS
REQUIRED

In

Memory

of

Dawn Barto

By Ellen Hart
Published by Ballantine Books:

NO RESERVATIONS REQUIRED

A Culinary Mystery

ELLEN HART

BALLANTINE BOOKS • NEW YORK

No Reservations Required is a work of fiction. Names, characters, places, and incidents are the products of the author's imagination or are used fictitiously. Any resemblance to actual events, locales, or persons, living or dead, is entirely coincidental.

A Fawcett Books Mass Market Original

Copyright © 2005 by Ellen Hart

Published in the United States by Fawcett Books, an imprint of The Random House Publishing Group, a division of Random House, Inc., New York.

Fawcett Books is a registered trademark and the Fawcett colophon is a trademark of Random House, Inc.

ISBN 0-449-00732-4

Printed in the United States of America

Ballantine Books website address: www.ballantinebooks.com

OPM 9 8 7 6 5 4 3 2

To my Sweet Gang of Muses:
Rufess, Mr. Beau, Sassy, Murphy,
Lilly, Commander Molly, Mimsy,
and "The Boys"—Busby and Newton.

Much Madness is divinest Sense—
To a discerning Eye—
Much Sense—the starkest Madness.

—EMILY DICKINSON

CAST OF CHARACTERS

SOPHIE GREENWAY: Owner-manager of the Maxfield Plaza in St. Paul. Restaurant critic for the *Minneapolis Times Register*. Bram's wife.

BRAM BALDRIC: Radio talk-show host for WTWN in the Twin Cities. Sophie's husband. Margie's father.

RUDY GREENWAY: Sophie's son. Food editor at the *Minneapolis Times Register*.

MARGIE BALDRIC: Wedding planner. Bram's daughter.

BOB FABIAN: Owner and publisher of the *Minneapolis Times Register*. Valerie's husband. Andy's half brother. Phil's brother-in-law.

PHIL BANKS: Owner of Banks Construction. Bob's brother-in-law.

CHRISTINE (CHRIS) PARILLO: Phil's girlfriend. Ex-chef.

VINCE PARILLO: Viet Nam vet. Head chef at the Rookery Club.

LYLE BOERICHTER: Pilot for Sunrise Airlines.

DEL IRAZARIAN: Investigative reporter at the *Minneapolis Times Register*.

ANDREW (ANDY) GLADSTONE: Bob's half brother. Anika's husband. Editor at the *Minneapolis Times Register*.

ANIKA GLADSTONE: Andy's wife. Assistant food and beverage manager at the Maxfield Plaza.

KENNETH LOY: The man who broadsided Valerie Fabian's car, killing her.

HENRY AND PEARL TAHTINEN: Previous owners of the Maxfield Plaza. Sophie's parents.

AL LUNDQUIST: Detective with the St. Paul Police Department. Old friend of Bram's.

NATHAN BUCKRIDGE: Sophie's high school sweetheart. Owner of Chez Sophia, a restaurant in Stillwater, Minnesota.

No Reservations
Required

1

Mid-October

When Ken Loy left his house for the last time, it was just beginning to turn dark. His bicycle, a LeMond with a superlight Reynolds 853 mainframe, was leaning against a stack of firewood in the garage. Ken loved riding at night, loved drawing the fresh, cool air into his lungs after being cooped up inside an office all day. He worked such long hours at Miller & Gustafson that his evenings were the only time he had for exercise and relaxation.

Ken Loy was the divorced father of two teenage daughters. He saw his kids mostly on weekends when he'd take them to a movie or a sporting event— whatever was around that interested them. During the past summer, he'd finally met a woman he liked a lot, but he had so little free time that the relationship had pretty much died on the vine.

That had been the problem in his marriage, too. Ken never seemed to have enough hours in the day for everything that needed to be done. But how was a guy supposed to get ahead if he didn't keep his nose to the grindstone? Ken had never believed his wife when she insisted that his job came first, last, and in between. But now he was beginning to wonder if she wasn't right. If—God forbid—his life should end tonight, he wouldn't have much to show for it other than a bank account and dozens of empty prescription bottles of Prilosec.

After checking his water bottle, Ken hopped on. He tightened the strap on his helmet—making sure his earphones were perfectly positioned in his ears—then turned on his CD player, adjusted the sound, and finally pumped off down Raymond Avenue.

It took only a few minutes to reach his destination—Shepard Road. Sailing along the bike path on the double highway, with railroad tracks on one side of him and the Mississippi River on the other, Ken felt happy for the first time all day. The air was a tonic, and Rod Stewart, his favorite singer, blasted all the cobwebs out of his brain.

Although the year hadn't exactly been a banner one for Ken Loy, he was doing his best to put the horror of last fall behind him. Exercise was a big part of that, and tonight it felt especially good to be alive.

Rush hour was long over. Now that the sun was almost down, the traffic had thinned to a trickle. He could see the headlights of cars behind him strike the road ahead, then whoosh past. Downtown St. Paul shimmered in the distance, the last rays of the setting sun hitting the tall buildings and turning them a fiery gold. Ken loved St. Paul, couldn't imagine living anywhere else. Even though he'd never used it, his undergraduate degree from the University of Minnesota was in Urban Studies. If any city in the United States had suffered from a complete lack of urban planning, it was St. Paul. The last governor of Minnesota once commented on national TV that the city had been platted by drunken Irishmen. The uproar the statement had created would dog the poor man to his grave.

The truth was, the planners probably were drunk, although Irish was by no means the only ethnic group to be evicted from the military compound at Fort Snelling and dumped on the shores of a spectacular bend in the upper Mississippi, shortly to be known as St. Paul. For good or ill, the town had been carved out by bootleggers, French Canadian fur trappers and traders, dishonored soldiers, Swiss refugees—a jumble of assorted outcasts, misfits, and murderers. Ken felt comfortable in that company. Nobody in that lot could judge him and find him wanting.

Ken always pointed out interesting buildings to his girls, peppering his conversation with the history he'd learned in school. Since the divorce, he had grown closer to his daughters. He called them more and more lately, looking for ways to engage them. As he thought about it now, gazing up at the glowing antique streetlamps that lighted this section of Shepard Road, there was so much he wanted to show them, so much he wanted to see again through their eyes.

Up ahead, Ken spied a construction site he'd been hoping to get a closer look at. He cycled past it almost every night, but a few of the crew always remained and he didn't want them to think he was snooping. Tonight, the area was empty of trucks. The new construction was part of a large condo complex on the river. The house he bought after the divorce was so big, he never felt he had enough time to take care of it. A small condo might be the perfect solution. If he lived here, he could even walk to work.

Before turning off onto a dirt road to take a closer

look, Ken glanced over his shoulder and saw bright headlights approaching. He hung a quick right as Stewart's voice belted out "Downtown Train" in his ears. The breeze off the river ruffled his hair. It was hard to see the building in the darkness, but if he just got close enough . . .

Suddenly, Ken felt a blow from behind, projecting him up and over the handlebars with such force that the bike went one way and he went another. He slammed into the dirt on his right shoulder, feeling a bone in his arm snap. Dazed and in pain, he tried to get his bearings. He twisted around just as a vehicle moved up next to him. The headlights were off. The motor was idling. All the windows were closed.

Ken's fright turned instantly to fury. "You shit-head!" he screamed. "Look what you did! I'm hurt! For God's sake, help me!"

The passenger's window opened. An arm eased out.

Ken's eyes locked on the gun. "Hey," he said, scrambling backward. "No! Stop! Please!" he pleaded. "You've got the wrong guy! My name's Loy. Ken *Loy*."

The gunshots to Ken's head had all the earmarks of an execution. In the end, the police would find that it was.

2

Valerie. It was always Valerie. Her image in his mind. The dream of drifting downward into her soft brown eyes. Tonight was the first anniversary of her death.

Bob Fabian had always known what he wanted out of life, and in large measure, he'd attained it. From his days at West Point through his two tours in Viet Nam, he always knew he would be a success. But the day his wife died, Bob's world ended. He kept on walking around, kept on eating and talking. What else could he do? Friends knew he was suffering—their kindness meant a lot—but every time he took Valerie's picture out of his wallet and sat down to look at it, he would dissolve into a trance.

It might sound melodramatic, it might even *be* the stuff of melodrama, but for Bob, all he wanted was the woman in the photo. Without her, life had no meaning. He listened to his friends, who assured him that time would heal his wounds. They told him that at fifty-six, he was still a young man. He'd move on. Find someone else. He wouldn't always feel this way. Bob had been waiting for the day his passion for living would return. But it hadn't. And he knew, deep in his heart, it never would. Valerie was everything to him. But Valerie was in heaven now. And Bob was alone.

It was just after eight thirty when he pulled into his driveway. He sat for a few moments gazing through the darkness at his house. It looked strange to him now—almost as if he were viewing it for the first time. He'd expected to feel different, but not like this. The world was brighter, bigger, sweeter tonight. All of his senses were dialed up to high. Maybe this was what it felt like to be on LSD—except his perceptions weren't altered, just intensified.

After switching off the engine, Bob waited a moment longer, listening to his heart hammer inside his chest. Maybe he lacked imagination, but how could a man not have a certain aching nostalgia for what had once been but would never be again. Was he frightened? Yes, but also excited.

What he wanted now was to be alone with his thoughts, maybe listen to some music or look through old picture albums. He had tranquilizers in his medicine chest that would help him get to sleep. He simply had to make it through the next few hours.

Just as he was about to climb out of his car, a head popped up right next to him.

"Lord," said Bob, rearing backward, away from the window. "You asshole. You trying to give me a heart attack?"

"Sorry." The man backed up and let Bob get out.

"It's not a good time for me right now, Sonny." Bob caught a whiff of Sonny's breath. "Do us both a favor. Go home and sleep it off."

Sonny didn't catch the edge in Bob's voice. Either

that, or he didn't care. "This can't wait." He looked as if he were about to burst.

"You win the lottery?"

"Better than that." In a whispered voice, he continued, "Let's go inside. We need some privacy." He looked over his shoulder, his grin fading to wariness.

Bob locked the car. On the way across the lawn, he glanced up at the sky as the heavens rumbled with thunder. He felt a droplet hit his forehead. It was starting to rain.

Sonny followed Bob through the two-story stone entry into the foyer. Without asking, he headed straight for the bar in the living room and poured himself a shot of bourbon.

Removing his suit coat and tossing it over a dining room chair, Bob switched on a few lights. He hadn't changed a thing in the house since Valerie died. He glanced out the front window as lightning lit up the night, but didn't see Sonny's car. "Where'd you park?"

"Around the corner. Hey, close the curtains, okay?"

"Don't get comfortable. You're not staying." This wasn't the way he intended to spend what was left of the evening. He'd be polite, but not patient if the conversation lasted more than five minutes. "Okay," he said, sitting down on the couch, spreading his arms across the back of the cushions. "What's up?"

Sonny downed the shot in one neat gulp. "I did it!" he said, an odd fire in his eyes. "I took care of him."

"Him who?"

"It was easy. I mean, I knew where he lived. I've been watching him for months."

"*Who?*"

"Loy! Who the hell do you think?" He leaned both arms on the bar. "The bastard was riding that bike of his down Shepard Road, just like he always does. If I believed in fate, it was like . . . like I was *supposed* to do it tonight, because everything just tumbled into place. He turned off at this construction site. You know the one—those new river condos? And there weren't any other cars around, so—" He drew his arms wide. "I did it."

Bob just stared at him.

"I shot him."

"If this is a joke—"

"No joke. Ken Loy is *history*."

Bob rose from the couch. He'd always suspected Sonny had a screw loose somewhere. But murder? "Are you telling me—"

"You think I made it up?"

"I hope like hell you did."

"I put a bullet right between his eyes, Bobby."

Now it was time to panic. "Sonny, this is insane!"

"It's payback. He murdered Valerie. You said so yourself."

"I was upset when I told you that. It was an accident, Sonny. An *accident*."

"Yeah, right. Maybe you never took me seriously before, but you will now."

Whether it was the booze, or just Sonny's addled brain, he wasn't being rational. "You killed a man in cold blood?"

"*Executed*. There's a difference."

"Are you sure he's—"

"Dead? Well, maybe he squirmed around a little at first, but he's dead. Trust me. I know what I'm talking about."

Bob had to get to a phone. And he had to do it someplace where Sonny couldn't hear him. "Give me a minute, okay? I need to use the bathroom."

"Can't take it, huh? No guts."

"Yeah. That's it." Bob covered his mouth and ran from the room. Rushing into the bedroom, he shut the door carefully behind him, then grabbed the cordless off his nightstand and punched in 911. It seemed to take forever before someone finally picked up.

"There's been a murder," Bob said, keeping his voice low. "Or an attempted murder. You've got to get paramedics to him right away. It's possible he's still alive."

"Are you all right?" asked the 911 operator.

"Me? No, *no*. This isn't about me."

"You're not hurt?"

"*Listen* to me."

"What's your location?"

"Not *here*," he whispered. "The shooting happened on Shepard Road—near that new condo construction site. That's all I can tell you. You've got to hurry!"

"What's your name?"

"Fabian. Robert Fabian."

"And you live at 9418 East River Road? Robert and Valerie Fabian?"

"Yes, but you're not listening to me. You've got to get some help to this guy right away! It's a matter of life and death."

"An EMT is on the way, Mr. Fabian. Can you tell me how the shooting occurred?"

"What?"

"Do you know who did the shooting?"

"Well, ah . . . see." The words stuck in his throat. "This isn't easy."

"Can you give me a name?"

"It was . . . he's, like . . . see"—he took a deep breath—"like . . . my brother—"

The door to Bob's room burst open.

"What's going on?" demanded Sonny. "What the hell are you doing?"

Bob's eyes focused on the gun in Sonny's hand.

"Who are you talking to?"

"Just calm down, okay?"

"Hang up the phone," demanded Sonny. His eyes had turned into two hard steel balls. Bob had never seen him look like that before. He tossed the phone on the bed, but he didn't cut the connection.

"You made a mistake, Bob. A big one."

"Put it down, okay? Come on. Don't get crazy on me." His voice was shaking.

"I thought you cared about Valerie—about *me*. We're family, damn it! As soon as I turn my back, you call the cops on me?"

"I wasn't doing that. I swear."

"This really sucks, Bob. Really freaking *sucks*."

"Just let me explain!"

Sonny glared at him. Raising the gun and pointing it at Bob's chest, he said, "You've got thirty seconds. Make it good."

3

The Rookery Club was at its peak of popularity in the late 1990s. That's when Sophie and Bram had joined. Though the price of admission was steep, it seemed the right thing to do—not only because it was one of the most prestigious private clubs in the Twin Cities, boasting a membership that included some of the best-known chefs in the area, dozens of restaurateurs, and hundreds of homegrown foodies, but also because it was the *only* truly gourmet club in town. At the time they'd first joined, Sophie wrote an occasional restaurant review for the *Minneapolis Times Register.* Her presence at the club seemed an important professional connection. Now that she was the full-time restaurant critic for the paper, her presence was a necessity.

The club was named after the building in which it was housed. The Rookery was an old brick mansion on Prince Street in one of the more colorful areas of Lowertown in downtown St. Paul. Built by James S. Peables in the late 1890s, the three-story brick building, a combination of Gothic architecture with hints of Richardson Romanesque, became the official home to the Rookery Club in 1968 after it was renovated by Taylor M. Wackenhut, a local entrepreneur and

the club's first president. After the renovation, Wackenhut donated the building to the club with the proviso that the club forever after bear the building's
name.

While no one was quite certain how the mansion
came to be called the Rookery, there was no dearth of
speculation. Some said it was because of the iron
birds that capped sections of the wrought-iron fence
surrounding the building. Others pointed to the pi-
geons that always nested on the south section of the
roof. Still others pointed to the fact that the building
had been an infamous bordello in the 1920s. All
made a certain sense, although none was definitive.

Sophie had once looked up the word "rookery" in
the dictionary. She was surprised to find it had so many
meanings. A rook was a chess piece—an essential and
highly powerful defender of the king—otherwise called
a castle. A rook was also a kind of European crow, a
gregarious bird that liked to congregate in groups.
And finally, a rook was just another name for a
swindler. Webster, in his usual helpful fashion, de-
fined "rookery" as "a colony of rooks." Thus, Sophie
assumed that the Rookery in downtown St. Paul was
either the gathering place for highly social birds, er-
rant chess pieces, or crooks.

"Kind of a wide variety when you think about it,"
said Sophie, gazing at her husband over the rim of a
martini glass.

"You actually looked it up in the dictionary?"

"You saying I don't own one?"

Bram grinned, grabbing a few peanuts and tossing
them into his mouth.

They were sitting at the ornate bar on the Rookery
Club's first floor, directly across from the main dining

room. Their dinner reservations had been for eight o'clock, but as soon as they arrived, they were told that the kitchen was running behind, and were offered a complimentary drink in the Wackenhut room—the bar—if they didn't mind a short wait. That was half an hour ago, but Sophie didn't care. She'd hardly seen her husband all week and tonight she had him all to herself. No ringing phones, no Margie—Bram's daughter—barging in and demanding that they listen to her ramble on and on about herself for hours. They'd left their cell phones back at the Maxfield, so the night belonged to them.

Sophie and Bram owned the Maxfield Plaza in downtown St. Paul. Sophie's parents had bought the hotel back in the early '60s, when it was a run-down dump just waiting for the wrecking ball. Like Taylor Wackenhut, Henry and Pearl Tahtinen wanted to preserve a piece of St. Paul history. The Maxfield had been built toward the end of the 1920s and was a wonderful example of Art Deco architecture. Just the idea that a building like that would be razed to accommodate a new parking garage made her father seethe. After years of hard work and lean times, the Maxfield Plaza had risen from the trash heap of inner-city urban blight to take its rightful place as downtown St. Paul's premier hotel.

Several years ago, Sophie's parents retired and sold the hotel—for one dollar—to Sophie and Bram. They wanted to keep it in the family, and so did Sophie. Bram already had a full-time job as a radio talk-show host for WTWN, so the running of the hotel fell to Sophie. Several weeks after the hotel's title was officially transferred, her parents wished her well and left for a two-year, round-the-world tour. They were home now, back in their apartment at the top of the hotel's north tower. Sophie had assumed that when they returned, her father might still take some interest in the family business, but she wasn't prepared for how constant his presence would be.

Before she and Bram had left tonight, Sophie stopped by her office to make a couple of notes for her meeting tomorrow with the food and beverage manager. She'd found her father sitting behind her desk, smoking one of his rank cigars, going through the September stats on her computer. So much for turning the reins of the hotel over to his daughter.

"Dad's driving me nuts," said Sophie, holding up her glass and nodding to the bartender for another martini.

"I made a bet with you—remember?—that as soon as he got back, he'd make your life miserable. Is he smoking those nasty cigars in your office?"

"Do I smell like smoke?" Sophie sniffed her sleeve.

"You smell wonderful." Bram moved over and kissed her cheek. "But spend a few more hours with those stogies and you might as well get a job as a prizefight promoter."

"He says he's got a list."

"What kind of list?"

"He never really says. He just keeps threatening me that he's got a list, and that we're going to talk about it soon."

Sophie's father was in his seventies. Sophie herself was nearly fifty. She'd always looked young for her age. So young, in fact, that in her early forties, people still referred to her as "perky." No woman in her forties wanted to be called perky. Perhaps it was her short stature—just over five feet—or her short, strawberry blond hair—untouched by bleach or dye. Bram often called her his "sexy Peter Pan." The sexy part was okay, but Peter Pan, à la Mary Martin, wasn't exactly Sophie's dream image. Even the fact that they knew who Mary Martin *was* dated them in a big way. They were getting old, no doubt about it. But there was still life in dem bones, and Sophie intended to prove it to her husband later tonight.

"You know," said Sophie, looking around at the crowd in the bar, "this place isn't exactly crawling with young faces."

"Your point?"

"That the Rookery Club is a little stodgy."

"Yeah, I've noticed that, too. Not that I'd include either of us in that stinging generalization. I mean, *I'm* not stodgy."

"Certainly not." And he wasn't. Bram was a handsome older man with an urbane wit that had garnered him a huge following for his afternoon radio show. He was broadcast in eight markets around the country now—soon to be nine when St. Louis came on board in January.

Out of the corner of her eye, Sophie saw the short, squat Sheldon Larr, the club's maître d', approach. Sheldon walked with a slight limp, and had a thin David Niven mustache. In Sophie's book, he was a character.

"Your table is ready," said Sheldon softly, with a small, dignified bow. He was wearing a tuxedo, just as Bram and virtually every other man in the bar was, only Sheldon's had a broad red band across the chest, like the king in a period movie. Sheldon also affected a British accent. That, combined with his very real Southern drawl, made him occasionally hard to understand. It didn't matter, though. His intent was always obvious: he was there to serve—in his hyper-class-conscious Southern mind—the upper crust of Twin Cities society. When he wasn't working, he fussed around the club, making sure everything was spit and polish. Dinner at the Rookery Club was always a formal affair. Perhaps that was another reason the members tended to be older. What twentysomething wanted to rent a tuxedo just to go out to eat?

On the other hand, Sophie and Bram liked dressing up and there were few opportunities to do so in Minnesota, the land of the terminally casual.

Sliding off the bar stool with as much grace as she could muster, Sophie straightened the neckline of her dress. "Sheldon, will you have the bartender bring my martini to the table?"

"Will do, madam," he said before turning and limping out of the room.

On the way through the front foyer, Sophie excused herself, telling Bram she'd join him in a moment.

The women's room was down the hall. As Sophie passed the lounge, she noticed that Anika Gladstone, the assistant food and beverage manager at the Maxfield, was sitting on a wing chair near the fireplace, just staring into space. The rest of the lounge was empty, except for a couple who faced the other direction on the other end of the room. Sophie wouldn't have interrupted the younger woman's reverie except that, as she passed the archway, Anika looked up and their eyes met.

"Anika, hi," said Sophie, pausing under the archway.

The young woman stood, fidgeting with her shoulder bag, her gold necklace, and finally her hoop earrings. She was in her midthirties, a pretty blonde with light blue eyes and a deep tan, but in her current attire—a thin jacket and jeans—she obviously hadn't stopped by for dinner.

"Sophie," said Anika, her gaze bouncing around the room. She wasn't the kind of woman to be rude, especially to her boss, but she clearly didn't want to have a conversation right now.

"I'm here with Bram," said Sophie, hoping to put Anika's mind at ease. "We're just about to eat."

Anika's smile was strained. "Oh. That's nice."

Not exactly her usual snappy patter. "Is something wrong?" asked Sophie.

"Wrong? What could be wrong?"

Several million things, thought Sophie, though she didn't say it out loud. "Is Andy with you?" Andy was Anika's husband. He also happened to be one of the senior editors at the *Times Register*—and the half brother of the owner and publisher, Bob Fabian. Bob was an old friend of Sophie's. He'd hired Andy after his last job had gone bust, and then leaned on Sophie to give Anika a job. The couple had moved from Marquette, Michigan, to St. Paul so that Andy could take the job at the paper, but Anika hadn't been able to find anything in her field. Since Sophie had just lost her assistant food and beverage manager, she was glad to do Bob a favor. She'd just hoped that Anika would work out. Thankfully, she had. Sophie could honestly say that, over the past year and a half, they'd become good friends.

"No, he's not," said Anika. "You haven't seen him here tonight by any chance, have you?"

Sophie shook her head.

"I stopped by hoping to find him, but"—she shrugged—"no such luck."

"If I run into him—"

"Don't bother," said Anika, not even trying to hide the disgust in her voice. "He's got his cell phone with him, but he's not answering. So what else is new, right?" She tried another smile, but her lips trembled. She looked on the verge of tears. Sitting back down, she said, "You know, Soph, I need to make a phone call. I'm sorry—"

"No, that's fine," said Sophie. "I'll, ah . . . see you tomorrow?"

"Right," said Anika.

On her way to the women's room, Sophie couldn't get the look on Anika's face off her mind. She'd never heard her speak unfalteringly about her husband. That bit about the cell phone was a definite slam. Sophie had always thought of Andy and Anika Gladstone as the perfect couple. Attractive. Intelligent. Devoted. She'd heard some recent gossip at the paper that hinted at a growing tension between Bob and Andy. Sophie didn't know what it was about, but maybe whatever it was had leaked over into Anika and Andy's marriage. She hoped that wasn't the case. Marriages were delicate organisms, easily damaged. If anybody knew *how* delicate, it was Sophie.

4

The call came in to the dispatcher at ten to nine.

"There's been a murder," said a hushed male voice. "Or an attempted murder. You've got to get paramedics to him right away. It's possible he's still alive."

"Are you all right?" asked the 911 dispatcher.

"Me? No, *no*. This isn't about me."

"You're not hurt?"

"*Listen* to me."

She read the name on the screen in front of her, scrutinized the address, then started to assess the situation. "What's your location?"

"Not *here*," the man whispered. "The shooting happened on Shepard Road—near that new condo construction site. That's all I can tell you. You've got to hurry!"

"What's your name?"

"Fabian. Robert Fabian."

"And you live at 9418 East River Road? Robert and Valerie Fabian?"

"Yes, but you're not listening to me. You've got to get some help to this guy right away! It's a matter of life and death."

"An EMT is on the way, Mr. Fabian. Can you tell me how the shooting occurred?"

"What?"

"Do you know who did the shooting?"

"Well, ah . . . see . . . this isn't easy."

"Can you give me a name?"

"It was . . . he's, like . . . see . . . like my brother—"

In the background, the dispatcher could hear another voice—an angry, demanding, male voice—but she couldn't make out what he was saying. "Mr. Fabian? Are you still there?"

"Just calm down, okay?" said Fabian. There was a fumbling noise.

The dispatcher ordered two squad cars—lights and sirens—to the address.

The next time Robert Fabian spoke, his voice was muffled: "Put it down, okay? Come on. Don't get crazy on me."

The dispatcher continued to try to get him back on the line. "Mr. Fabian? Are you all right? Can you tell me what's going on?"

"I wasn't doing that," Fabian cried. "I swear . . . Just let me explain!"

The dispatcher could hear him talking, but she couldn't make out his words. She assumed he'd moved farther away from the phone. "Mr. Fabian?" she kept calling. "Are you all right?"

A gunshot rang out.

"Mr. Fabian? Are you still there?" She waited. Five seconds, ten seconds, fifteen. But all she heard on the other end of the line now was silence.

5

Five days later, at the same hour but in different parts of the Cities, Kenneth Loy and Robert Fabian were laid to rest. Sophie and Bram didn't know Ken Loy, but they did attend Bob's funeral. As the whitest sunlight descended from the bluest sky, Pastor Clarence Ewald led the assembled crowd in reciting the Lord's Prayer.

Sophie held on to Bram's hand and bowed her head. It was a sad day in the Twin Cities. Bob had been a friend to so many people. Several hundred mourners stood around the lake at the west end of Lakewood Cemetery, their whispered voices joined with those closer to the casket.

Just a little over a year ago, Sophie and Bram had come to this same cemetery for Valerie Fabian's funeral. Valerie had been a joyous, vibrant woman, an artist whose paintings were exhibited at galleries and bought by private collectors all over the country. Sophie had served on the board of a number of charity events with her and knew her well. She'd accomplished a great deal in her forty-six years, but nothing was more important to her than her marriage. When Bob lost her, the light went out of his eyes. Grief made him ill, created a barrier around him that he couldn't seem to escape and others couldn't enter, no matter how hard they tried.

Valerie's sudden death came as a complete shock to everyone. She'd just left an appointment with her lawyer on the west side of St. Paul, when she failed to stop her VW Beetle at a stop sign and was broadsided by another car. The man in the second car, Kenneth Loy, was talking on his cell phone at the time. Both cars were badly damaged, but while Loy walked away from the accident with only a bruised shoulder and a sprained ankle, Valerie was taken to the emergency room with life-threatening injuries. She died two days later.

Even though Valerie was the one who'd failed to stop, Ken Loy was deemed, at least by Valerie's friends and family, to be partially at fault. If he hadn't been talking on the cell phone, with his attention compromised, he might have been able to stop in time, thus preventing her death. No criminal charges were ever brought against him. Valerie's older brother, Phil Banks, had begun a civil lawsuit, hoping to sue Loy for every dime he had, but nothing had gone to trial so far. And now that Ken was dead, it never would. Both Ken and Bob had been murdered the same night—and, according to the police report, the same gun had been used in both shootings. It was the talk of the town.

When the Lord's Prayer was over, Sophie looked up and saw Andy Gladstone, Bob's half brother, wipe a hand across his eyes. Andy stood with his arm around Anika, all trace of the irritation Sophie had seen the other night on Anika's face now gone.

Andy was a gentle-looking man with a brooding ethereality that made women want to mother him and men want to dismiss him. His sweet, pale face was surrounded by softly curling hair as black as boot polish. He was in his early forties, but looked ten years younger. Standing beside him, Anika seemed sad but radiant, her honey gold skin and wheat blond hair a lovely counterpoint to her husband's darkness. Together, they made a striking couple.

Charles Andrew Gladstone was now the owner of the *Minneapolis Times Register*. Bob and Valerie had no children, and Andy was Bob's closest relative. Andy had been an editor at the paper for the past two years. Sophie wasn't entirely clear on the details of his journalistic background—Anika never wanted to talk about his past—but if Bob had left the paper to him, he clearly not only loved but trusted him.

Sophie sensed that Andy was a good man, but she wasn't sure he was up to running a large metropolitan newspaper, especially one with a national reputation for being a political pressure cooker. The ownership seemed to sit heavily on his shoulders. He looked worn out. Sophie knew for a fact that he'd been having almost round-the-clock meetings with the editorial staff. One minute he was an editor himself, and the next he was in charge. His head must be spinning— his *and* Anika's. Not only had they inherited the paper, but Bob Fabian was a multimillionaire. After living a middle-class existence, Andy and Anika were suddenly wealthy. Andy had yet to call a full staff meeting, although Sophie expected it would come soon. The employees at the paper were starting to wonder what changes he might make—and whether it would affect their jobs. Not a great working environment.

Phil Banks, Valerie's brother, stood on the other

side of Anika. He'd brought his latest girlfriend, Chris Parillo, to the service. Phil hadn't repeated the Lord's Prayer with the rest of the crowd, but instead had looked around, apparently more interested in who had come to mourn than in a show of piety. As far as Sophie could see, he was the only man at the funeral who wasn't wearing a suit. Sophie didn't know him well. He was a building contractor with financial interests in several restaurants in the Twin Cities. With his floppy silver pompadour and his well-muscled, leather-jacket-clad body, he looked like an aging movie star. But where Valerie had been cultured, Phil struck Sophie as crude.

Chris was the niece of Vince Parillo, kitchen manager and executive chef at the Rookery Club, and a cook in her own right. Bram told Sophie that Chris was a line chef at one of Phil's restaurants when she and Phil first met. Bram had gotten to know her because she liked to spend time with her uncle Vince at the club, liked to help out in the kitchen. Bram thought the world of her.

"And now, may the Lord bless you and keep you," said Pastor Ewald, repeating a familiar benediction as he raised his arms to the heavens. "May the Lord make His face shine upon you and be gracious unto you. May the Lord lift up His countenance upon you and give you peace."

"Amen," said the crowd.

"Amen," repeated Sophie, closing her eyes. She was still unable to get her mind around the fact that Bob was gone. When she looked up, she saw Vince and Lyle Boerichter standing by the coffin, their heads still bowed. Lyle was a pilot for Sunrise Airlines. Vince, Lyle, and Bob had all served together in Viet Nam.

Bob once told Sophie that Lyle and Vince were like brothers to him.

"Look over there," whispered Bram, bending down close to Sophie's ear and pointing to a tree at the top of a small rise.

"Who is it?" asked Sophie, shielding her eyes from the sun.

"Al Lundquist." Al was a homicide cop, an old friend of Bram's.

"What's he doing here?" asked Sophie.

Bram scanned the crowd, then put his arm protectively around Sophie's shoulders. "My guess is, he thinks one of Bob's friends or family may also be his killer. He's here to check out the suspects."

As they walked back to their car, Sophie couldn't help but shiver.

6

Most weekdays, before his afternoon radio show, Bram took several hours to peruse various newspapers—from the *New York Times* to the *Minneapolis Times Register*, and dozens of other papers from all over the country. Now that his program was in so many national markets, he couldn't just talk about Minnesota anymore. Nonetheless, like Garrison Keillor, Bram had developed a certain "Minnesota take" on national and world events.

With his deep, expressive radio voice, Bram hosted several daily features. One of the most popular was a segment called "The Bold and the Bashful," a rundown of colorful local news stories. There was no dearth of those in the land of ten thousand lakes— and ten billion mosquitoes. Bram put his usual ironic spin on each. He also had two running characters: Ole Bumquist, an old sugar beet farmer who gave advice to the lovelorn, and Senator Gunder Tweet. Gunder allowed Bram to comment on one of his major interests—local and national politics. What had Bram currently dialed up to high dudgeon was the Minnesota legislature's decision to allow the good people of the state to carry concealed weapons—at the same time extending bar hours and cutting law enforcement budgets. If that didn't say it all about conservative politics, nothing did.

Bram also spent one of his three on-air hours interviewing a guest. Today he would interview an expert from the Bureau of Criminal Apprehension in St. Paul, a man who'd written a book on Internet crime. He expected it to be a lively hour.

Bram had just put down the *Detroit Free Press* and was ready to dive into the Milwaukee whatever when he heard a knock on his office door. It wasn't much of an office, and what there was was cluttered with books, magazines, and old newspapers. Although he was organized, Bram never made anything other than chaos out of his dusty chamber.

"Enter at your own risk," he shouted.

The door opened and Al Lundquist, his buddy the homicide cop, stuck his head inside. "The coffeepot on?"

"Isn't it always?"

Al had been a friend of Bram's since childhood. Both men had grown up on Chicago's South Side. Al looked like it, even cultivated the toughness, while Bram had tried hard to leave the rougher parts of his childhood behind.

Several years ago, Al advanced to the rank of lieutenant in the homicide division. He was plainclothes now, strictly an off-the-rack kind of guy. In that, he and Bram also departed company. Whereas Bram spent an inordinate amount of money on his appearance, Al had only one look: cheap. He was tall and lanky, with sandy blond hair, a long face, and innocent blue eyes that probably conned the hell out of evildoers everywhere.

As he entered, Bram nodded to the table next to the window. His office might be a dump, but he always kept good coffee on hand—one reason Al visited him so often. That and the stash of gourmet cookies Bram always kept in his top desk drawer.

"What's the brew of the day?"

"Ethiopian Harrar. The bean that started the world on its coffee craze."

"You amaze me, Baldric. You do everything with such style." He poured himself a mug, then sat down on a threadbare chair in front of Bram's desk. "So, tell me again, why don't you get someone to clean this pit up?"

"I like it like this," said Bram, tossing a sack of fresh chocolate chip macadamia nut cookies across the desktop. "It helps me think."

"Right. I should take some photos when you're not here and sell them to *Minnesota Monthly*. They'd love to skewer Mr. Suave with the real deal."

"Is that a blackmail threat?"

Al cracked his knuckles, then opened the sack. "Maybe. I hear you're interviewing Joel Hellstrom this afternoon. Internet crime." He dunked the cookie in the coffee.

"You heard right."

Al took a bite, then leaned back and made himself more comfortable.

Bram eyed him for a second. "I don't suppose you'd like to tell me everything you know about Robert Fabian's murder." It had been *the* topic of conversation around his house since the night it happened.

"Can't."

"You mean you won't."

"I'm involved in an ongoing investigation, Baldric. Meg Corrigan and I are the primaries on the case." Al crossed one long leg over the other. "I took charge of the crime scene at Fabian's house. Meg was over at the Shepard Road scene. I assume you've heard that Fabian and Loy were shot with the same gun."

"I don't spend my days in a hermetically sealed vault, Al. Yes, I've heard. With Fabian's connections to the community, you're probably getting leaned on pretty hard to come up with an arrest. Sophie adored him, you know. She's been listening to the news every night hoping to hear more details. Got any hot suspects?"

Al coughed into his fist. "All I can say is what I've told everyone else. The matter is under investigation."

"Al, it's *me*. Your old buddy. Whatever you say won't leave this room."

"Sorry."

"Okay, then I'll talk. You listen. I've got a few ideas. Why don't I tell you what they are. You might learn something."

"Sure, pal. Whatever you say." He finished his first cookie, then started on a second, pushing the sack back across the desk.

"One of the reports I read said Bob's house hadn't been broken into. That means he must have let his killer in, so he probably knew him."

"Could be."

"Might have been a friend, or a member of his family."

"Okay."

"That's it? You won't confirm *anything*?"

"Nope. Can't."

Bram drummed his fingers on the desk for a second. "All right. Let's change gears, then. Who had a motive for Loy's murder?"

"It's your dime, Baldric. You tell me."

"Valerie Fabian's family, that's who. They all thought Loy was responsible for her death."

"It's kind of a stretch to suggest that this family member, whoever he was, was so angry that he was willing to whack Loy."

"*He?* It was a man? A male relative?"

"No comment."

But Bram could see he'd struck pay dirt. "All right, let's just say for a moment that whoever shot Loy went straight to Bob's house. Maybe Bob was in on it. Maybe he *paid* this guy to do it. Whatever the case, they got together and they got into a fight. Suppose our bad boy walked in and announced what he'd done, and Bob thought, Hell, I've got to call the police. Maybe he threatened to turn the murderer in."

"Possible."

Bram watched Al's face for hints that he was going in the right direction. "So this man, this . . . relative . . . shoots Bob."

"Someone sure did."

"Bob's taken to the emergency room, where he dies of the gunshot wound."

Al just stared at him.

"What?"

"I didn't say a word."

Bram could tell he'd taken a wrong turn, but couldn't for the life of him figure out what it was. "I'm missing something."

"You're missing a lot."

"Have you talked to any of the suspects yet?"

"No comment."

"Come on, Al. Give me a crumb. What would it cost you?"

"Well, let's see. My job?"

"You've got to be all over Bob's family. You're the one who's always saying that the colder the trail becomes, the harder it is to nail the perpetrator."

"Don't repeat my words back to me, Baldric. It's not nice."

"I suppose if Bob's murderer *was* a relative, fingerprints, fibers, that sort of thing are all useless because there would be a reason why those people—men— would have been in the house. They're family."

"I wish it were that simple. This is the most convoluted case I've ever worked on."

"Why? Two murders, both tied together. One perpetrator."

"I wish."

Now Bram was confused. "More than one shooter?"

"No. Just one."

"Then—"

"I can't talk about it. We're not sure what we've got yet. It's more complicated than what you're reading in the papers."

"In what way?"

Al lowered his eyes.

"*Use* me, Al. I'm here for you."

The cop gave him a disgusted grunt.

"Want another cookie?" Bram rattled the sack.

"Save the charm, Baldric. It doesn't work on me."

But he grabbed the sack. "Okay, look. You'll find this out in a matter of hours anyway, so I might as well tell you. I learned a few hours ago that somebody leaked one of our main pieces of evidence to the press. We're in possession of a taped 911 call Fabian placed the night he was shot. He called to report a murder down on Shepard Road."

"Loy."

Al nodded.

"Did he say who did it?"

"He was about to, but somebody stopped him. There was another man's voice on the tape in the background, but it was garbled, so we don't know who it was."

"That had to have been Bob's killer."

"No comment."

"But Bob must have said something to give you a lead."

"Maybe."

"Will that be in the newspaper or do I have to beat it out of you?"

Al studied Bram for a moment, then took a sip of coffee. "It sounded like Fabian was about to say his *brother* killed Loy."

Bram whistled.

"But he didn't finish his sentence. So, for all we know, he may have been going somewhere else with it. A good defense lawyer could drive a truck through a hole that big. And even if he did mean to say that his brother was the one who killed Loy, that still leaves us with a problem. Which brother? Fabian's brother-in-law, Phil Banks, or his half brother, Andy Gladstone."

"Was the entire 911 tape leaked to the press, or just the fact of its existence?"

"We've got the tape locked up. Nobody's got access to it but us. But yeah, I think the press has a transcript."

Bram tapped a finger to his lips. "I saw you at Bob's funeral the other day. I figured you weren't there just to pay your respects."

"You saying I got no compassion?"

Bram spread his arms wide. "Why don't you haul Andy and Phil in, shine a bright light in their eyes, and apply your thumbscrews?"

"You watch too many dumb movies."

"But you've talked to them, right?"

"Like I said, it's complicated." Al took the last cookie out of the sack.

"And I wouldn't understand."

"No, you'd probably get it, but I can't talk about it. I've already said too much."

"You eat all my cookies and then you have the nerve to hold out on me?"

"Guess so," said Al, crunching up the sack and tossing it at Bram's chest.

Bram thought he'd had the real story nailed, but now he wasn't so sure. What the press had reported so far must be only the tip of the iceberg. Glancing at his watch, he saw that he had a little over a minute to get to the sound booth before his program started. "Between you and me, just give me a hint."

"Between you and me?"

"Goes no farther than this room."

Al rose from the chair, dropping the last cookie into his side pocket of his suit coat. "Okay. Listen carefully, pal. I'm only going to say this once." He placed his hands on the desk, bent closer to Bram, and whispered, "Rosebud." Then he winked.

"Asshole."

"No comment."

7

Chris walked out of the bedroom, toweling her long, curly brown hair dry. As she stood on the balcony that enclosed a section of the second floor, she looked down into the living room. Phil was crouched low next to the front windows, gazing at the street in front of the house through a crack in the curtains. "What's going on?" she asked, curious about what might be happening outside.

"It's that damn car again."

"What car?"

"The one that followed us home last night."

"I didn't see a car."

"That's because you weren't looking. I'm being tailed. Have been for several days."

This was the first Chris had heard of it. "By who?"

"The cops."

"Why?"

"They've got to nail somebody for those two murders."

Chris was aghast. "But you were nowhere near those locations that night. I should know."

"You think that matters to *them*?" He jabbed his forefinger at the curtain. "They just need a warm body with a potential motive."

"What motive? You liked your brother-in-law. And the idea that you'd ever hurt someone—it's ridiculous."

"Tell that to the plainclothes jerk out in the car."

"Fine," said Chris, marching down the stairs into the living room. "I will."

Phil turned around and grabbed her by the waist just as she steamed past him toward the front door. "God, but you're a sexy woman." With one flick of his hand, he untied her robe. He slipped his arms around her naked body, running his palms up and down her back.

"And you're my guy. I gotta protect you."

"I'll handle the cop."

Chris had dated only casually before meeting Phil, and she'd never been in love before. Phil told her right off that he was used goods. He'd been divorced twice, and freely admitted that the problems in his marriages had been mostly his fault. That admission only made Chris love him all the more. Honesty was important to her, and Phil might not be perfect, but he was an honest man. He was her silver fox, a super-confident older guy who would never let her down. None of the younger men she'd dated could hold a candle to him. The difference in their ages didn't matter a bit to her. He was in better shape than most twenty-year-olds.

Chris was the second child of a hardworking mom and a father who'd dumped her before she was even born. Her first memories were of an apartment over a dentist's office. Tiny rooms. A TV set that didn't work. Lots of canned spaghetti for dinner. When she was nine, she and her mom and her older brother had moved to another apartment, this one above the Lakeside Pavilion in South Minneapolis. It was a cheap dollar theater that, in the '80s, before VCRs were in every home, had made money showing old movies. Chris had grown up watching Montgomery Clift and Elizabeth Taylor, Bette Davis and Jimmy Stewart. Her favorite was Errol Flynn. When she was twelve, she got a job helping the manager at the theater clean up between showings. By the time she was fifteen, she was working the concessions. At sixteen, she manned the ticket booth. One of the perks of her job was a free pass to any movie she wanted to see—and she wanted to see them all. It was a glamorous world totally unlike her everyday life. She always suspected that when she met "the" man, it would be incredibly romantic, just like what she saw in the movies. It turned out that she was right.

Two summers ago, she'd been jogging around Lake Harriet early one morning when she'd turned into Super Klutz, tripped over a rock, and landed in a bush. A man who'd been sitting on one of the benches came over and helped her up. Branches had scraped her legs, but other than that, she was fine.

"If you hadn't been checking me out so carefully, you would have seen the rock," he said. When he grinned at her, she saw that he had a beautiful smile. He looked just like Errol Flynn.

She smiled back at him. And that was how it started. She sat down on the bench and they began talking. He told her he owned a construction company. She said she worked for Cafe Aldo as a line chef. He laughed, said it was a small world. As it turned out, he was part owner of that restaurant. And that's when they realized they'd met before. He'd walked through the kitchen one day a few months before and asked her to grill him a steak. She remembered thinking he was handsome, but that was as far as it went.

They couldn't seem to stop talking that first morning. He invited her to have breakfast with him. She had the day off, so she took him up on his offer. Later, they ended up in Hudson at another restaurant for lunch—one more cafe in which he had a part interest. They spent the afternoon antiquing along the St. Croix, the evening sitting on Phil's deck, and then she stayed the night.

The next morning, Phil asked her to move in with him. He told her he'd never been so powerfully attracted to anybody before in his life, both physically and intellectually. He couldn't let her get away now that he'd found her. He said he felt he'd finally found his soul mate, and even though she wasn't an impulsive person, Chris felt the exact same way.

And still, she hesitated. The apartment she lived in wasn't fabulous—nothing like his home in Woodbury—but it was hers. She'd worked hard to get where she was. When she tried to explain it to him, he said he understood—it wasn't a problem. He'd pay the rent on the place as long as she liked. He just wanted her to give their relationship a try. She brought some of her clothes over the next day.

Phil didn't like schedules. He preferred to make spur-of-the-moment decisions on what they would do each day. Sometimes he'd go to work; sometimes he wouldn't. Six months ago, she'd quit her job. It was a major source of contention between them. Phil would want to do something fun, and she always had to go to work. It just didn't make sense. He said he had enough money to last him a lifetime—and he wanted to share it with her.

A month after quitting, she gave notice at her apartment. The little furniture she owned wasn't as nice as Phil's, so she sold it. All she brought with her were the rest of her clothes and some personal stuff she'd collected over the years. Her mother and her uncle lived in the Twin Cities, but because Phil didn't like her spending time away from him, her relationship with them had become somewhat strained. Chris felt bad about that, but she figured that once she convinced Phil she was completely committed to him, his possessiveness would mellow to more manageable levels. She could hardly deny him her time when he'd been so generous to her. She had a beautiful home, new jewelry, lots of romantic trips to the "Mexican Riviera," as he laughingly called it. Puerto Vallarta. Acapulco. Mazatlán. Phil was everything Chris had ever wanted—and more.

"Why don't you make us some lunch?" said Phil, returning his attention to the window and the cop outside.

"Sure," said Chris. She watched him clench and unclench his fists. "What are you going to do?"

"I'd like to go out there and beat the crap out of that guy."

"But you won't." She knew he had a terrible temper because she'd seen it, but she'd never seen him this wound up before.

"Hell I won't." He turned suddenly and stormed toward the door.

"Take it easy, Phil." She followed him, then stood on the front steps and watched him stomp across the street. He banged on the driver's-side door with his fist.

"Open the goddamn window," he shouted.

The window eased down.

"Listen, jerkoff, you want to ask me something, you come into my house and ask it. But don't follow me around. I don't like it."

The man in the car got out. He was tall and lanky, wearing a baseball jacket over a blue dress shirt and tie. He and Phil talked quietly for a few moments, and then both men headed for the house.

Chris, wearing only a robe, quickly dashed upstairs to put on a pair of jeans and a tank top.

When she returned to the living room, Phil introduced her as his fiancée, Chris Parillo. That shocked her a little because Phil had never talked about marriage. She sat down on the couch next to him and he draped his arm across her shoulders.

"Detective Lundquist here seems to think I had something to do with Ken Loy's murder. I assume he'd like to peg me for Bob's, too, but he's being cagey. He likes to play games. I've already talked to his partner. But it seems that doesn't count. He says *he* wants to talk to me now. Think I should do it?" He looked at Chris.

Phil could sound so arrogant at times. His personality put people off. He was smart and he didn't mind letting others know it. Chris was drawn to his confidence, although she knew not everyone was. "Sure. Why not? You've got nothing to hide."

The detective's gaze swept over the living room, then rose to the second-floor balcony. "Nice house," he said. He was sitting on a leather chair across from them. Chris could see the bulge under his jacket, the shoulder holster where he kept his gun.

"Glad you approve." Phil turned to Chris. "Al wants to know where I was the night Loy died."

"You were with me," she said. It was the truth.

The detective's quick blue eyes dropped to her.

"We'd gone out to eat at Pazzaluna, and then we drove over to the Grandview theater and saw *The Hours*. Phil didn't like it. He fell asleep."

Detective Lundquist removed a small pad from his pocket and started to take notes. "What time was that?"

"Well, our dinner reservations were for five thirty. I know because I made them. The movie started at seven fifteen."

"Do you have ticket stubs, anything that would prove you were actually there?"

"I put the dinner and the movie on my credit card," said Phil. "That should be plenty of proof. Look, I already told all this to your partner."

"And you never left the restaurant or the theater at any time?"

"No," he said, tightening his grip around Chris's shoulders.

"Is that correct?" asked the detective, looking directly at Chris.

She nodded. "He was with me the entire night."

Returning his attention to Phil, the detective asked, "You'd filed a civil lawsuit against Ken Loy, isn't that right?"

"I did," said Phil. "I was suing him for the wrongful death of my sister, Valerie Fabian. Now I'll just have to sue his estate. If you want to know what I thought of the guy, I'll tell you. He was a worm. He didn't deserve to live after what he did. It was criminally negligent homicide. The guy was on his freakin' cell phone and he wasn't watching the road. I'm not sorry he's dead. As far as I'm concerned, he got what was coming to him."

"Those are strong words."

"Strong words aren't against the law last I checked."

"Do you own a gun, Mr. Banks?"

"Several. I have permits for all of them."

"Can you describe them to me?"

"I have a Smith and Wesson J Frame .38 Special. A Steyr nine-millimeter semiautomatic and a Springfield Armory semiautomatic .45."

"That cover it?"

"I also own a couple of hunting rifles."

"Are you a hunter, Mr. Banks?"

"A lethal hunter, *Al.*"

Chris wondered why Phil was talking like that. He was almost baiting the cop, daring him to prove he was guilty.

"You get along with your brother-in-law?"

"Sure. Bob and I weren't best buddies or anything, but he was family. He was good to my sister. We stayed in touch after her death. Had drinks or dinner together every now and then."

"He supported your lawsuit against Loy?"

"Absolutely."

The detective changed gears. "What can you tell me about Andy Gladstone, Robert Fabian's half brother."

Phil narrowed his eyes. "What's he got to do with anything?"

"Are you a friend of his?"

"I know him."

"What about his relationship with Fabian?"

Phil shrugged, looked at Chris. "They seemed friendly enough. Andy struck me as kind of a suck-up, but a lot of people acted like that around Bob. He was a powerful man."

"Was Mr. Gladstone upset over Valerie's death?"

"Sure. We all were."

"What did he think of the lawsuit you were bringing against Loy?"

"He thought it was a good idea. Hell, we all wanted to see Loy rot for what he did. If I was the kind of guy who believed in 'an eye for an eye,' I would have driven over him with one of my cement trucks. But I'm not. I chose to take my revenge *within* the law."

"And Andy Gladstone. Did he ever say anything about getting back at Ken Loy?"

"You ask me, you guys are really reaching. He's about as milquetoast as they come."

"Mind answering the question?"

"No. Not that I remember."

The detective pulled a card out of his pocket and handed it to Phil. "If either of you should recall anything you think is important, my number's at the bottom."

Phil stood, ripped up the card, and flipped it in the air. "I've answered all your asshole questions. Anything else you want to know, talk to my lawyer. Now get the hell out of my house and don't come back."

8

In newspapers across the country, the name Jayson Blair could cause an editor's blood pressure to skyrocket and reporters to break into a cold sweat. Blair was the *New York Times* reporter who had been fired for plagiarizing and fabricating major news stories. The fact that this sort of journalism existed was a growing scandal, a damaging bullet the *Minneapolis Times Register* had always taken great pride in dodging.

And that was why, only a few days after Bob Fabian's funeral, Sophie was so surprised to hear the Blair name repeated again and again—never directly to her, but as she passed people talking in small clumps in the hallways at the Times Register Tower, the name was definitely being invoked. Reporters looked scared and she wondered why.

Sophie had come to the office on Monday to finish writing a restaurant review of the recently renovated Heartland Grill in Mahtomedi. As she entered the office she shared with her son, Rudy, she saw that he was on the phone.

Sophie was the main restaurant reviewer at the paper, but because she was already running a major hotel in downtown St. Paul, she'd taken the job with the proviso that her son be hired as her assistant. In truth, Rudy did most of the work. In early September, he'd been offered the job of food column editor and he'd accepted.

Sophie loved working with her son—it was one of the main reasons she took the job at the paper in the first place. Rudy had graduated from the University of Minnesota with a degree in Theater Arts, but like his mom, he had a great interest in all things culinary. At first Sophie wasn't sure he would be content to work for the *Times Register*, but she'd been wrong. In the past year, he'd really grown, both in his writing ability and in his passion for food. Sophie was incredibly proud of him.

Their shared office was divided into two cubicles, with a small outer area that served as a waiting room. As he continued to talk on the phone, Sophie entered Rudy's cubicle and gave him a kiss on his cheek. He was a handsome young man. At least, his mother thought so. They both had strawberry blond hair and great smiles. Rudy was also small, like his mother, but he worked out regularly. Sophie could tell he was talking to John Jacoby, his partner. John was a fine artist who supported himself by working for a local brewery. Rudy and John had been together for nearly three years.

Feeling that she might be interrupting a private conversation, Sophie sat down behind her desk, took out her notes, and began to work on the review. When Rudy was done with his conversation, he came into Sophie's cubicle and sat down in the chair in front of her desk.

"Hello, Mother of mine," he said, tapping the

eraser end of a pencil against the side of his head. "John found a dog."

She looked up from her computer keyboard. "What kind of dog?"

"A mutt. We've seen him roaming around the neighborhood for the past few days. Brown and black, maybe twenty pounds. He's obviously lost. He's got no tags on him, no collar. John thinks maybe he was dumped. But he's a really cool little guy. We brought him in last night, gave him a bath, and he slept on a pillow next to our bed. He even seems to be house-trained." Rudy folded his arms over his chest and leaned back in his chair. "He kind of looks like a cross between a hedgehog and a fox."

"Have you talked to your rental agent? Can you have a dog in your duplex?"

"John left a message for him. We're waiting to see what he says. You working on the Heartland Grill review?"

"It's almost finished. Look, Rudy, I'm curious about something. Why are so many people around here talking about Jayson Blair? Has something happened that I don't know about?"

Rudy wagged his finger at her. "If you spent more time here, you'd know."

"Know what?"

"Irazarian. Our homegrown golden boy."

Del Irazarian was a reporter who had bagged two of the hottest news stories of the last year—an in-depth report on airline safety at Twin Cities International, and another one on drug addiction among Minneapolis police officers. The drug addiction series won him an award.

"What did he do?"

"I don't know all the details, but he's about to be fired."

"When?"

"Today. The scuttlebutt is that he fabricated sources, made up quotes, statistics, cited research papers that didn't exist. The whole nine yards."

Sophie put her head in her hands. That's when a thought struck her. "Wasn't his editor—"

"Yeah. Andy. I don't understand how he let Irazarian get away with it. I mean, Andy's good. Better than good. If anything, he's a little too conservative when it comes to sources. It doesn't make any sense."

"Who'll fire Del?"

"Probably Fred Scott. But it came down from Andy. We're printing a full page of retractions tomorrow morning."

"I wonder . . ."

"Hmm?"

"Well, you know that Anika Gladstone works at the Maxfield. We've become pretty good friends. She mentioned to me a few weeks ago that Andy and Bob weren't getting along."

"You think it was about Irazarian?"

"It's possible. Anika said it—whatever *it* was—was killing Andy. He idolized Bob, always tried to do everything he could to please him."

"They were brothers, right?"

"Half brothers," said Sophie. "They had different fathers. Bob was, oh, maybe a dozen years older than Andy. I think Andy's had kind of a spotty job history. Bob was taking a chance by hiring him, but then, from what Anika said, Bob was extremely pleased with his work."

"Until a few weeks ago."

She nodded.

"Well," said Rudy, tipping his chair back and clasping his hands behind his head, "whatever went down between them, Bob Fabian didn't change his will. Andy still inherited the paper. You ask me, he's in way over his head."

Sophie had to agree.

"The fallout from what Irazarian did is going to hit this paper like a sledgehammer. If any heads were about to roll, I would imagine Andy's would have been at the top of the list. Now he owns the paper. He sure got lucky, if you ask me. If Bob hadn't died when he did, Andy would be working as a checkout guy at Home Depot."

Sophie glanced up, caught the look in Rudy's eyes, and knew what he was thinking. She knew because she was thinking the exact same thing.

9

Sophie was out on the balcony grilling salmon when Bram got home from the station. It was a warm October evening, what people often referred to as Indian summer. She called out to him to grab himself a beer and join her. She was already on her second. It had been that kind of day.

Sophie had spent the morning with her father, enduring his smelly cigars and his disgruntled comments as he made broad hints about "the list" he was working on to improve the hotel. Even though she owned the Maxfield now, she could hardly ignore her father's requests, although she had a feeling that his ideas might be a tad out there. On the round-the-world trip he and Sophie's mom had just returned from, he'd learned a thing or two about running a hotel *right*, he said. Sophie could tell they were headed for a major clash. The economy was far worse now than when he'd been running the Maxfield, but he didn't seem to grasp that. If he continued to constantly look over her shoulder, he would force her to take a stand. For now, Sophie decided to let him dangle "the list" in front of her. Maybe, in time, he'd remember that he trusted her to take over the running of the hotel and that *that's* what he should do.

Bram came through the double screen doors onto the balcony. He'd already removed his sport coat, socks, and shoes. Two years ago, when they'd moved to the Maxfield Plaza, they couldn't seem to get enough of ordering in room service from the Zephyr Club, the gourmet restaurant on the top floor of the south tower. Now that Bram was watching his diet due to a recent heart surgery, they prepared their own food more often.

"How was your day?" asked Bram, giving her a peck on the cheek.

She groaned. "Better now that you're home."

"That sounds ominous." He stood for a moment looking down on downtown St. Paul. "God but I love living up here. I feel like we're on top of an urban mountain." Their apartment was sixteen floors above the ground.

Sophie smiled at him as she basted the salmon with a fresh basil and balsamic marinade.

"What's for dinner?"

"I made a cold orzo salad with lots of radicchio, roasted eggplant and red peppers, green onions, and pine nuts. The salmon goes on top. And I whipped up a quick coconut sorbet mixture and put it in the ice-cream machine, so we'll have that for dessert with biscotti and coffee. We have to live a *little*."

Bram snuggled up behind her. "Why don't I open a nice pinot noir and we can sit out here and you can tell me all about how much your dad is driving you crazy."

"You're a mind reader. Actually, it's more than that. I may have spent the morning with him, but this afternoon, I went over to the paper to work on a restaurant review. Rudy was there and boy did I get an earful about a scandal that's just about to explode."

"Oh, goody," said Bram. "I love a good scandal. Be right back."

When he returned, he carried two half-filled wine-glasses and the open bottle. Handing a glass to Sophie, he clicked his to hers. "To us."

"To us," she repeated. It felt good to be back on track with her husband. All the insanity with Nathan Buckridge was finally behind her. Thank God she'd kept the worst of it to herself.

"Now," said Bram, sitting down on the chaise, "tell me about the scandal. Don't leave out any of the gory details."

As Sophie basted the salmon again, she filled him in on everything she'd learned about Del Irazarian.

When she was done, Bram sat for a few seconds, digesting the information. "You know, I can't believe someone at the paper didn't catch him in one of his lies. Who was his editor?"

"That's the worst part. It was Andy."

"Boy, talk about being asleep at the switch."

Sophie flipped the salmon. Staring at it for a moment, she asked, "Bram? What if Andy felt his position was threatened? Not only his position, but his future."

"You saying he had a motive to murder his brother?" Bram shook his head. "I've never met a guy who seemed more intent on making a good impression. If I were to put it less charitably, I'd say Andy did everything he could to brownnose. He wanted to please Bob at all costs."

Sophie had noticed it, too. But she found it genuine. She felt strongly that Andy cared deeply about his brother, and about Valerie.

"Andy would have jumped through a ring of fire if he thought it would score him points with his brother."

Turning her back to the grill, Sophie looked down at her husband. "Remember the night Bob and Ken Loy died? We were at the Rookery Club having dinner. It must have been right around the time it happened."

"Sure I remember. Shepard Road is a stone's throw from the club."

"I saw Anika in the lounge that night. I didn't mention it because, well, something she said bothered me so I put it out of my mind because I wanted to have a relaxing dinner with my handsome husband."

"You really think I'm handsome?"

"Don't fish for compliments, dear. It implies desperation."

"I'll remember that."

"But now I'm wondering what was going on." She sat down on one of the chairs. "Anika had come to the club hoping to find Andy. He wasn't there. She said she'd tried his cell phone, but he wasn't answering. Her exact words were, 'So what else is new.' As if he made a practice of not answering her calls."

"Huh," said Bram. "That surprises me. They always seemed like the last word in happy coupledom."

"So where was Andy that night? Why wouldn't he take her call?"

"Maybe he had his cell phone turned off."

"Maybe."

Bram took a sip of wine. "Soph, you can't honestly

think Andy had anything to do with those two murders. He seems so . . . gentle."

"I agree, but what's underneath the gentleness?"

"More gentleness?"

Sophie looked up at the cloudless fall sky. "I hope you're right."

"Of course, I learned something pretty interesting this morning myself. Now that I think of it, it adds some credence to your theory."

"Learned what?"

"That the police have a tape of a 911 call Bob made just before he died. He was calling to report a shooting on Shepard Road. And, although I don't have all the details, he seemed to indicate that the shooter may have been his brother."

Sophie was stunned.

" 'Course, he didn't finish his sentence, so he could have been about to say brother-in-law."

"Phil Banks?"

"Or maybe he was headed somewhere else with the sentence. The police won't know for sure until they figure out who was responsible for the two homicides."

"I just don't see Andy with a gun. Anika wouldn't have allowed one in the house."

As Sophie got up to check the salmon, the doorbell chimed.

An instant later, Margie, Bram's daughter, breezed through the screen doors out onto the balcony.

"Hey, Dad. What's up?" As an afterthought, she added, "Hi, Sophie."

Sophie's heart hit the floor. She'd been looking forward to a relaxing dinner with her husband, and then, well, the night was young.

Margie had moved into one of the apartments at the Maxfield right after she returned home from Texas. Bram wanted her to be close, and Margie was only too happy to take the offer of the apartment, with the rent paid by her father. Bram assured Sophie that when Margie and her friend Carrie got their wedding planner business off the ground, that Margie would be able to take over paying the rent. But she was still living at the hotel free of charge, even though her business already seemed to be booming.

Bram also assured Sophie that Margie's continual presence in their lives, barging in anytime she felt like it—which was always at the most inopportune moments—would end when she reconnected with old friends and made new ones in the Twin Cities. That hadn't happened either. Margie spent four or five nights a week at their apartment, sometimes arriving for dinner, more often banging on their door late at night, then letting herself in with her key. She would hold them captive in the living room as she went on and on and on about some minutia in her life. Sophie had tried hard to like Margie, but she couldn't shake the feeling that Margie wanted to see their marriage crumble. If nothing else, it was likely to hit the skids from lack of sleep.

Margie could stay up talking until the wee hours and still make it to work the next day. Bram could sleep late because he didn't need to be at the station until late morning. But Sophie had to be up bright and early. Now that her father was home, breathing down her neck, it was more important than ever that she be in her office downstairs by eight.

"I ran into Henry downstairs on my floor," said

Margie, lighting up a cigarette, then tossing the match over the railing.

"Henry" was how Margie referred to Sophie's father.

"Oh?" said Sophie.

"Yeah. He was replacing a lightbulb in one of the hallway wall sconces. Don't you have maintenance men who can do that? I mean, God, that guy's pretty old to be hauling such a *gargantuan* ladder around."

Sophie knew that, where Margie was concerned, she was way too sensitive. But she felt as if Margie was accusing her of parent abuse. "Yes, we have a full maintenance staff." As Margie well knew. She used them constantly, more than anyone else who'd ever lived in one of the Maxfield's six rental units. The head of maintenance thought she was a pain in the ass. "She acts like she owns the place," he often said. And that was part of the problem. Sophie felt strongly that Margie did see stars in her eyes when she looked at the hotel. She knew this was a community property state. If Bram and Sophie divorced, Bram would inherit half the hotel. And that meant that one day, Margie would be half owner herself. Bram had no other children.

"You look pretty snappy tonight," said Bram, nodding to Margie's new red dress.

Margie twirled around. "Just got home from work. Carrie and I met with this family out in Deep Haven. Very wealthy couple. They want to give their daughter a *huge* wedding and they hired us to do it."

"Congratulations," said Bram, reaching up and squeezing his daughter's hand.

"This is the break we've been waiting for. If we do

this right, it will serve as a *humongous* entrée to other upscale jobs."

Sophie detested Margie's use of hyperbole. And yet, even the fact that she noticed it made her uncomfortable. It made her feel like a snippy schoolmarm. And that was another thing. Sophie hated the way Margie made her feel about herself. She wasn't snippy, or nasty, or super-judgmental, or, as Margie put it once, "tight-assed." But when she was around Margie, that's exactly how she behaved.

"The bride-to-be picked out these, like, *hideous* colors for the wedding, but between Carrie and me—and her mother—we were able to talk her into something more elegant. I mean, green just *kills* a person's complexion. Makes even the youngest skin look *totally* cadaverous." Margie glanced over at Sophie and saw that she was wearing a jade green sweater set. She smiled.

Sophie thought it was more of a smirk.

"Hey, Dad, I thought maybe we could go for a swim before dinner."

Dinner! thought Sophie, leaping up. "Oh Lord," she said, seeing that she'd just incinerated the salmon.

"Oh, honey, don't worry about it," said Bram, climbing off the chaise. "It's no problem. We'll just have the orzo salad."

"You really go for Italian food, don't you?" said Margie, looking at Sophie.

Sophie was still so upset about the burnt salmon that she didn't pick up on Margie's drift.

"Speaking of Italian food," continued Margie, "I saw that friend of yours downstairs this afternoon. It was just before I left for my meeting in Deep Haven."

"What friend?" asked Bram.

"Her old boyfriend. What's his name. Nathan?"

Sophie turned around in time to see Bram stiffen.

"I thought you didn't see him anymore," said Margie, tapping some of the ash from her cigarette over the railing.

"I don't," said Sophie.

Nathan Buckridge was Sophie's high school sweetheart. He was also a chef with a restaurant just outside of Stillwater. He'd come back into her life shortly after she'd taken over the reins of the hotel, after an absence of some twenty-five years. She'd been dismayed, and also more than a little flattered, to find that he was still attracted to her. Actually, it was more than that. He'd asked her to marry him. The fact that she was married didn't seem to matter. Nathan insisted that he'd found her first, and if it hadn't been for a series of stupid mistakes, they'd be married.

Sophie had never confessed to Bram what had really gone on between them two summers ago. It was over and done with, so, in Sophie's mind, there was no point in discussing it. And yet, even though she'd never given Bram the details, he apparently sensed that Nathan was a threat. Bram wasn't normally a jealous man, but when it came to Nathan Buckridge, he reacted with the part of his mind that wasn't entirely civilized.

"Maybe he found out my parents were home from their trip," said Sophie, "and he wanted to say hi."

"I suppose they thought of him as a son once," mused Bram.

"Well," said Sophie. "Yes, I think they did."

"Nope," said Margie. "When I saw Henry in the hall, I asked him if he'd seen Nathan. He said he hadn't."

"Ah," said Bram. "Well then, maybe you better give him a call. Find out what he wants. Or maybe you can just talk to him tomorrow when he stops by. I assume he usually drops in when I'm at the station."

"Don't do this, Bram. Nathan doesn't stop by. There's nothing between us but friendship." That wasn't entirely true. Nathan did drop in from time to time, even sent flowers occasionally, though Sophie rarely spoke to him for more than a few minutes, never alone in her office—and she always made it clear that it was over between them. She tried to be tactful, hoping he'd get the message, but he never seemed to give up. He'd been dating one of Sophie's friends for a while, but he still couldn't seem to let go of the notion that, one day, he and Sophie would be together. It was starting to worry her a little, although Nathan was a good, sensible man. She put it down to simple stubbornness.

"Then I guess Margie saw an apparition this afternoon," said Bram.

"Maybe she did." It wouldn't be the first time Margie had brought up Nathan just to sour her father's mood.

"Oh, right," said Margie, tossing her cigarette over the rail. "I've got twenty-twenty vision, you know. I know who I saw. But hey, I shouldn't have mentioned it. Dad, chill the hell out, okay? Sophie didn't do anything wrong."

Just what Sophie needed. Margie torpedoes the evening, then comes off looking like a saint by defending the guilty party.

Bram took a deep breath, then let it out. "Maybe you're right. I'm sorry, Soph, but I just get a little crazy when that guy's name is mentioned."

"Kind of like Pavlov's dog," said Margie.

"You can shut up now," said Bram.

The phone rang.

"I'll get it," said Bram, grabbing the cordless off one of the glass tables. "Baldric." He listened for a moment. Then, glancing at Sophie, he handed her the phone. "It's for you."

"Who is it?"

"Who else? Your boyfriend."

This couldn't be happening. "Bram—"

"Take it!" he ordered, shoving the phone at her. "Margie, why don't I buy you dinner. There's a place I've been wanting you to see."

"Bram, no," pleaded Sophie. "This will just take a second."

"Oh, no," said Bram, opening the screen door and waiting until Margie walked through. "I wouldn't dream of rushing you. And this way, you two will have complete privacy."

"I don't want privacy."

"Well, you got it."

10

Bram and Margie walked the six blocks to the Rookery Club in total silence. Margie tried to introduce a couple of subjects on the way down in the elevator, but Bram couldn't concentrate on anything other than what had just happened. He loathed himself when he responded like a jealous jerk. He knew Sophie loved him, but what he didn't know—what he'd *never* really known for sure—was how deep her feelings went for Nathan.

It was hard for Bram to shake the sense that Sophie wasn't being totally honest with him. From what Bram could tell—and he'd talked to Nathan personally only a few times—he appeared to be everything Bram wasn't. Rough around the edges, but appealingly rough. A poet in his youth who'd become the picture of the rugged outdoorsman. An internationally respected chef. And more to the point, Sophie's first love. First loves, especially when they were never resolved, still had power. And it was that power, the lure and romance of unrequited love, that Bram feared.

As they passed Rice Park, Margie slipped her arm through Bram's and said, "I hate Sophie for what she's doing to you."

"Don't hate her, honey. We'll work it out."

"Why doesn't she just make a clear decision about Nathan and then let it go?"

"She says she has."

"Then why's he always hanging around?"

"I don't know that he is."

"Well, I've seen him twice in the last week. That must mean something."

"Was he with Sophie?"

"No. But why else would he come to the hotel?"

Why indeed, thought Bram. If he'd stuck around instead of blowing a gasket, he might not be so completely in the dark right now.

"I just think you deserve better."

"I already have the best, honey. If I have to fight Nathan for her, I will."

"God, that is so totally Neanderthal, Dad. You're like a gorilla in a forest making *uhga uhga* sounds to prove you're the alpha male."

Bram laughed. "Nice image."

"My father is more evolved than that."

"Don't kid yourself. When it comes to love and war, nobody's evolved."

They continued on in silence.

As they passed through the wrought-iron gate and headed up the steps to the club, Margie asked where they were.

"You've heard of the Rookery Club, right?"

"Not really."

Bram briefly explained the history. Once inside, he stopped to talk to Sheldon Larr, the maître d', to see if they could get a dinner reservation. Sheldon told him there would be a twenty-minute wait.

"Well," said Bram, looking around, "do you want a drink or a guided tour of the building?"

Margie glanced into the Wackenhut room. "Omigod, there's Mrs. Josefowicz. We did her daughter's wedding last month." She waved and plunged into the crowd. "Mrs. Josefowicz, hi! It's Margie Baldric!"

Bram smiled. Margie was just like him—a born schmoozer.

Seeing that Margie was already talking up a storm, Bram decided to check out the action in the De Gustabus room, a large pantry off the kitchen that Vince Parillo had turned into a dining room.

Within the Rookery Club were smaller groups based on specific gastronomic interests. For instance, there was a wine club that met the third Wednesday of every month. Then there was a bread-making club, an Italian food lovers club, a coffee and tea tasting club, and on and on. The strangest group of all was De Gustabus. So strange in fact that it had only three members—two now that Bob Fabian was dead. The reason for the limited interest was the kind of cuisine De Gustabus pursued.

Bob Fabian, Lyle Boerichter, and Vince Parillo had met in Viet Nam. What drew them together years later was a love of, well, just plain weird food—food that most Americans would find not only disgusting but downright dangerous. All three men traced their love of odd cuisine to the years they spent in Southeast Asia.

Bram had done a tour in Viet Nam himself, but he'd never much liked the local food. He had grown up eating tuna noodle casserole, hamburgers, and grilled cheese sandwiches. As a young army grunt, he was by no means a culinary adventurer, although he found that he was fascinated by it now. Not that he wanted to eat pygmy iguana paté, snake soup, or lamprey stew, but the menus never failed to intrigue him. So much so that he often dropped in on the De Gustabus room to see what new loathsome beast the men were eating.

Above the door to the small dining room, Vince had placed the sign NO RESERVATIONS REQUIRED. That was obvious. There was no stampede to get a seat at the table, only to be served a chocolate cricket torte. Vince was not only the head chef at the club, he was also the culinary inspiration for most of the De Gustabus dishes. The "normal" club members forgave him his culinary idiosyncrasies because he was such a marvelous chef.

Tonight, when Bram entered, he found only one man present. Lyle Boerichter was an airline pilot for Sunrise Airlines. He was husky, maybe five-nine, with thinning red hair and a florid, bulldog face. The lights in the room were turned low. At the end of the long table was a picture frame with black crepe paper draped around it. Bram squinted to get a better look. It was a picture of Bob Fabian.

Lyle sat with a bottle of rye whiskey in front of him. His head rested on his hand, elbow on the table, and in the other hand, he held a shot glass. When he looked up and saw Bram standing in the doorway, he gave a faint smile. "Hey, Baldric. Sit down. Join me." He lifted his glass.

"You and Vince not having dinner tonight?" It was Monday, their regular night to dine together—if you could call it dining.

"Vince is in the kitchen making us some sashimi. It was Bob's favorite. We thought we'd eat, hoist a few rounds, wish him Godspeed on his heavenly journey, wherever the hell that is."

Bram pulled out a chair and sat down. "You're not a religious man?"

"Nope. Not after what I've seen in my life. I don't believe in heaven and I don't believe in hell—unless you call this life hell."

He seemed depressed. "I'm sorry about Bob. He was a great guy."

"The best," said Lyle, pouring himself another shot. "Now, Bobby, he believed in heaven. No doubt in his mind. He said Valerie was there just waiting for him to join her." Tipping his head, he tossed back the drink. "God love him, I hope he was right."

Vince burst into the room through the swinging kitchen door. He was carrying a small oriental platter. "Baldric, hi. You joining us tonight?"

Bram shrugged. He liked sashimi. Why the hell not. "Sure."

"Cool," said Vince, glancing at Lyle with an amused smile on his face. "You want a glass of wine? Beer?"

"I'm fine," said Bram. He glanced at his watch. "I'm here with my daughter. We've got dinner reservations in a few minutes."

"Well, then consider this your appetizer." Like Vince's, Lyle's smile grew amused.

Bram wondered what the hell was so funny. "What's the sauce?" he asked, hoping it wasn't pulverized pig genitals.

"Soy sauce," answered Vince. "Chopped chives and grated radish."

Vince was one of these lean, sinewy types who could eat anything and never gain a pound. Bram hated him on principle. But Vince was also totally bald, his head shaped like a hundred-watt bulb. Bram's hair, although starting to gray around the temples, was still thick and chocolate brown. Maybe that evened the score.

Vince grabbed a wine bottle off a small buffet table, pulled a corkscrew out of his pocket, and began to open it. "Did Lyle tell you we're putting together a reward?"

"Reward?" repeated Bram.

"For information leading the cops to Bob's murderer," said Lyle. "Unless I find him first. In that case, the bastard's history. His body will never be found."

Vince shot him a cautionary look. "We've already got close to twenty-five thousand dollars. You want to donate, just let Sheldon Larr know. He's keeping the kitty."

"Sure," said Bram. "Thanks for telling me."

"I guess we were the last two people to see old Bobby alive," said Lyle, his head sinking back down on his hand. "Except for the guy who gunned him down."

"You were?" said Bram.

"We had a kind of spur-of-the-moment meal here at the club," said Vince. "Nothing special. It was a hard night for Bob. It was the anniversary of Valerie's death. He didn't want to be alone, so he called Lyle and we arranged a dinner. If we'd just kept him here awhile longer, maybe—" Vince looked down at the bottle in his hand. He'd cut himself somehow. Blood oozed from a gash in his thumb.

"Shit," said Vince. He pulled a work cloth off his apron and pressed it against the cut.

"Any idea who did it?" asked Bram.

Lyle grunted. "Police asked me the same question."

"You talked to the police?"

"We both did," said Vince. "We were the last people to see him that night, so that automatically made us 'persons of interest.'"

"Jesus," snapped Lyle. "All that new government terminology. We've turned into a friggin' Fascist state, but nobody sees it. The St. Paul PD has been all over Vince and me. Like we would have shot Bob. *Us*. His best friends. I hate this government."

"You're ranting," said Vince.

"So what if I am? What did they ever do for me?"

"They taught you how to fly."

"Well, there is that, yeah."

"Here," said Vince, pushing the plate closer to Bram. "Try some."

Bram dipped a piece of the sashimi in the sauce and took a bite. "It's good. The fish is kind of chewy."

"That's because there's no fat in it," said Vince.

"What kind of fish is it?"

"Like we said, it was Bob's favorite," said Vince.

"But what *kind* is it?" Bram was getting a hinky feeling in the pit of his stomach.

"Japanese," said Lyle. "Actually, this one isn't precisely Japanese, but it's a hugely popular fish in Japan. A delicacy. In Tokyo alone, there are hundreds of restaurants that specialize in this dish—for those who can afford the price."

Vince nodded. "Did I ever tell you that in my late twenties, I was trained as a chef in a Japanese restaurant? Big honor. They thought I had real talent. I used to go to the Haedomari Market in Shimonoseki every morning, where most of the country's catch was sold. Boy, that was a trip."

"No, you never told me," said Bram, gazing warily at the plate. "You also haven't given me the name of the fish."

"It's called fungu," said Vince, pouring himself a glass of wine.

"Fungus?"

"No, *fungu*," said Lyle. "It's a type of blowfish."

"I thought blowfish were poisonous."

"Some are," said Lyle.

"But this one isn't."

"No," said Vince. "It's highly poisonous. That's part of the allure. In Japan, fungu is the ultimate edible. In the wrong chef's hands, this fish can kill you. It's all in how you carve it up. See, the toxin starts by blocking nerve impulses, and then it quickly shuts down the entire nervous system. Death usually follows shortly thereafter. Kind of a horrific death, too, when you think about it. Lots of dizziness, nausea, stomach pain, then comes the convulsions and on and on. Actually, you know you've been poisoned when you feel a little numbness in your lips and the tip of your tongue."

Bram was seized with dread. "How come you guys haven't eaten any?"

"We were waiting to see if you had any reaction," said Vince, casually sipping his wine.

Bram swallowed hard, then stared at them.

"We're being cautious," said Lyle.

"Feel any tingling?" asked Vince.

"You guys are nuts!" said Bram.

"Millions of people eat this every year and never have a problem," said Vince, scratching his bald head.

"Yup," said Lyle. "I've eaten it dozens of times."

"You have?" said Bram. Was that a tingle he felt in his upper lip?

"Sure. Here." Vince took a big bite. "You passed the test, Baldric."

Lyle lifted his shot glass. "You're one of us now, pal. We die together, or we die alone." He dropped one of the little rolls into his mouth. "We'll expect to see you every Monday."

"What's on the menu next week?" asked Bram.

"Well," said Vince, spreading a napkin in his lap, "we're starting out with crudité and a peppery meal-worm dip. And then the main course will be deep-fried field rat with rice pilaf and a hearty jellyfish salad. I think I might make some ground cricket sugar cookies if I get the time."

"Oh, I love those," said Lyle, stifling a burp.

Bram glanced at his watch. "I, ah—" He pushed away from the table and got up. "I'll have to think about it. I better go now. My daughter will be wondering what happened to me."

"Remember," said Lyle, smiling up at him. "No

reservations required. Come to think of it, that exactly sums up my philosophy of life. How about you, Vince?"

"Oh, yeah. Those are definitely words to live by."

11

Sophie closed the grill cover so she wouldn't have to look at the burnt salmon. "Nathan, you promised you'd never call me at home. We've already had this discussion."

"Just hear me out, okay?"

Sophie could tell he was smoking. He'd stopped years ago, but now that he was dating Elaine Veelund, one of Sophie's oldest friends, he'd started again. "And you can't just drop by the hotel. You know it upsets Bram, and when that happens, it upsets me."

"Then you'll be happy to hear the news. I wanted to tell you this afternoon, but when I bumped into Margie, she said you weren't around. I figured it was the kind of news you'd want to hear in person, but now I've got no choice. You need to hear it from me first."

"Hear what?" She sat down on the chaise and picked up Bram's half-finished glass of wine.

"I'm getting married."

For a moment, she was knocked off balance. "You're serious? To Elaine?"

"Are you happy for me?"

Sophie wanted to shout "No!" Elaine Veelund was the last person she wanted to see marry Nathan. Not that Sophie didn't think the world of her, but when it came to men, Elaine was a horror show. She ground men up and spat them out. She'd already been married four times. She'd started dating Nathan when she was on the rebound from her last divorce. Didn't he have a brain in his head? "Have you proposed to her?"

"Tonight. I've got the ring and I've even got the honeymoon all planned."

Sophie had no business meddling in his affairs. If she felt proprietary about him now, it was just because he was a friend. She'd warned him about Elaine, so what more could she do? "Well then, that's . . . wonderful."

"You really think so?"

"Sure. If it's what you want."

Silence. "You already know what I want, Sophie. But I'm never going to get it, right?"

"What is this? You're calling to give me one last chance to accept your proposal?"

"What if I said yes? That no matter how hard I try, I still can't get you out of my heart."

"Nathan, I love my husband. How many ways can I say it?"

"But you love me, too."

"Not the way you want. Not anymore."

More silence. "Okay. Then I guess I'll marry Elaine."

"You make it sound like you're standing at a candy counter, deciding which candy bar to buy. Have you really thought this through?"

"Of course."

"You don't have to marry anyone, you know."

"But I want to. I'm sick of being alone. I'm settled

here now. I have a great restaurant and I want to share my life with someone."

"And Elaine and I are interchangeable?"

"I didn't say that. I care about Elaine, but I'll never feel for her what I feel for you."

"You're aware of her track record with men."

His voice grew hard. "Your concern is touching, but I can take care of myself."

This was a guilt trip, pure and simple. But it was so obvious, it was pathetic. He was calling so that Sophie could save him from the clutches of an evil femme fatale. But the only way she could do that, the only way he would change his plans, was for her to choose him over her husband. In the past year, Sophie had thought long and hard about her feelings for both men. The conclusion she'd come to was clear and firm: Bram was the only man she wanted. Perhaps the only man she'd ever really loved. The feelings she had for Nathan were all wrapped up in teenage angst and adolescent melodrama. She couldn't even say she knew him—not as an adult.

Nathan's voice suddenly brightened. "Elaine said that your stepdaughter is a wedding planner. She just started a business."

Now Sophie grew wary. "That's right."

"I may contact her."

"Nathan, I'm not sure that's a good idea."

"Why not? Might as well give her the job. Keep it in the family, so to speak."

"Nathan—"

"I was also thinking that getting married at the Maxfield might be cool."

"You've got to be kidding."

"No? Well, I'll find someplace else, then. Listen,

Soph. I've got to get back to work. I'll call and let you know if Elaine accepts my proposal."

"Please, Nathan, don't call me here."

"Well, I'll catch you one way or another." He laughed. "Freudian slip. Bye, Sophie. Wish me well."

12

It was the eye of the storm. Anika was certain of it. Ever since Bob's funeral, her life had become unnaturally still. While events swirled furiously around her, nothing touched the silence that had become her world. In the last few weeks, Andy had retreated into a sullen shell. The distance she'd felt growing between them before Bob's death had seeped suddenly into every part of their relationship. For months, Anika had been thinking about asking Andy for a divorce. But asking him now would be like throwing a drowning man an anchor.

When Andy had proposed eight years ago, he'd insisted that he didn't want a traditional wedding. Specifically, when they said their vows, he wanted the words "for better or for worse, until death do us part" replaced with the phrase "as long as love is good." Perhaps he'd had a premonition. Anika didn't know. But what she did know was that their love had ceased to be good a long time ago.

She traced the disintegration to Andy's first week as associate editor at the *Minneapolis Times Register*. Bob had offered him the job out of kindness, out of the desire to help his brother through a rough patch, and probably as a way to get to know him. Andy had grown up in Ann Arbor, Michigan, and had attended Northern Michigan University in Marquette on a journalism scholarship. He'd received his degree in 1987. For the next few years, he'd worked as a reporter at various small-town papers across the country. He hated big cities, and working in small towns allowed him to become a big fish in a small pond. It provided him with a chance to really make a name for himself.

Andy craved success. But the first paper he worked for folded after only a few months, and the next was sold after he'd been there a little over two years. Andy lost his job to a relative of the new owner. The third job he took paid so little that he subsisted on Kraft macaroni and cheese and peanut butter sandwiches for the duration—just under a year. After his fourth job ended because the owner of the paper died suddenly and no one else in the small town had any interest in keeping it going, Andy moved back to Marquette. It was the spring of '94, and he was depressed, exhausted, and penniless.

One day, while having a cup of coffee at a shop on Milford Street near NMU, he'd run into an old buddy of his who was seriously considering a start-up publishing company. Rick Lostine had the money, but what he didn't have was a good editor—a partner, really. Rick was the same age as Andy, also from Ann Arbor. They'd been friends since grade school. Rick's enthusiasm was so contagious that Andy said he'd kill for a chance to be that editor. He explained that he was sick to death of newspapers where he had to do everything from editing and reporting to paying the light bill. He couldn't finance the plan, but he'd developed considerable editing skills over the past six years, and he promised he'd work not only gladly but tirelessly to make the idea a success. Thus, Lostine & Gladstone Publishers was born.

Anika met Andy for the first time that spring. He was so passionate about what he was doing, so upbeat, focused, and energized that Anika thought that's who he was. Andy Gladstone was a man on fire, a man who loved books as much as she did. Watching the publishing house take shape was almost as exciting as falling in love. Maybe it was all part of the same fabric. It was certainly hard to separate the two in her mind now.

Lostine & Gladstone started out slowly, publishing only two books that first year. But five years later, they were publishing twelve books a year, both fiction and nonfiction. As far as Anika could see, Rick and Andy had done everything right. They'd taken their time, learned through trial and error the best ways to approach various publishing problems. Andy had the capacity to throw himself into his work with total single-mindedness. And yet he always had time for Anika. Andy was a romantic. He loved to bring Anika little gifts, plan romantic trysts. He'd never been in love before, and Anika and the publishing house quickly became his whole world. He seemed to have endless energy, staying up late, getting up early. He never appeared to get tired those first few years.

After they were married, they bought a little house on Colby Avenue and settled down. Anika had a degree in hotel management and worked at one of the top hotels in Marquette as an assistant food and beverage manager. Everything was going wonderfully. They were even talking about having a baby. And then the roof fell in.

In the summer of '99, Rick acquired a book called *White Sails*. It was a memoir, one man's account of his eight months sailing the Great Lakes. The author, Whitby Armstrong Sellers, was a professor of English literature at Princeton, and a modern-day adventurer and raconteur. The book was brilliant—beautifully written and observed, hilarious and touching, full of suspense and good old-fashioned adventure. Everyone told Andy and Rick that this memoir would be huge. It would put Lostine & Gladstone on the map.

They published the book in September of 2000. The initial print run was a modest six thousand copies, but when it sold out almost immediately, Andy okayed another five thousand copies to be printed. As soon as the major book chains got wind of the memoir's growing popularity, orders came in from all over—in such huge numbers that Rick and Andy had to borrow money to print more books to meet the demand. This happened several times over a two-month period. Before they knew it, all their assets, both personal and professional, were in hock to *White Sails*. But Andy told Anika not to worry. The chains wouldn't order such large quantities if they couldn't sell them. These were smart businessmen. It would just take a little time.

Thanksgiving rolled around and people began their Christmas buying. Rick and Andy expected that *White*

Sails would sell like crazy, especially in the Midwest. Professor Sellers was supposed to be interviewed on NPR's "Fresh Air" in early November, but due to scheduling difficulties, the interview fell through. Not to worry, said Andy. The *New York Times* was reviewing the book. But somehow, that never happened either.

And then, in late February, booksellers began to return the books. It was just a trickle at first. The chains had obviously miscalculated and hadn't sold as many copies as they'd anticipated. But there was still time. The memoir had received a great review in *People* magazine in late January and that was surely a magic bullet if there ever was one. That one review alone would sell thousands of copies, just as soon as people went back to the stores—or so Rick and Andy thought. Book buyers were tapped out after Christmas, but in the spring, sales would pick up. And Professor Sellers had hired himself a publicist. He felt certain he'd get on a major morning network show soon.

But in the end, that fell through, too. By the end of March, the floodgates had opened as books poured back into Lostine & Gladstone, with very few orders going out. Of the 220,000 copies that were printed, only 40,000 sold. By May, most of the unsold copies were sitting in a warehouse gathering dust. The book that was supposed to be Lostine & Gladstone's breakout bestseller had bankrupted them. A bigger press might have been able to absorb the loss and go on, but for a small press, the major interest from the big chain bookstores had ultimately sunk the publisher.

The day their bankruptcy was officially finalized,

Andy came home and closed the door to his study. Anika knocked several times, wanting to comfort him, but each time Andy said he needed time alone. She could hear him crying, but by then, that wasn't new. He'd been crying a lot the last few months as he watched his dreams once again turn to ash.

Shortly after they moved out of their little house into an efficiency apartment, Andy got a call from Bob Fabian. Bob was twelve years older than his half sibling. They shared the same mother, but had different fathers. Andy was six when Bob had gone off to West Point. Their mother had died two years later, and Bob had never returned home again after that. He'd never gotten along with Andy's father, Merle Gladstone. From what Anika had been able to piece together, neither had Andy. Merle had come to their wedding, but he'd remarried shortly thereafter and hadn't invited any family or friends. His father had called it "eloping," but Andy said it was just a way for him to cut people out of his life. He always referred to his dad as "the old bastard"— that is, when he referred to him at all, which was seldom.

Andy never wanted to discuss his childhood. At first, Anika had pressed him about it, but she'd learned quickly that if she didn't want to spend the evening with a sullen, quietly furious fiancé, she should drop the matter—and fast. She'd looked through his family photograph album, and nothing looked amiss to her. The house, the Christmas dinners, the swing set in the backyard all looked pretty normal. There were far fewer pictures after Andy's mother had died. Apparently, Merle wasn't into photography. In Anika's family, her mother had always taken the pictures and videos at family events, so it didn't seem that odd to her. Still, she wished she knew more about Andy's childhood. It might help her make sense out of a man she found nearly inscrutable these days—a man she'd once loved deeply and perhaps still did, but someone who'd changed so much in the eight years that they'd been married that she hardly recognized him anymore. His sweetness, his desire to make her happy, his humor and his unassuming kindness had all vanished. In its place, she found she was living with a man of mercurial temperaments, one whose own internal darkness, something she'd never really comprehended before, had virtually swallowed him whole.

But the question remained. Should she ask him for a divorce, or should she wait? Maybe there was still hope for them, although in her heart, she knew the bright, happy man she'd married was not the same one she was living with now. Andy seemed haunted and frightened. Anika had no idea why that should be. For the first time since the publishing debacle, his life was back on track. More than on track. Overnight, they'd both become millionaires. And yet she'd recently seen not only fear register in his eyes, but panic. He no longer talked to her the way he once had, sharing his triumphs and tragedies, his ups and downs—*himself*. Especially during the last year, he'd grown secretive, short-tempered, self-centered. They were strangers living in the same apartment. Except Anika wasn't sure Andy saw it that way. He treated her, when he talked to her at all, as if everything were fine between them.

The phone rang just as Anika came into the kitchen. She picked it up and said hello, but received only silence in reply. She knew someone was on the other end because she could hear street noises in the background.

"Hello," she said again. "Who's calling, please?"

The line clicked.

As she placed the receiver back on the hook, she heard Andy's key in the front door. Their current apartment was much larger than the house they'd lived in when they were first married. Andy's salary was almost triple what it had been during his days at the publishing house. And since coming to Minnesota, Anika had found another job as assistant food and beverage manager, this time at the Maxfield Plaza in St. Paul. After Bob's death, she'd taken a leave of absence. She wouldn't return to work for another few days. She was going stir-crazy in the apartment by herself, but felt she should be available for Andy if he needed her.

He hadn't.

"Honey," called Andy from the living room. "I've got some great news."

In spite of herself, Anika kept hoping that Andy's gloomy distance might finally evaporate and in its place her old husband, the man she thought she'd married, would return. "I'm in the kitchen."

He walked in and set his briefcase down on the glass-topped table. "Come here."

"Why?"

"Just come here."

She moved cautiously toward him.

He folded her in his arms, kissing her hair, running

his hands up and down her back. "I love you, babe. Have I told you that lately?"

She could feel her body stiffen, but Andy didn't seem to notice. "Not really."

"Well, then I should be drawn and quartered."

"I've considered it."

He stood back, holding her by her shoulders. "It's been a hard year, honey. For both of us. But all that's going to change." He leaned back against the counter, his right hand jingling the change in his pocket. "I got a call this afternoon. You'll never guess who from."

Anika sat down at the kitchen table.

"Rick! He's been offered a job at Simon and Schuster in New York. He's got two weeks before he has to start, so he's flying out here to stay with us for a few days."

"That's great news," said Anika. And it was. They hadn't heard from Rick since he'd moved to New York six months ago. "What kind of job is it?"

"Publicist. He'll be working with their children's book line—or something like that. He can tell us more about it when he gets here."

"And when will that be?"

"End of the week." He glanced at the clock on the wall. "I talked to the movers this afternoon. They said they'd be here first thing in the morning."

"Movers?"

"Sure. You didn't think we were going to stay here, did you? We're millionaires now, babe. I want to be all settled into Bob's house before Rick arrives."

Anika was shocked. She'd never considered that Andy would want to move into Bob's place.

"Come on. Don't give me that look. There's no point staying here when we own that incredible piece of property."

The idea of living in a house where a man she'd loved had been shot to death repelled her to her very core. Surely that revulsion must be written all over her face. But Andy went on as if her agreement were a given.

"I feel like celebrating. I mean, I'm not trying to dance on Bob's grave or anything like that. What happened to him is horrible and it goes without saying that I'll do everything I can to help the police find the man who murdered him, but I'm sick of being down in the dumps. We've got a chance at a new life. A new beginning. I know I haven't been the best husband lately. Well, even longer than that. You were such an angel when I hurt my back last year. I probably never thanked you enough. And you're still my angel. Come on, sweetheart. What do you say? Should I call and make reservations at the Rookery?"

He knew the restaurant at the club was her favorite. Was he really holding out an olive branch, or was this just another one of his moods? Anika was so war weary, so battered and bruised by his ups and downs, she didn't even know how to judge it anymore. "Sure. I guess."

"Great!"

As he reached for the phone, his cell phone gave two quick trills. Retrieving it from the inner pocket of his suit coat, he flipped it open. "Gladstone." He paused. "Oh, hi." He turned his back to Anika. "What? No. I was in a meeting so I turned it off." He listened a moment more. "Now?" He lowered his head. "Yeah. My thinking exactly." He checked his watch. "Where?" Another pause. "Okay. Ten minutes."

Andy turned back to Anika, running a hand through his unruly dark hair. "It's still early. I've got something I need to take care of, but it won't take me long. Why don't you call and make reservations for eight thirty? Then put on something pretty. Something sexy." He grinned.

"Who was that on the phone?"

"Nobody important."

"Then why are you meeting with him?"

"Just some business. Nothing you need to worry about. Look, I'll be back in a flash, okay? I can tell you need some serious cheering up. I've got my work cut out for me tonight, but I'm up to it. By the end of the evening, we'll be laughing again, just like old times. You know what they say. Laughter's the best medicine."

As he breezed out of the kitchen and the front door shut behind him, Anika continued to sit at the kitchen table. If anything in the past few weeks had convinced her that her marriage was in desperate trouble, it was Andy's last comment. *Laughter is the best medicine?* Had he totally lost his mind? Did he really think their problems could be solved with a romantic dinner and a few good yuks?

Anika stared straight ahead as the silence in the apartment engulfed her. It was the eye of the storm, all right. Valerie's car accident, Bob's murder, Ken Loy's murder, their inheritance, all the millions of dollars flowing into their bank accounts, Andy's drift away from her into a private hell she couldn't begin to understand—it was all connected somehow. She wanted to believe that the swirling darkness all around her was just a metaphor. Nothing real, just words. But she knew better. When the storm finally swept over them, she wasn't sure who would be left standing.

13

The Minnehaha Creek zigzags its way across south Minneapolis from the western edge of the city, all the way east to the Mississippi River. The parkway is a piece of quiet beauty in the midst of a thriving metropolis, filled with bike and walking paths and quaint footbridges. The section that lies between Nicollet and Lyndale is sparsely traveled during the day, and even less so at night.

Andy parked his RAV4 in the shadows far from the streetlamp. He eased out of the front seat and looked over both shoulders as he opened the back hatch and took out a briefcase. The agreed-upon meeting spot, one they'd used many times before, was under the Nicollet Avenue Bridge. Andy had ferreted out the darkest, deepest hole in the city in which to meet with Irazarian. It was imperative that they not be seen, particularly tonight.

A gusty October wind blew off the creek, causing Andy to pull the collar of his suit coat up around his neck. To anyone watching, he probably looked like a character in a le Carré novel, a spy meeting his operative under the cover of night.

Irazarian was already there, waiting for him, pressed against the inside of one of the pillars. He was smoking a cigarette. Andy could see the glowing tip as he approached through the darkness.

"What took you so long?" Irazarian stepped away from the pillar, dropping the cigarette to the pavement and grinding it out with the heel of his shoe.

"I'm here now," said Andy.

"The money?"

Andy handed him the briefcase. "It's all there."

"It better be."

"I want you out of this city tonight." He reached into the inner pocket of his coat and pulled out an airplane ticket. "Your flight leaves at nine. I don't care where you go or what you do after you get to L.A.—just stay lost. You've got enough money there to start a new life wherever you choose. I never want to hear from you again, is that clear?"

Andy could smell Irazarian's acrid sweat. It made him want to gag.

"Don't you want the stuff? You could act a little grateful, you know. It took some doing."

"You want thanks?" Andy was incredulous. "After what you've done?"

"Hey, you're the editor."

"You nearly cost me everything!"

Irazarian dropped the briefcase and came at him, pinning him to the concrete pillar with the force of his body. He outweighed Andy by a good hundred pounds, had played defensive tackle for the Golden Gophers once upon a time. As far as Andy was concerned, he was an educated thug.

Pressing his forearm hard against Andy's throat, he whispered, "You're a weasel, Gladstone. You may think you're a big man now, but you're a loser. You'll always be a loser." His breath stank of booze and cigarettes.

Andy knew enough not to show weakness around a bully, even though Irazarian terrified him. If he told what he knew, Andy would go to jail for sure. His life would be ruined. He had a second chance now, and he wasn't about to blow it.

Irazarian pinned him a moment longer, then backed up. In the darkness, he looked like a refrigerator wearing a raincoat. He was huge. Andy's knees felt wobbly. He had a gun in his pocket, but he'd only brought it in case of an emergency. He didn't want to threaten Irazarian. Instinctively, he knew that would be a mistake.

"Look," said Andy, "take the money. Go make yourself a life somewhere else."

"I'm a writer, a reporter. That's what I *do*."

"It's what you did," said Andy. "You could be prosecuted for fraud if you stay here. There are people at the paper who want your blood. I'm trying to protect you from them."

Irazarian laughed. "*You're* protecting *me*?"

Even a few inches away, it was so dark that Andy could barely make out Irazarian's face. And yet he could feel the man's sneer as if it gave off waves.

"We need each other, asshole," said Irazarian. "Don't forget it." He handed Andy a package and Andy handed him the ticket.

"Just leave," said Andy. "And don't ever come back." He waited for Irazarian to go, but instead of returning to his car, he just stood there.

Andy didn't know what to do, so he took off running. When he was a good hundred feet away, he glanced over his shoulder and saw that Irazarian had walked across the street and was standing directly under a streetlamp.

Andy got in the SUV and started the motor. His hands shook so hard, he could barely get the key in the ignition. He told himself to breathe, that it was almost over. When he tore past the streetlamp, Irazarian reached up and pantomimed tipping his hat. But it was the smile and the spooky intensity in his eyes that caused something bitter and abandoned to rise up in Andy's throat. As he was driving away, that old bitterness nearly choked him.

14

Early the next morning, Sophie pulled back the blankets and swung her feet out of bed.

"What time is it?" mumbled Bram.

"It's early," said Sophie. "Just after six."

"Why are you getting up? Did the alarm go off?"

"I can't sleep. I thought maybe I'd putter in my office for a while."

Bram flipped over on his side, tucking the covers up under his chin. "Don't putter at anything I wouldn't putter at."

She smiled. "I won't." She stroked his hair for a moment. "You go back to sleep."

"I couldn't possibly. I'm wide awake." A few seconds later, he started to snore.

After showering and dressing, Sophie took Ethel out for her morning ablutions. Ethel, their old black mutt, never wanted to walk very far. She was the hotel mascot now, and she took her job seriously. If she wasn't on her large paisley pillow in the Maxfield's first-floor lounge by eight A.M., she descended into a funk. Of course, it was hard to tell if Ethel was in a funk because her normal demeanor wasn't all that lively. Still, having lived with Ethel for so many years, Sophie could read her eye twitches.

After getting Ethel settled on her throne, Sophie headed for her office. As she rounded the bend in the corridor, she spotted her father at the other end of the hallway. He was down on his hands and knees.

Sophie felt her blood pressure rise. "Dad," she called softly, "what are you doing?"

He looked up and waved.

Sophie could see now that he had a portable tool chest next to him.

"This piece of carpeting was coming loose," he said. He searched through the chest until he found what he was looking for. A hammer. Placing it on the floor, he continued his search.

"You can't repair that now. You'll wake the guests."

"One tack," said her dad. "That's all it will take. Two at the most."

"Dad?"

"Then you can join me for breakfast—after I replace a lightbulb on nine."

"Dad, we have a full maintenance staff."

"So? You think I'm too old to swing a hammer?"

"No, of course not, but—"

"I had to get out of the apartment, Soph. Your mother is driving me batty. She thinks she's Agatha Christie."

"Excuse me?"

"She's up at the crack of dawn every morning to read the newspapers. She's been following that Bob Fabian–Kenneth Loy murder case. She has this crazy theory, and I'm sick of hearing about it."

"What's the theory?"

"Oh, no," he said, holding up a box of carpet tacks as if he'd found the Holy Grail. "You wanna hear about that, go talk to Miss Marple."

He'd piqued her curiosity. "Actually, I've been following it myself."

"Go," he said. He reached into his shirt pocket and took out a cigar.

"You can't light that in here."

"I know, Officer. I just chew on it for moral support. Makes me feel purposeful and manly, like I'm Winston Churchill."

Just think, thought Sophie as she walked away. Her mother was one of the most famous women writers of all time, and her father was the Prime Minister of England. She hated to think what that made her. Napoléon, no doubt.

Sophie joined her mother in her parents' bedroom. She sat in a bright yellow chintz-covered armchair while her mother made the bed.

"I'm surprised your father mentioned my theory," said her mother, fluffing a pillow before she spread the chenille bedspread over it. "Tell me the truth. Did he call it Pearl's 'crackpot' theory? I know he did."

"Well—"

"Don't bother putting a pretty spin on it. He thinks I've lost my mind."

"Why?"

"Because I don't believe Bob Fabian is dead."

Sophie's mouth dropped open. "You what?"

"See, you think I'm crazy, too."

"No, I . . . well—"

"It's okay."

"But you were at the funeral."

"So? I was at the wake, too. And if memory serves, there was no open casket. Who's to say he was in there? Can you prove it? I can't."

"But Mother, he was shot in his home—by the same person who shot Kenneth Loy. He was taken to the emergency room, where he died. That's all been verified by the police."

Her mom opened the closet and began sorting through her father's suit coats. "You're correct up until the point where they say he died. None of the police reports said the bullet killed him. The reporters merely inferred that."

"Of course it killed him."

"Then why haven't the police ever stated that?"

Sophie couldn't believe what she was hearing. Her mother had to be wrong.

"You want to look at the newspapers? I've saved all the clippings. I thought it was strange right from the start. That officer what's his name—Lundquist—he hedged every time the questions turned to Fabian's death. He just kept saying no comment, that it was all under investigation. If Fabian died from that supposed gunshot wound, why wouldn't he just admit it?"

"I don't know."

"Because Bob Fabian isn't dead, that's why."

"Then where is he?"

"I'm still working on that part." Her mom found a chewed-up cigar in one of her father's vest pockets. She held it by the tip, as if it were made of plutonium, and dropped it into a small wastebasket next to the dresser. "Filthy thing."

"I guess maybe I'd like to look at those clippings."

"Sure," said her mother. "You'll see. I'm not wrong."

Sophie followed her out to the living room.

"Here," said Pearl, lifting a manila folder off the coffee table. "You look, read for yourself, see if your old mother isn't smarter than the average bear."

Sophie took the folder, smiling weakly.

"And then you come back and we'll figure out where Bob Fabian is. Every good sleuth needs a side-kick. You can be my Dr. Watson."

"Gee," said Sophie.

"Yeah, it's cool. We'll show your father, Mr. Doubting Thomas, what's what."

Several hours later, Sophie was sitting at her own breakfast table reading through the clippings when Bram finally emerged from the bedroom. He looked sleepy, his chocolate-colored hair rumpled as he sat down at the table, tying his midnight blue silk robe snugly over his pajamas.

Ducking his head sheepishly, he said, "I'm sorry about last night. I acted like a jerk."

Sophie had gone to bed around eleven. Bram didn't get in until much later, so they hadn't talked yet about Nathan's call, or his unexpected appearance yesterday at the hotel.

"I'm not involved with Nathan Buckridge in any way," said Sophie. "I don't know how I can be more clear than that."

Bram rubbed the sleep out of his eyes. "I believe you. But why can't he just fade away? Every time I start to think he's gone from your life, he pops back up."

"He's getting married, honey. To Elaine Veelund."

That snapped him to attention. "That's why he called?"

"He wanted to tell me in person, but when I wasn't around yesterday, he decided to phone. That's all, Bram. I can't make him disappear off the face of the earth, but I don't love him. I care about him, but that's it. I'll admit, when he first came back into my life, after not seeing him for so many years, there were unresolved feelings. But I've worked through all that. You're the only man I want in my life."

Bram grinned. "Music to my ears."

"So, can we be done with Nathan now? No more jealousy?"

Bram crossed his chest and held up his hand. "Promise."

"Good. Now, you can help me figure this out." She pushed the manila folder across to him. Next, she pushed the morning paper. "Just like your buddy Al Lundquist told you, there's an article this morning that talks about that 911 tape."

Bram glanced down at the *Times Register*, scanning the front page. "Boy, if that doesn't narrow the suspects, I don't know what would. Sounds to me like Bob's murderer was either Andy or Phil Banks." He opened the folder. "What's all this?"

"It's every article Mother could find about Ken Loy's and Bob Fabian's murders. Except, get this. She thinks Bob is still alive."

Bram looked up, stared at her a moment, then burst into laughter. "You've gotta give Pearl credit. She's not afraid to take the road less traveled. But this time, I think she's stumbled off a cliff."

"I thought so, too, but then I read all the clippings."

"Sophie, get real. We saw him buried."

"I used the same argument, but Mother contends that none of the official reports actually say that Bob died from that gunshot wound."

Bram sat back, shaking his head. "She's got to be wrong."

"She's not. Look at the folder."

"But I talked to Al myself. Yesterday. He said it was complicated, but he never said Fabian was alive. No, Sophie, your mother can't be right. He was shot, taken to the emergency room, and he died."

"Well, if he's dead, then why all this hedging whenever the subject of the gunshot comes up? Read it for yourself."

Sophie could see the wheels turning inside Bram's mind. She was hoping he'd have some information to counter her mother's claim. "What did Al say to you? Specifically."

He thought another few seconds. "Come to think of it, he was a little evasive. Hell, he wasn't just a little evasive, he was a whole lot evasive. But I never got the sense that Fabian was still among the living."

"Then what's going on?"

"No idea. Al did say it was the most convoluted case he'd ever worked on. I asked him why. I mean, it seems pretty straightforward. One gun, two dead bodies, one killer."

"What did Al say when you said that?"

"He said, and I quote, 'I wish.'"

Sophie sat for a few moments, staring into her coffee cup. "Well, if Bob is alive, all I can say is, somebody better tell Andy."

Bram was about to get up, when there was a knock on the front door. "I'll get it."

A few seconds later, Sophie could hear Margie's voice as she greeted her dad.

"Look who's here," said Bram, returning to the table. "Want some coffee, honey?"

Margie shook her head. She was all decked out today in leather. Black leather pants. Leather jacket. Not biker leather, but designer leather. She looked great. She had the same brown hair and green eyes as her father, but on Margie, the features were arranged to create a much different effect. Which was good. Not many young women were dying to look like an aging Cary Grant.

"What's up?" asked Sophie. She could tell Margie was bursting to tell them something. Sophie dreaded the revelation. In Sophie's opinion, Margie rarely brought good news.

"This is *so totally* cool," she said, dropping down into a chair.

"What is?" said Bram, returning with a mug.

"I just got a call. It's another wedding for Carrie and me to plan."

"That's wonderful," said Bram, giving her a kiss. "Bravo."

"And guess whose wedding."

Sophie knew what was coming. She braced herself. There was only one thing that could put that kind of gleam in Margie's eye—the chance to stick it to Sophie

"Who?" asked Bram.

"Nathan Buckridge. He wants me to handle all the details. And this will be another big one. Expensive. He wants the best of everything."

Sophie studied Bram's face. She could tell his emotions were at war. He was happy Nathan was getting married, but not pleased that he'd pulled Margie into it. Then again, it was a wonderful opportunity for his daughter, but if it meant that Nathan's presence would touch their lives in any way, was it worth it? Sophie could see that the answer was no. But Bram wouldn't let Margie see that. "That's fabulous," he said. "Wow. Really . . . amazing."

"We're meeting with him and Elaine later today at the hotel."

"This hotel?" said Bram.

"It's easier for Elaine," said Margie. "She's planning to be in town this afternoon, and didn't want to drive all the way out to Stillwater."

"Where are they going to be married?" asked Sophie.

"Not sure," said Margie, tapping her fingernails on the table. She'd come to drop her bomb and now she'd dropped it. But she wasn't satisfied. She'd been hoping for a bigger, more negative reaction.

Life was full of disappointments, thought Sophie. She was warmed to think she'd provided Margie with one.

"Look at the time," said Bram, checking his watch. "I've got to be over to the Rookery by ten. There's a board meeting this morning."

Bram had served on the board of directors for the past year.

"I'll walk you over," said Margie. "That way, I can tell you more about Nathan's ideas for his wedding. They're *totally* spectacular."

Surely Margie knew that even the mention of Nathan's name made her father suffer. And why didn't

Bram put a stop to it? Didn't he see how manipulative she was?

"Sure," said Bram. "Give me ten minutes and I'll be ready."

Ten minutes, thought Sophie. What *would* she and Margie talk about for ten whole minutes?

15

Chris carried a breakfast tray into the bedroom and set it on the bed, then crawled back in, snuggling down next to Phil. He'd fallen asleep while she was in the kitchen making them scrambled eggs, bacon, and toast, but as soon as she touched him, he woke and turned around to encircle her with his arms.

"Good morning, Mr. Banks," said Chris, happier than she'd ever been in her life. And it was all Phil's doing.

Yesterday had been a whirlwind. Right after the detective left, Phil had gone out, saying he had some business to take care of and would be back in a couple of hours. But he hadn't returned until nearly four. Chris called her mother and talked to her for a while. Her mom never failed to remind Chris that she'd made a big mistake, moving into Phil's house so fast. Chris told her it was *her* life, and that she trusted Phil. She loved him and he loved her. That's what mattered. Chris could still hear her mother's words. "But he's old enough to be your father, honey. And he's been married twice before. You'll never get what you really want from a man like that."

Chris lied, said that marriage wasn't important to her. So what if Phil wasn't interested in marriage anymore? Was that so odd? He'd been burned twice. He took the blame for both of his failed relationships, said his wives were good women, it just didn't work out. But Chris knew the truth. Both his ex-wives were terrible people, selfish and slutty women who didn't deserve a man like Phil. She knew because, every now and then, he'd let something slip about one of them. She tried to make her mother understand. Phil had been unlucky in love—until now.

Her mother always countered with the same old warning: if a man has been that unlucky in love, there has to be a reason, and it can't always be the other person's fault.

But Chris knew that's exactly what it was. Phil was simply too good for his first two wives. They took advantage of him, took him for granted. They used him and then kicked him out, hoping to get big fat settlements. But Phil had outsmarted them. That's why they were so mad, even now, after many years of being apart. He said that sometimes his two ex-wives scared him. They both had a violent streak. How could they be so blind? thought Chris. Phil was handsome, smart, funny, charming beyond belief, and he was incredibly sensitive. He cried sometimes after they made love. He said he was so grateful he'd found her. He'd almost given up hope of ever finding any lasting happiness in life.

When he finally returned home yesterday afternoon, he sat Chris on the couch. Again, he told her he loved her and that he couldn't imagine a life without her. And to prove it to her, he handed her a huge diamond engagement ring. And then he asked her to marry him.

Chris wanted to shout for joy, to call her mother

and tell her she was *wrong wrong wrong*. Her mind went into overdrive, imagining the wedding they would have, all the guests they would invite.

But Phil said no. They needed to be married right away. Now that he'd realized how pigheaded he'd been, he wanted to rectify the situation. He needed her to be his wife, no prenups, no lawyers, just the two of them and a judge—a friend of his. He told her to go upstairs, put on her prettiest dress, and get ready to become Mrs. Phil Banks.

Chris was disappointed. She tried hard to hide it, to act like this was what she wanted, too. She'd always dreamed of a wedding at the St. Paul Cathedral, with her brother there to give her away, maybe her uncle Vincent as one of the groomsmen. She imagined her husband-to-be in a handsome morning coat, lifting her veil after they'd said their "I dos" and kissing her with such passion that it made all the women in the church wish they were her. The sanctuary would be filled with flowers, and then afterward, they'd have a big wedding dinner, gorgeous catered food that she and her mother would agonize over for months. Maybe there would even be a rock band, or better yet, a country-western one, something fun for entertainment and dancing. And finally, the wedding night. It would all be so incredible.

In the end, they were married in the living room of Judge Warren Wilson's home. He was a high school buddy of Phil's and lived in Edina. It was a nice enough house, but not exactly a cathedral. His wife had played several classical pieces on the piano, and Phil slipped a simple gold band on her left hand before he kissed her. She'd been right about the passion in his kiss. But instead of a fancy hotel, they went home and made love. Phil had covered their bed with red rose petals. He was trying to please her. He simply wasn't the kind of man who liked everything planned out. She would just have to get used to it. On the way home, he'd bought a bottle of French champagne to celebrate with, and while they were drinking it, they'd ordered a pizza. All in all, her wedding had been crazy and silly, even a little tacky at times, but also meaningful and loving, something she'd remember until her dying day.

"Good morning to you, *Mrs.* Banks," said Phil, pulling the breakfast tray closer to him. "What should we do today?" He picked up a slice of toast, gave her the first bite, then finished it. "I know I didn't say anything about a honeymoon. That's because I'm not sure when I can get away. Actually, I should probably go in to work this morning and look at my schedule. Then we can talk about it. Hey, we could rent a yacht and sail the Caribbean. Have you ever been on a yacht?"

She shook her head.

"Think you'd like it?"

"Sure!"

"Or," he said, kissing the side of her neck, "we could fly to Paris for a few days, then head south and spend some time on the Riviera."

Her eyes were filled with stars. She never thought she'd ever have enough money to do anything like that.

"Well, we'll talk about it later, okay?"

She laid her head on his chest and closed her eyes. "Say it again."

"What?"

"*Mrs.* Banks."

He tipped her chin up and kissed her softly. "I adore you, *Mrs*. Banks. Get used to it. You're going to hear that a lot from now on."

The moment Phil left, Chris was on the phone to her mother. But her mother wasn't home. This wasn't the kind of news you left on an answering machine, so she decided to call back later. Or maybe she'd stop by her mom's apartment, tell her in person. And if she did that, she could show off her new rings.

Chris was still sitting with the phone in her hand when it rang. Thinking it might be Phil, she answered it without checking the caller ID.

"Hello?"

"Phil Banks, please." It was a male voice. One she didn't recognize.

"He's not here. But I'm his wife. Can I take a message?"

"His wife, huh? What's your name?"

"Chris."

"So tell me, Christine—it *is* Christine, isn't it?"

"Yeah, but I prefer Chris."

"What's Phil's cell phone number?"

She didn't like the man's tone. Phil had told her more than once never to give strangers information about him. "He's out. That's all I can say."

"Out where? Is he at work? I tried over there a few minutes ago and he wasn't in."

"Who's calling?"

"When will he be back?"

"I don't know."

"You're his wife and you don't know when he'll be back?"

Now she was getting angry. "Look, if you'd like to leave a message—"

"Okay, okay. Don't get all hot and bothered. Just tell your husband *Del* called. Oh, and while you're at it, tell him I know what he's got stored on Old Mill Road. That should get his attention. If he doesn't want other people to find out, he better be home the next time I call."

"What's on Old Mill Road?"

"Gee, Christine. I don't know. I can't say. I have temporary amnesia, just like you."

"What do you want?"

"Actually, to give you a small warning. Be careful, Christine. Your husband's not a nice man. In fact, he's a very very *bad* man."

"What do you mean?"

But it was too late. He'd already hung up.

16

Sophie spent the next couple of hours in her office at the Maxfield. The work stacked up on her desk was enough to keep her busy for the next year, but Rudy phoned around ten and said that Andy had called a full staff meeting for all newspaper employees at eleven. He figured it was something Sophie might not want to miss.

He was right. She quickly returned to her apartment, changed into her power clothes—fitted black skirt and blazer, and three-inch heels, the shoes that helped her feel less like a shrimpy twelve-year-old and more like a mature woman. She retouched her makeup, fluffed her short strawberry blond hair and put in her gold hoop earrings. After spritzing herself with her favorite perfume, she was ready to deal with anything the day could throw at her.

The drive to Minneapolis took just over ten minutes. After parking her Lexus in the lot across from the Times Register Tower and entering through the glass front doors, Sophie was surprised to find Nathan sitting in one of the chairs directly across from the elevators.

"What are you doing here?" she asked, backing up as he stood and walked toward her.

"Sophie, we've got to talk. You have to let me apologize about yesterday." He seemed truly distraught.

He was wearing a chef's coat and jeans. He looked tall and rough, just as he always did. And he'd recently regrown his beard. "Did you drive all the way here from your restaurant?"

"I had to. I couldn't stop thinking about last night, that I made an ass of myself when we spoke."

"Did you ask Elaine to marry you?"

"Yeah." He didn't look happy.

"Did she say yes?"

He nodded. "Do you forgive me?"

"Nathan, forget about me. I'm not mad at you. Enjoy your engagement to Elaine. That's what you should be concentrating on now."

"You're right. I know you're right."

"I just wish you hadn't involved Bram's daughter in your wedding plans."

"Do you?"

"I thought I made that clear."

"But she's a wedding planner, Sophie. Why not use her?"

"Because she's Bram's daughter. Don't you get it? We need to separate our lives, not interweave them. There are tons of good wedding planners out there."

"Yeah, but I thought . . . I mean, since you and Elaine are good friends, and since her mother is gone now, I thought you'd want to help her with some of the planning. And if I hired Margie, it would only make it that much easier all the way around."

Where did he get these ideas? "Nathan, you've got to listen to me." She pulled him aside, away from the elevators. "Are you listening now? Really listening?"

"Don't treat me like a four-year-old."

He could be so exasperating sometimes. She might have found it endearing once, but she didn't anymore. "I love my husband, and it upsets him when my old boyfriend seems to be continually hovering around me. That's why we have to put a stop to it. We can't see each other, not even casually. I won't be eating at your restaurant again. And you can't stop by the Maxfield anymore, okay? Do you understand? You can't call. We have to live separate lives."

Grudgingly, he nodded.

Watching him, she had a chilling sense that this was all for show, that he was marrying Elaine not out of love, not with the intent to end his relationship with Sophie, but as a way to keep it going. Elaine was just a means to that end. "Do you really want to marry Elaine?"

"Sure."

"Nathan? Look at me."

He didn't seem to want to look her in the eye.

"What?" he mumbled.

"Why do you want to marry Elaine?"

"I care about her. She's a wonderful woman."

"Really?"

"You think I'm lying?"

Sophie wasn't sure anymore. "Are we clear on this? On our living separate lives?"

"You want me to fire Margie?"

"No." She sighed. "That would only cause more problems. But I won't be helping Elaine with your wedding. I wish you two only happiness, Nathan. You know that."

"Yeah, I do. You're the greatest person I've ever known. And don't worry. I'll make sure you and

Bram get a wedding invitation. Maybe you two would like to sit at the head table with us."

For some reason, he wasn't tracking. He just didn't seem to get it. But standing here arguing with him wasn't doing any good. Sophie glanced at her watch. It was already after eleven. If she didn't get up to the auditorium on the fourth floor, she'd miss the meeting. "Nathan, I need to get upstairs."

"But . . . I was hoping you'd have time for a cup of coffee."

He hadn't heard a word she'd said.

"Don't look at me like that, Sophie. I understand. I was just hoping we could have a civil conversation. Just one last time."

"I've got a meeting."

"Okay. I suppose I should get back to the restaurant. I shouldn't have left, but I had to see you." He bent his head close to hers.

She backed up, but before she realized what was happening, he'd kissed her square on the lips.

"Nathan!"

"I'm a cad. What can I say?" He grinned and then took off out the glass front doors.

By the time Sophie reached the auditorium, it was standing room only. She pushed into the back and leaned her shoulder against the wall. With her diminutive height, there was no hope of being able to see over the tall shoulders in front of her, so she closed her eyes and listened. Andy was talking.

"Public speaking isn't one of my strong points, so I'm going to make this short and to the point. I know that a number of you have been worried about staff changes. I'll address that first. I don't plan to make any changes right now in the daily running of the paper, and that includes the staff. The *Minneapolis Times Register* is one of the finest daily papers in the country, and with your help, I hope to make sure it remains that way. I subscribe to the simple notion, If it ain't broke, don't fix it. I know that may be a little folksy for some of you, and I suppose I could find a more sophisticated way to phrase it, but that's the bottom line.

"As for Del Irazarian, I accepted his resignation yesterday afternoon. He is no longer employed by this paper, and I hope to God that no other newspaper in this country will ever employ him again. As you all know, we printed a series of retractions this morning concerning two of his series, as well as apologies. I was Del's editor when the stories were published. For the record, let me just say that although I've always discouraged the use of anonymous sources, sometimes it's the only way to get the story. In Mr. Irazarian's case, it was a judgment call. I believe my failure was in trusting a man I felt was not only scrupulously honest, but brilliant. The matter has been turned over to our legal department. Let me assure you, and I underscore this, that the only one who will take a bullet for this debacle is Mr. Irazarian himself. I'd like to tell you this will never happen again, but I suspect that, in the long run, newspapers are and will always remain at the mercy of clever liars."

From the rear of the audience, a man's voice shouted, "What about the rumor that federal prosecutors are considering filing criminal charges against Irazarian?"

Andy waited until the murmurs quieted down before answering. "To my knowledge, that hasn't happened, nor do I expect that it will."

A woman's voice rose, this time from the front of the crowd. "The *New York Times* appointed several ombudsmen to handle the fallout from the Jayson Blair scandal. Will you do the same?"

Andy quickly responded, "I've spoken with Dean Peterson. You all know and respect him. For a trial period of six months, he will serve as our new standards editor, a sort of internal ethics czar. As the new publisher, I plan to work closely with him in an effort to make sure this kind of scandal never happens again on my watch. I also plan to appoint a twelve-person committee to look into the atmosphere and attitudes in our newsroom. I realize that what Mr. Irazarian did to the paper will have some far-reaching effects. It's a shock to our system, to our morale, and to our reputation. But it also presents us with an opportunity to change old ways of doing business that no longer work. Mr. Peterson's door will always be open to you, as will mine. I intend to be a very hands-on publisher."

Sophie wondered if this comment was a veiled slam at Bob Fabian's management style, one that tended to spread out authority, not keep all power at the top.

"I realize that we may have some flawed structures and processes at the *Times Register*. Since I came to the paper two years ago, I've often heard people talk about editors' failure to communicate. I've also been told that staffers have felt intimidated, afraid to speak out. That's something I want to change."

The crowd broke into cheers and applause.

"We have an amazing amount of talent at this paper, and I want to use it, not stifle it."

More applause.

After a few parting comments, it was over. Sophie backed out of the doorway and stood to the side as people walked out. Everyone seemed pleased that Andy had come to them directly to discuss what had happened. In all Sophie's years at the paper, she'd never known Bob Fabian to call a meeting like this. Then again, he'd never been faced with this kind of scandal. Still, in Sophie's opinion, Andy had ignored some serious issues. He'd mentioned that Del Irazarian had used anonymous sources, but he never talked about the nonexistent studies Del had cited again and again—studies that, if Andy had taken the time to verify them, would have landed the articles in the trash. A big question mark still floated above Andy's head. Why had he let it happen? He certainly knew better. As owner of the paper, he would try to sweep his part in it under the rug now, but the taste would still remain. In many ways, Andy was as culpable as Irazarian, and everyone knew it. But he'd just been handed the keys to the kingdom. All power resided in him, so nobody would challenge him outright. The grumbling and anger would move underground.

Sophie looked for Rudy, but when she couldn't find him, she assumed he'd ducked out one of the side doors. She'd catch him later.

On her way back to her car, Sophie pushed out through the front doors just as Andy was about to get into a waiting limo.

"Sophie, hi," he said, reaching for her hand and giving it a squeeze. "What did you think?"

He'd put her on the spot. Just as everyone else probably had, she told him what he wanted to hear.

"It was a good speech." It wasn't a lie, just not the entire story.

He nodded. "Thanks. Hey, since you're here, I should thank you for being understanding about Anika taking time off from her job at the Maxfield."

"Not a problem."

"Our lives have changed so much so fast. Actually, I'm not sure Anika will return. There's no reason now. We have more money than we'll ever need. Who would have thought, huh?"

"Life never runs in a straight line."

"No." His expression darkened. "If you read the St. Paul paper this morning, you'd probably find yourself wondering if I was the one who shot my brother."

"I read the story," said Sophie.

"But that 911 tape doesn't prove anything. Not really."

"No."

"I would never have hurt my brother. I respected and loved him probably more than anyone I've ever known."

"Did the police talk to you?"

"Yeah, the day after it happened. I was a basket case. But thankfully, Anika and I were together the night Bob died, so I had an alibi. It disgusts me to even think I needed one."

Sophie's ears pricked up. "You and Anika were together that entire night?" She knew it was a lie.

"Yup. Just think, I could have been out driving around with no alibi at all, and then where would I be?"

"Where indeed," said Sophie.

"Well, sorry to run off, but I've got a meeting down in Hastings. I don't want to be late."

"Give my love to Anika."

"I will. And thanks again, Sophie. You're a good friend."

17

Bram stepped inside the Wackenhut room at the Rookery Club and looked around the empty bar. Backing out immediately, he nearly bumped into Sheldon Larr. Sheldon had just emerged from the kitchen carrying an extra-large vase of fresh-cut flowers for the table in the front foyer.

"I thought there was a board meeting this morning," said Bram, tucking a lily he'd inadvertently knocked sideways back into the mix.

"It's tomorrow," said Sheldon, limping his way toward the front table.

"Tomorrow," repeated Bram. How had he gotten that wrong? "Must have been a senior moment," he called to Sheldon's retreating back. Now what was he going to do? He had several hours before he had to be to the station and no particular plans. He stood for a few seconds and watched Sheldon set the vase in the center of the round, polished mahogany table, then adjust the bouquet, making sure every individual strand was perfect. Bram was so used to seeing Sheldon in his evening tux that it was strange to find him in a normal business suit and tie. Bram imagined that even with jeans and a T-shirt on, standing in a ditch digging a trench, Sheldon would look both immaculate and formal. He had a classic touch with clothes. This morning, he wore a pink rose in his lapel that exactly matched the color of his tie.

Looking up and seeing that Bram was watching him, Sheldon limped back toward the bar. "I understand your daughter is a wedding planner."

"That's right," said Bram, wondering how Sheldon had heard about it. Perhaps he'd talked to Margie last night. "It's just getting off the ground, but knowing my daughter, she'll make a success of it."

"She's stopping by this afternoon."

"She is?"

"One of our newest members, Nathan Buckridge, is getting married soon and he's reserved the Rookery for the event. Sometime in December I believe." He stroked his thin mustache.

Bram'd had no idea Nathan had become a member.

"Your daughter is coming by with Mr. Buckridge and his fiancée to look at the facilities."

Nathan was like a sticky piece of gum Bram just couldn't scrape off the sole of his shoe. He was sick to death of hearing his name, but he also knew he needed to resign himself to the fact that his daughter was about to plan the man's wedding. Things could be worse—he could still be chasing Sophie.

"Would you like a table?" asked Sheldon. "Breakfast is served until eleven thirty."

"No thanks," said Bram. He was hungry, but he usually liked to eat an early lunch. He wished Sheldon a good day and drifted back to the De Gustabus room. Glancing up at the sign above the door, he laughed to himself, thinking what a crazy bunch of guys Vince, Lyle, and Bob Fabian had been. *No reser-*

vations required. It was a play on words, one that appealed to Bram's own eccentric sense of humor.

Vince was sitting at the table going over some papers when Bram entered.

"Baldric. How's the digestion?"

Bram grimaced. "After you guys tried to poison me last night, I guess the best thing I can say is, I'm still alive."

"Would I feed you something that could kill you?"

"I don't know. You tell me."

"Hey, speaking of culinary adventure, I've got some roasting camel eyeballs in the oven. Lyle's coming back tonight for dinner and I'm planning to serve them cold—as an appetizer on toast points. Want to taste one?"

The idea of gagging down a camel eyeball nearly sent Bram over the edge.

"You're looking a little green this morning, Baldric."

"I was fine before I came in here."

Vince smirked. "Have a seat. There's fresh coffee in the carafe."

"Just *plain* coffee?"

"Yeah, Baldric. Just the regular stuff." He nodded to a sideboard. "Help yourself."

Bram poured himself a cup before he sat down. "I thought the board was meeting this morning."

"Nope," said Vince, signing his name at the bottom of one of the papers. "Tomorrow."

Bram's gaze wandered to the photo of Bob Fabian still sitting at the end of the table, draped in black crepe paper. "You know," said Bram, taking a sip of coffee, "this may seem totally crazy, but my mother-in-law thinks Bob's still alive."

Vince looked up, his expression startled.

"I know, I know. There's no way that could be. But she's been following the story in the papers. Seems the police never actually said the bullet Bob took killed him. I mean, it doesn't make any sense. They've got this 911 tape of the phone call Bob made the night he died, the one reporting the shot taken at Ken Loy. I suppose it's possible the gunshot they heard on the tape never actually hit Bob. But he was taken to the emergency room. Why do that if he wasn't injured? Makes no sense."

Vince just shook his head.

"Who set up the funeral?"

"Andy Gladstone. Lyle and I were pallbearers."

"Right. I remember that now." Bram tapped his fingers on the table. "Did you ever see Bob . . . after he died? Was the casket ever opened?"

"Not when I was around."

Bram stared at him a moment, then said, "Nah, can't be. A guy might want to fake his own death, but the entire police force would have to go along with it."

Vince seemed reluctant to weigh in on the subject, which Bram found odd. Vince was usually full of opinions on just about everything.

"You don't know any reason why Bob would want to fake his death, do you?" asked Bram.

"Nope. And I don't mean to speak out of turn, Baldric, but maybe your mother-in-law needs to get herself a life. Bob's dead and gone. I hope to God he's in heaven with Valerie. That's what he wanted."

"Yes," said Bram. "That's what I think, too." He took another sip of coffee. "But it is strange that the police keep hedging about it. One of the detectives on the case is a friend of mine. He told me this is the most convoluted case he's ever worked on."

"Really?"

"Al Lundquist. You talked to him yet?"

Vince's eyes dropped to the papers in front of him. "His partner came by a couple days after Bob died."

"You and Lyle were the last two people to spend time with him that night—other than his killer."

"True."

"Did he seem depressed, anxious, or upset about anything?"

Vince shook his head. "On the contrary. I'd say he was upbeat."

"This past year must have been a hard one for him. The fact that he died on the anniversary of Valerie's death is . . . well, even you've got to admit it's kind of coincidental."

"I suppose."

"If he *did* die." Bram watched Vince's face. His reticence made Bram itchy. He was sure there was something Vince was holding back.

"He's gone, Baldric. Off floating somewhere on a cloud, enjoying the view. Forgive me if I'm overstepping again, but I'll bet your mother-in-law loves conspiracy theories. She believe Oswald shot Kennedy?"

Bram laughed. "Hell no."

"My point exactly."

"Yeah," said Bram, stretching his arms over his head. "And it's well taken. All I can say is, if I were Phil Banks or Andy Gladstone, I'd be watching my back right about now. I assume you saw the morning paper. You know that 911 tape points the finger at one of them in Loy's murder."

"So I hear."

"Your niece is dating Banks, right?"

"Temporary insanity."

"I like Chris. I wouldn't want to see her get mixed up in any of this."

Vince frowned. "You and me both. Banks should stick to women his own age. Leave the kids alone."

"Chris is hardly a kid. Early thirties, right?"

"She's still a kid in my book."

Just as Bram got up to warm what was left of his coffee, Chris stuck her head inside the door. "Hi, you two. You up for some company?"

"Hey," said Vince, his mood instantly brightening. He stood to give her a hug. "You're a long way from home."

"I thought I'd drive in and give you the good news in person." She grinned at Bram. "You can both be happy for me."

"Happy about what?" asked Vince, pulling out a chair for her.

She held out her left hand.

Bram's eyes popped at the sight of the diamond ring and the gold band.

"Banks?" said Vince, his smile evaporating. "Are you two engaged or something?"

"Married," said Chris, her heart-shaped face beaming with happiness. "Yesterday."

"Congratulations," said Bram, filling up the silence her announcement had created. He could see Vince was having trouble knowing what to say.

"Aren't you happy for me, Uncle Vincent?"

"Yeah. I guess."

Chris sat down. She tugged the edges of her varsity coat together over her chest. "I know you don't like Phil, but that's because you don't know him."

"He's been married twice, and he's old enough to be your father."

It was water off a duck's back. Chris was head-over-heels in love. Bram could see it in her eyes. You couldn't talk someone who was in love out of that love. If Vince tried, he was in for a fall. Although Bram didn't know Vince all that well, he knew he'd never been married. Occasionally he'd talk about one of the women he'd lived with over the years, but he never struck Bram as the romantic type. In his late fifties now, Vince probably spent his spare time watching ball games or fishing. Bob Fabian and Lyle Boerichter were his two best friends, perhaps his only real friends. But Vince clearly loved his niece. And it was obvious he thought she'd just made a big mistake.

Bram had no particular opinion about her marriage one way or the other. He might be able to recognize Banks if he saw him in a crowd, but that was about it. If Chris was happy, that was good enough for him. Chris was a sensible young woman. She'd grown up poor but loved, so she'd turned out to be a fine, levelheaded woman. Maybe she *was* looking for a father figure in a husband—and financial security—but that didn't necessarily mean the marriage was doomed. Pop psychology be damned.

"Only thing is," said Chris, fingering her rings, "since I quit my job, I'm kind of bored. Not when Phil's around, but he has to work a lot and then I'm left at home with nothing to do. Phil tells me to go shopping, but you can only shop for so long before that gets boring, too."

"You want a part-time job cooking, you've always got one here at the club," said Vince, rubbing his balding head.

"Thanks. But Phil wants me home when he gets home. I need a gig with flexible hours."

"He sounds like he's from another century," Vince grunted.

She shrugged.

"Hey," said Bram. "Something just occurred to me. I'm interviewing Victoria Svensvold this afternoon. You might be able to help her."

Victoria Svensvold was a big name in the cookbook world, and an even bigger name in Minnesota. She'd written the definitive work on American regional cookery and was now tackling the food of Scandinavia. She'd spent the last two years traveling back and forth between Norway, Sweden, and Denmark.

"She's working on a new cookbook," said Bram. "That's what we're talking about this afternoon."

"Gee," said Chris. "How could I help her?"

"She's at a point with the book where she's tested all the recipes herself, but she's looking for another tester, someone who has some cooking experience who can take the recipes and make them in their own home kitchen, then give her written feedback on what might not work. She used to employ a woman who was in her early seventies, but she's pretty much retired now, so Victoria's on the lookout for a new recipe tester. It would be the perfect job for you. You could do it around Phil's schedule."

Chris's eyes glowed with excitement. "Do you really think she'd consider me?"

"If I put in a good word for you, you bet I do. Look, why don't you come with me to the station. We could stop somewhere and pick up some lunch, and then when Victoria arrives, I can introduce you to her."

"Deal," said Chris. "This is incredible. I just married the best guy in the world, and now maybe I've just snagged the best job in the world. I never thought I'd get this lucky."

Half an hour later, Bram and Chris walked into the Speakeasy Cafe, a new restaurant in Fridley, not far from the radio station. Bram had been wanting to give it a try for months, and this seemed like the perfect opportunity.

Because the word of mouth was so good, the dining room was crowded. Bram and Chris were shown to a table in the back, near the large open kitchen. The smell of wood-fired ovens filled the room with the wonderful aroma of applewood and pizza.

"I could eat a horse, I'm so hungry," said Chris, tucking a leg under her as she sat down.

The hostess gave them each a menu.

"If you're in the mood for horse meat," said Bram, "you should have stayed at the club. I'm sure your uncle could have whipped you up a horse meat stir-fry, or something along those lines."

Chris rolled her eyes. "Yeah, he does have unusual tastes. I walked in on one of their totally gross dinners a few months ago. There was this pot sitting in the middle of the table. I made the mistake of asking what was in it."

Bram wasn't sure he wanted to know.

"It was a curried hog testicle stew. I guess hog testicles taste really good with sweet potatoes and peppers."

Bram grimaced. "Did you try it?"

"Do I look stupid?"

Bram checked her over. "No, you look pretty intelligent to me."

"Thank you. Those three guys. When you were with them, they were a total hoot. They were always laughing or joking about something. I feel so sad for Uncle Vincent."

"They were really tight, huh?"

"Yeah, well, except, the last time I saw them together, Mr. Boerichter—he's the pilot—and Mr. Fabian didn't seem to be getting along. Lots of heavy stares, withering looks. You know the deal. It seemed pretty intense."

"Do you know what it was about?"

She shrugged. "I asked my uncle about it later, and he just said they'd been arguing politics. Both Uncle Vincent and Mr. Boerichter are totally liberal. Mr. Fabian was an old-school conservative, so I guess I can understand it. I'd heard them argue politics before, but I'd never seen Mr. Fabian or Mr. Boerichter get that worked up. I mean, they'd talk back and forth, call each other names, but it was, like, always with a twinkle in their eyes."

When the waiter arrived with the water, Chris ordered a Speakeasy Burger—flame-grilled ground beef with sautéed porcini mushrooms and cipollini onions, covered in provolone. Bram ordered a small pizza Margherita—Italian tomato sauce, fresh mozzarella, fresh basil, all drizzled with a spicy green olive oil. And they both ordered Cokes.

"You know, my uncle made a pizza once for his culinary club. He put bugs and worms on it. It looked normal, with the cheese on top and all, but it smelled kind of funky." She shuddered. "No wonder they have that sign over the door. Who needs reservations? It's not like there'd ever be a stampede to the back room."

They talked for a few more minutes, and then Bram excused himself to use the restroom. When he returned, he saw that the waiter had brought their Cokes. Chris had taken out a pen and was doodling on the napkin. Bram glanced at it as he sat back down and saw that she'd been practicing writing her new names: "Mrs. Phil Banks," and "Christine Banks."

"You're really happy with that guy," said Bram.

Chris grinned and nodded, her eyes still on the napkin. "I can't believe how lucky I am. I wish my mother and my uncle would lighten up a little. You'd think I was ten years old and Phil was some lech trying to lure me into the back of his car with a candy bar."

Bram laughed. "Well, they're protective. They love you."

She glanced around the room. "If they'd just give Phil a chance, they might—" She stopped.

"What?" said Bram. He didn't immediately understand the change in Chris's expression. She seemed startled—or maybe a little shocked. "What is it?"

"It's . . . Phil," she whispered, her eyes narrowing.

Bram turned to look.

Phil Banks had just entered the restaurant with a woman. He had his arm around her shoulders and appeared to be whispering something amusing into her ear. The woman was blond and good-looking, much older than Chris and far better dressed, the kind of woman who probably got stared at a lot.

When Bram swung his gaze back to Chris, he could tell she was confused and angry, and probably a dozen other emotions she couldn't define. "Do you know who the woman is?" asked Bram. He couldn't exactly pretend he hadn't seen them.

Chris shook her head. "He told me he had to work today."

"Maybe she's a client."

Chris's stare hardened.

"Don't jump to conclusions."

"You mean, I should ignore the fact that he just kissed her?"

"He did?" Bram whipped his head around, but it was too late. They were already being seated at a booth near the front windows.

"That bastard," she said, looking away.

"You've got to give him a chance to explain."

"Right. Sure."

The waiter arrived with their food.

"I just lost my appetite," said Chris.

"Do you want to leave?"

She started doodling again on her napkin. "I don't know."

They'd driven separately. "Look, I can get this stuff wrapped for takeout and you can meet me at the station. We can eat lunch there. Maybe sticking around here isn't a good idea."

"Yeah. Maybe."

"Lunch is on me, kiddo. Do you know how to get to WTWN?"

She shook her head.

Bram borrowed her pen and quickly drew a map on his napkin. "I'll meet you there. Are you okay to drive?"

"Fine."

But she wasn't fine, and they both knew it.

Bram watched her pick up her purse and leave the table. He wondered if she'd walk over and confront Phil, but instead, she skirted her way around the edge of the room and left without saying a word.

Bram felt immensely sorry for her. He called the waiter over and asked for the food to be boxed up. As he waited, he pulled Chris's napkin over in front of him. She'd drawn an X through "Mrs. Phil Banks." Underneath, she'd written the name "Del." And then the words "Stored on Old Mill Road." Bram wondered what that was all about. It was probably meaningless in the scheme of things, but all the same, he slipped the napkin into his pocket.

18

Chris drove to the station in a fog of incomprehension. In her heart, she couldn't believe that Phil would cheat on her, but with her own two eyes she'd seen something else—something terrible but true. He was with another woman, and not just in a friendly way. To Chris, the woman looked hard and old, and most definitely cheap. Oh, she was wearing expensive clothes, but she seemed easy and even a little desperate, like Mrs. Robinson in *The Graduate*.

Chris sat in an uncomfortable chair waiting for Bram, but she just couldn't concentrate. She'd for sure make a mess of it if she met Victoria Svensvold today. She was already way beyond nervous to meet such an icon of the cooking world. Chris felt as if she might break into tears at any moment—and wouldn't *that* impress a potential employer. No, there was no use waiting around. She wrote Bram a note, telling him that she was still interested in the job, and maybe she could meet with Ms. Svensvold another time. She told him she was really sorry, but seeing Phil with another woman had upset her and she needed time to get herself together. She thanked him for lunch, and for being such a good friend, and said she'd be in touch.

What Chris needed to do was go back to the restaurant and wait for Phil to come out. And then, well, she'd play it by ear. Maybe she'd confront him, or maybe she wouldn't. What she wanted more than anything was to see them together again, to confirm in her mind what she'd just seen.

Once back at the Speakeasy Cafe, Chris quickly located Phil's black Corvette in the restaurant's lot. Parking her Escort across the street, and making sure she had a clear view of the front door, she waited. Forty minutes later, Phil and the woman emerged into the bright afternoon sunlight. Phil was chewing on a toothpick, his hand on the back of the woman's neck as they walked to his car. There was no more kissing or whispering in her ear, but they were obviously an intimate pair. Phil had placed his hand on Chris's neck in exactly the same way when they walked around. Sometimes he'd lay his arm across her shoulders and she'd put her hand in his back pocket. She loved the closeness, the feel of his body against hers, the way they fit together so perfectly. Tears welled up behind her eyes, but she refused to cry.

Phil rolled his car to the edge of the lot, then headed east down Alton Road. Chris followed at a distance, careful not to lose them, but careful also to avoid being seen. A few minutes later, Phil turned onto Standish, then left onto Poke Avenue. He stopped in front of a small, one-story house in the middle of the block. Chris drove on down Standish, quickly circling the block. By the time she got back to the house, they'd gone inside.

More waiting. Chris parked at the end of the block and turned off the motor. She wished she could turn off her imagination as easily. Were they making love?

Was Phil undressing her, touching her the way he touched Chris? Did he love this woman? That seemed even more horrific than the idea that they were physically intimate. She knew men could separate sex and love. Was that what this was? Just a little afternoon roll in the hay? And if so, how long had it been going on? Did the woman know Phil was married now? Maybe Chris was supposed to put up with this kind of crap, but the idea that she could never trust Phil again, never truly believe him when he said he was going to work, made her sick to her stomach. She knew other women lived with men who cheated on them, but this wasn't the Hollywood romance Chris had envisioned. And she wasn't sure she could settle for anything less.

A little over an hour later, Phil came out of the house. She was too far away to see his expression, but at least the woman wasn't with him. He got into his Corvette, gunned the motor, and drove away.

Chris sat in her Escort, staring at the woman's house, deciding whether or not she should bang on the front door and demand to know what was going on. The hurt she'd felt just a short while ago had quickly changed to anger. If Phil was on his way home to feed her more lies, when he arrived she wouldn't be there. If he got mad, too freaking bad. She had somewhere else she wanted to go before she returned home.

Fifteen minutes later, Chris pulled into a gas station. She needed gas and a map. While talking to the guy behind the counter, she learned that Old Mill Road ran along the Mississippi River just across the Roberts Street Bridge in St. Paul. Checking the map, she saw that it wasn't a very long road. She scouted out the best way to get there, then got back on Highway 10, heading for downtown St. Paul.

Chris thought back to the conversation she'd had earlier in the day with the man named Del. He said that Phil was a "very very bad man." If Phil had secrets about the women in his life, maybe he had others. And that's what Chris intended to find out.

After crossing the bridge, she drove two blocks until she came to Old Mill Road. Hanging a quick right, she saw that she was heading into an industrial area. Del's message said that he knew what Phil had stored on Old Mill Road. But that could be anything. Phil's construction company owned lots of heavy equipment, and what they didn't own, they rented. This was exactly the kind of area where Banks Construction probably did a lot of business.

As she whizzed along, she glanced at the names of the businesses. And that's when she saw it. Old Mill Road Mini Storage. Could that be it? She hung a left and drove into the parking lot. The entire area was cordoned off with a high chain-link fence capped with razor wire. Two heavy gates, an entrance and an exit, flanked either side of the main building.

Chris got out of her car and looked around. She figured there must be over three or four hundred storage garages on the property. She'd heard about these personal storage places before, but she'd never seen one up close.

Entering the front office, she found a middle-aged man in jeans and a sweatshirt sitting at a beat-up desk behind a tall Formica counter. He was working at a computer. Everything in the office looked dusty and worn, as if nobody really cared about the appearance.

She cleared her throat to get him to look up. "Excuse me. Your name wouldn't be Del, would it?"

He squinted at her through the smoke from his cigarette. "Mike."

"Ah, hi. Does a guy named Del work here?" It was a guess, but she thought it was worth a try.

"Nope."

"Well, then, maybe you could help me."

"Maybe. What you need?"

"My husband, Philip Banks, gave me something he wants me to put in his storage unit. This is the right place, isn't it? He does rent a garage here?"

The guy turned back to the computer. "Repeat the name."

"Phil Banks."

"Phone number?"

"555-595-2098."

He tapped a few more times before turning back to her. "Yup—2298."

"How do I get in?"

"He give you the security code?"

"No. He said you would."

"Can't, lady. Against policy. It's all self-serve here. Out at the front gate, you type in the code, the gate swings back, and you're in. Same to get out. Everybody puts their own personal lock on the garage, so we got nothin' to do with that."

"I've got the key," she said, holding up the key she used on her locker at Phil's health club. "Just no access code."

"Sorry. You tell your husband he's got to give it to

you personally. You wanna call him, you can use our phone." He nodded to the one on the counter.

Chris had to think fast. "He's in a meeting."

"Well, then, I'd say you're out of luck."

"You mean there's no way I can get in? My husband's going to be really pissed at me if I don't do what he says." She set her purse on the counter and took out her billfold.

"Save it," said the guy, tapping the ash off his cigarette. "If I gave it to you, I could lose my job."

"But you don't know my husband."

"Nope. And sounds like I should keep it that way."

Realizing there was nothing else she could do, she thanked him and left. On her way to her car, it occurred to her that, at the very least, she'd proved what Del had alluded to this morning was true. Phil did have something stored on Old Mill Road. She was learning fast that Phil was the kind of guy who liked to keep secrets. One way or another, she intended to find that security code. And when she did, she'd be back.

19

Sophie spent the afternoon shopping at Manderbach's department store with her mother, hoping to find a baby gift for some friends who'd just had their first child. She returned to her office around five. Checking her voice mail, she found that Nathan had called. With a sinking feeling in her stomach, she listened to the message:

"Sophie, hi. It's me. Elaine and I met with Margie Baldric this afternoon. I thought I'd let you know that it went well. We're planning on doing the wedding in mid-December—over at the Rookery Club. I like that place. I understand you and Bram do, too. Anyway, Elaine wants this very formal affair, but I'm leaning toward something less grand. I thought maybe you could talk to Elaine and see if you can get her to back off on some of the formality. You know me, I'm just a country guy at heart. I'd get married in the woods if she'd agree to it, but hey, whatever makes her happy. Except, I don't want to wear a tux. I don't mean to put you in the middle between Elaine and me, but I could use the help. I'll keep you posted on how everything progresses. Great seeing you today, Soph. You looked fantastic in that outfit—very Jackie Kennedy. Very tailored and powerful. Oh, and sexy, too. Always that. What was the perfume you were wearing? I'd like to get some for Elaine. Later."

"Yuck," said Sophie, deleting the message. She had no intention of calling Elaine, and she wasn't interested in hearing Nathan's opinions of her. The whole situation was starting to make her uncomfortable. She was sick and tired of trying to spare Nathan's feelings. From now on, for his own good, she had to get tough with him. He needed to know that he was no longer welcome in her life on any level. Maybe he was the kind of guy who just had to hear it a few times—loudly—to get the point.

When she entered her apartment a few minutes later, she was surprised to find Ethel, her black mutt, lying on a pillow under the dining room table. Ethel was fast asleep, snoring audibly.

"Bram?" she called, wondering if he was home yet from the station.

"In here."

She followed his voice into the living room, finding him sprawled on the couch, reading a *Newsweek*. "How come Ethel's up here?" Normally, she stayed down in the lobby on her throne until early evening.

Flipping the magazine shut, he sat up. "There was an . . . incident."

"A what?"

He patted the seat next to him. "Come here." He narrowed his eyes and gave her a lecherous grin. "For a kiss you get the information you are seeking."

She matched his look. "You want a piece of me, huh?"

"We'll start with the kiss and then see what other pieces are available."

She sat down. After they'd said a proper hello, she asked the question again. "What *incident*?"

"Ethel barked."

"No."

"Yes. Wouldn't stop."

"Barked at what?"

"The bellboy who brought her up didn't really know. She just became terribly agitated and the concierge felt it was best to get her upstairs, away from the guests."

"But Ethel is the meekest, mildest, friendliest dog in the world."

"You mean she's generally too lazy to move anything other than her eyes, and she *tolerates* repetitive social interaction. *Nice little doggy. Are you a good little doggy? Can you sit up? Can you shake hands?*"

Ethel lurched her way into the room. She understood dog talk.

"Maybe it's her age," said Bram, watching her drop to the floor and begin to lick her paw.

"Meaning what?"

"Maybe she's becoming curmudgeonly."

"Not our Ethel."

"It happens."

Sophie couldn't believe it. If Ethel barked, she did so out of a sense of protection, of territoriality. "Someone frightened her. She has good instincts."

"She has terrible instincts. She adores your cousin Solo, who—forgive me for stating the obvious—is a sociopath with paranoid tendencies, and she won't go near your aunt Agnes, who is the dearest, sweetest woman in the world."

"Yes, well—"

"We may have to rethink our policy about having a hotel mascot."

"Look at her," said Sophie, her heart breaking.

Ethel's normally droopy eyes were even droopier. Her baleful expression bordered on melodrama. Ethel knew how to suffer. She was the Mildred Pierce of Dogdom.

"Not to change the subject," said Bram.

"No, please do."

"I'm not following that crisis at the *Times Register* as closely as I should. What was the name of the reporter who just got fired? Was it Del?"

She nodded. "Del Irazarian."

"I thought so."

"Why?"

"Oh, you know. Just curious."

"Andy called a meeting this morning for all the employees at the paper. He skirted his involvement in the whole mess, but he's going to institute some badly needed changes. Actually, I ran into him as I was leaving. Something he said, well, it really bothered me."

"About the 911 call?"

"Yes. In a way. He said he was glad he had an alibi for that night."

"And it was—?"

"He said he was with Anika."

"But . . . you ran into her that night at the Rookery Club."

"And she said she was looking for Andy."

"So he's lying."

"Without a doubt."

"But that doesn't necessarily mean he was the shooter."

"No."

"Sophie, look at me. You actually think he murdered his brother?"

"*If* Bob is really dead."

Bram groaned. "Are we still acting like your mother's newest theory has merit?"

Sophie snuggled next to him. "No. Not really." She'd been thinking about it all day. "Andy might have lied to the police because he felt he needed an alibi, even if he's not guilty."

"But why not simply tell the truth? I mean, isn't that always the best way to handle it?"

"I suppose," said Sophie. "But maybe we don't have the whole picture."

Bram put his arm around her shoulders. "So he got Anika to lie to the police for him. That's not smart. If he did kill Bob, it could make her an accessory."

Sophie hadn't considered that.

"You could blow his alibi out of the water."

"Apparently Anika has forgotten that little detail— or hopes I have."

"Maybe you better talk to her."

That's exactly what Sophie had concluded. "I thought I'd call, ask her to stop by."

"Tonight?"

"If possible, yes."

"What about dinner?"

"Let's order in. Whatever you want."

"Hey, how about I go get us some of that Thai food from that restaurant up the block? I'll make us a pitcher of martinis. And we can put a movie in the DVD."

"Sounds perfect." Too perfect, thought Sophie. Margie was always out there lurking, waiting to ruin an otherwise wonderful evening.

"Have I told you lately that I love you?"

"Not today," said Sophie.

"Well," said Bram, lowering his voice and whispering in her ear, "I'll remedy that later."

Anika agreed to stop by the Maxfield Plaza at six thirty. Sophie couched her request by saying they needed to talk about Anika's position at the hotel. Sophie explained that she had no time to meet tomorrow or the day after, but was free tonight and hoped that Anika would have a few minutes to get together. She never mentioned the real reason for the meeting.

Sophie had a few minutes to kill before Anika arrived, so she drifted through the hotel, checking the appetizer buffet for Maxfield Club members on eleven, the Fountain Grill on the mezzanine level, and finally the hospitality suite, otherwise known as the Lindbergh room, on the main floor. She wasn't exactly surprised to find her father polishing the brass knocker on the hospitality room's door.

"Hey, Dad," she said, giving him a kiss on his cheek.

"Don't tell me we have a staff to do these kinds of things. I know about the staff. I hired most of them. The fact that they don't do their job in a timely fashion isn't my fault."

Sophie sat down on the edge of one of the club chairs.

"That old boyfriend of yours was here again today."

"Nathan?"

"That's the one." As always, he chewed on an unlit cigar. "He had some sort of meeting with Margie. Elaine Veelund was with him."

"Nathan and Elaine are getting married."

Her father hooted. "Well, if two people ever deserved each other—"

"What do you mean by that?"

"Their mothers spoiled them both rotten."

Sophie stood up. "You liked Nathan. You always said that."

"Your mother liked him. Not me."

"You never said you thought he was spoiled before."

"You mean back when you two were teenagers? What good would it have done? You were head over heels in love with the guy. I was just your father. What the hell did I know?"

Sophie was aghast, but also intrigued. "Tell me more."

"Well, if I'd figured you were going to marry him, I would have sat you down and tried to talk some sense into you. But then you went off to that college in California, so there was no point. Nathan was history."

"He was a beautiful young man. Poetic. Sensitive. He worked hard for important causes."

"Okay, he was nice-looking enough. But hard work? Nah, I never saw that. In my day, we would have called a young man like him a playboy—and it wasn't a nice term. Nathan expected the whole world to be impressed with him, and if they weren't, he got mad. His mother gave him everything he ever asked for, didn't she? Can you think of one toy Prince Nathan didn't have?"

"*Prince* Nathan?"

"That's what Pearlie and I called him."

That was news to Sophie.

" 'Course, I heard his mom told him after you

dumped him to either get a job or go to school. He was moping around, not doing anything, and she finally put her foot down. I thought it was about time. But then he took off for Europe and she paid for him to go to some fancy school over there. You know, Soph, I'll bet you're the only girl who ever turned him down, and he couldn't believe it. It probably still eats at him."

"We loved each other."

"I'm sure you loved him. He acted like he *owned* you."

It was as if her father were talking about two entirely different people. Had Sophie been so infatuated with Nathan that she'd missed all that? Nathan had come back into her life when her parents were on their round-the-world tour, so this was the first time her father had weighed in on the subject of Nathan Buckridge.

"If you told him no," continued her dad, "say, you couldn't do something on a particular night, he'd show up anyway. If you said you had to study, he'd stand outside in the hallway and recite some stupid poem until you came out, until you gave in and went off with him. He never understood the meaning of the word no."

Amazingly, he still didn't, thought Sophie. How was it possible that she'd never seen that in him? Or perhaps she'd seen it, but she'd never realized how destructive it could be.

"If I were you," said her father, taking the stogie out of his mouth and studying the tip, "I'd watch out for that guy. He's not all there"—he tapped his forehead—"if you know what I mean. Okay, okay. So he's a big-time chef. So give the boy a cigar." He held his up. "He's grown up that much. But that doesn't give him the right to keep sniffing around my daughter's life. What the hell's he up to?"

"He's an old friend."

"Yeah, right." He snorted. "You're still blind as a bat, Soph. I been home, what? Two months? I got eyes, don't I? Stay the hell away from him or you'll be sorry. That's all I've got to say. Now get on out of here and let me finish my work."

20

Chris arrived home just after six. She knew Phil would be pissed if she didn't have something on the table, but she didn't care. Without time to think about what she wanted to say—and how to say it— she might ruin everything. She was hurt and angry, but she still loved him with all her heart. She'd come to the conclusion that there might be an explanation for what she'd seen. She couldn't imagine what it was, but she owed him the benefit of the doubt. She'd been married only one day. It was inconceivable to her that her marriage was already on the rocks.

When she walked into the house, Phil called to her from the back deck.

"I'm out here."

There was a hardness in his voice that chilled her. She moved through the living room into the kitchen and opened the sliding screen doors. Phil was sitting in the hot tub.

"Where the hell you been?" he demanded.

She sat down on the far edge of the tub. "Out."

"Out where?"

She shrugged. "Just driving around."

"Like hell you were. You were with your mom, right? Bet you couldn't wait to tell her we got hitched." His irritation faded, replaced by a grin.

"I called her, but she wasn't home."

"So . . ." He eyed her carefully, looking for clues. "Something's wrong—I can tell. What is it?"

She looked down at the roiling bubbles.

"Chris?"

She still didn't know how to say what she needed to say, how to ask the man she loved if he'd been unfaithful. "I, ah . . . I might get a job." It just came out. But it was as good an opening as any.

"A *what*?" He crossed his arms over his chest, his frown returning. "You know I don't want you to work."

"No, but see, it wouldn't be like before. I'd be testing recipes for a cookbook. I could do it at the house, totally around your schedule. It wouldn't be a problem. And it would give me something to do. I'm bored when you're not here."

"Read a book. Rent some movies."

"But I miss cooking, Phil. I'm good at it. And this would be a way for me to do it and not mess up any of our plans."

He spread his arms across the back of the tub. Thirty seconds passed. Then a minute. He watched her, his gaze full of unspoken criticism. Finally, he said, "Oh, all right. If it means that much to you." He smiled magnanimously. "Now take off your clothes and get in. I'm lonely in here all by myself."

Chris had a premonition. He hadn't really given

in; he was simply placating her. If she did get the job, he'd find some way to sabotage it. But why? Why didn't he want her to do something that made her feel good about herself? She'd just have to figure out a way to explain it to him so that he understood.

When she hesitated about getting undressed, he said, "*Now* what's wrong?"

She was a coward. She didn't want to say what she'd prepared. "Ah, actually, you got a call this morning after you left the house."

"Yeah? Who from?"

"A man named Del."

"I don't know anybody named Del."

"He left a message. He wanted me to tell you that he knows what you've got stored on Old Mill Road. And that he'll be in touch."

Phil roared up out of the water. "Say that again?"

She was surprised by the violence of his reaction, but she repeated it anyway, hoping he'd remember she was only the messenger.

"Did he give you a phone number?"

"No."

"That's all he said? He didn't say anything else?"

"He said . . . that . . . you were . . . a bad . . . man."

Phil leapt out of the tub, grabbed his robe, and threw it on. "Damn it to hell, woman. Why didn't you call me right away?" He slammed back the screen door and stomped into the house. "Which phone?"

"In the kitchen." She trotted after him. "What are you doing?"

"What you should have done. Hit star 69." He held the phone to his ear and listened. After a few seconds, he expression darkened and he threw the phone across the room. It hit the far wall and burst apart.

"What?" said Chris.

"He used a goddamn pay phone." He turned to her, grabbing her by her arm. "What else did he say? I want it word for word."

"You're hurting me." She tried to squirm away.

"Tell me!"

She'd never seen such rage in his eyes before and it terrified her. "I told you. He said he knew what you had stored on Old Mill Road. That you were a bad man. And that he'd be in touch."

"You're leaving something out."

"No . . . no, I'm not."

He struck her hard in the face with the back of his hand.

"Phil," she gasped.

When he let her go, she crumpled into a chair. She couldn't believe what he'd just done. It took her a minute to absorb the shock of the blow. When she finally looked up, she saw that he'd walked over to the screen doors and was standing, looking out at the hot tub. She wanted to ask him what it all meant, why he was so upset, but she was afraid to say anything, afraid she'd set him off again. She touched her eye, felt the puffiness and the bruise. "God, Phil." She started to cry.

He turned around. "Chris, I'm sorry. I didn't mean it. Please, I didn't mean it." The next second he was kneeling next to her, wrapping his arms around her. "Let me see your eye."

She looked away.

"Chris, you've got to forgive me. That call, it just made me crazy for a second."

"Who is he? What's going on?"

"Nothing I can't handle, sweetheart. Don't worry. God, look what I did." He touched her face. "Let me get you a cold washcloth."

"No. I'm fine."

"Chrissy, you have to understand. This has been a horrible day. I called my exes to tell them I'd remarried and they both went ballistic all over me. And then, hell, I find out my best project manager has been stealing me blind. For months. I had to fire him on the spot. It couldn't be worse timing. I'll have to pick up the slack until I can hire someone new, and that means more hours at work, less time with you. Honey, please say you forgive me. It will never ever happen again."

She didn't move. She wanted to believe him.

"Just promise me one thing. If that guy ever calls again, you tell me right away. If I'm not home, call me on my cell. It's *very* important, okay?"

"Okay."

"Chris, I love you. More than anything in this world."

"Do you?"

"How can I make it up to you? Just tell me." He stood up and pulled her into his arms.

She couldn't relax. Her body felt tight, unyielding.

Phil stood back, held her by her shoulders. "You're afraid of me."

"A little," she managed.

"Don't be, please. Oh, please," he pleaded. "Don't be."

"It's . . . all about trust, isn't it, Phil?"

He let go. "Come on outside. You need to unwind in the tub. I'll rub your back, just the way you like." Without waiting for her, he opened the screen, took off his robe, and climbed back in. "Come on, honey. Why don't you pour us each a glass of single malt."

Feeling like a zombie, she moved to the shelf where they kept the bottle, took it down, and poured them each a stiff drink. To steady her nerves, she tossed hers back, then poured herself a second.

Once out on the deck, she handed a glass to Phil.

"Are you going to come in?"

"I don't know." She stood looking down at him.

"Chrissy, you're my whole world."

"Am I?"

"Absolutely."

Inside, she began to shiver. "I went out to lunch with Bram Baldric this afternoon."

"Baldric? What the hell were you doing with him?"

"He's a friend. A good friend. He took me to the Speakeasy Cafe."

Now it was Phil's turn to be silent.

"I saw you with that woman, saw you kiss her. Do you love her, too, Phil?" She was taking a big chance. If he'd hit her once, he could hit her again. But she had to know the truth, had to stand her ground. "Who is she?"

"Just . . . somebody I used to date."

"*Used* to date? Seems to me you still do."

He shook his head—and kept on shaking it. "I never meant for you to see that."

She took another swallow of the Scotch. The liquid burned her throat, warmed her deep inside.

"Okay," he said, brushing a shock of gray fringe off his forehead. "So I was with her this afternoon. But I had to tell her about us, didn't I? About our marriage. And I wanted to do it in person. I care about her, Chris. But I don't love her, not like I do you. We had lunch. I thought, hell, why ruin a good meal? But then, when we were done, we went back to her house and I told her that I'd gotten married and we had to call it quits."

"Were you sleeping with her while I was living with you?"

"No. Never. Not once. I stopped right after you moved in. But I still saw her every now and then. It was casual, just friends. Lunch, or coffee. That's all. I swear it. Maybe she thought the relationship was headed somewhere else, but I never did."

"What's her name?"

"Barbara Kerwin. My company built an addition on her place, a bedroom, a few years back."

How convenient, thought Chris. But she didn't say it.

"You have no right to judge me, you know. You were out with Baldric. So what was all that about?"

"He's a happily married man, Phil. He promised to introduce me to Victoria Svensvold, the woman who might give me a job testing recipes."

"Never heard of her."

"She's very famous, writes cookbooks. I wouldn't lie to you."

"Meaning I've lied to you?" He spread his arms across the back of the tub again. "You know, Christine, don't get all hot and bothered on me now, but you could learn something from Barbara. She really knows how to take care of herself. She understands fashion and she looks damn hot for a woman her age. If you ask me, you could spruce up a little, go find yourself something to wear other than jeans and tank tops."

Chris was dumbfounded. "You never said before you didn't like the way I dressed."

"Well, I'm saying it now. As of yesterday, you're my wife. That gives you status in this town. Act like it. Do you think I enjoy walking around with a woman who looks like she's just come from a Grateful Dead concert? Go to a hairdresser and get your hair styled. Get someone to help you with your makeup. Buy yourself some new clothes. *Dresses*. I don't care what it costs. I want you to look good. Sexy. I want other guys drooling over you. Are we clear?"

She didn't know what to say. Suddenly, this was no longer about him; it was about her. Her shortcomings. He'd succeeded in making her feel small, ugly, diminished. In an attempt to hold back tears, she tilted her head away and shut her eyes.

She felt him move to the seat closest to her. When he touched her, she pressed her lips together and looked down at him. "If I'm such a loser, you shouldn't have married me."

"Oh, honey. Don't look so sad. You're the one who love movies, right? So look at it this way: I'm Henry Higgins and you're Liza Doolittle. Do what I tell you and everything will work out just fine—like a true movie romance."

In the last few hours, Chris had suddenly lost faith in the rosy picture those old movie favorites portrayed. Or maybe she'd just lost faith in Phil. But something had gone wrong in her world and she wasn't sure it would ever be right again.

21

Anika sat across the desk from Sophie in one of the Maxfield's comfortable club chairs. She looked tired as she crossed her legs and leaned back, trying to get comfortable. She was dressed casually in khaki chinos and a mulberry V-neck sweater. Sophie wondered if Anika had lost weight. She seemed even thinner than usual—and usual was just a shade this side of skinny.

As they talked, Anika pulled absently on the gold chain around her neck.

"I saw Andy this morning," said Sophie. "He spoke to a full house at the *Times Register*. All the employees. I think it was a good move. How's he doing? I can imagine he feels pretty overwhelmed at the moment."

Anika abandoned the necklace and moved on to examine a piece of lint attached to her sweater. "He's up and down. To be honest, it's been a rough year, Sophie. For both of us."

"I'm sorry to hear that."

"Yeah. Well. Whoever said this life was easy . . ." She laughed, but her face didn't register any amusement.

"Is there anything I can do to help?"

Anika folded her hands in her lap. "You're a good friend. I appreciate the offer, but I don't know what it would be."

"I assume that since you and Andy inherited Bob's estate, you'll probably want to quit your job here at the hotel."

"No," said Anika, looking startled. "That's not what I want at all."

"Well, I just thought—"

"I need this job. I intend to be back at the beginning of next week, just like we planned."

Sophie was baffled and couldn't help showing it.

"Work is important to me," said Anika. "I love my job here at the Maxfield. It's even more important to me now."

Sophie couldn't imagine why. The entire world was open to Anika now. She could buy her own hotel if she wanted to.

"I need to be . . . self-supporting."

"You do?"

She bowed her head. "The thing is . . ." She hesitated, then plunged in. "I've been thinking of asking Andy for a divorce."

Sophie couldn't believe what she was hearing. "I had no idea."

"No. Nobody does. But then nobody's lived through the last year with us. It hasn't been pretty."

"Have you talked to Andy yet?"

"No. I can't, not right now. He's been hit with so much. But as soon as he gets on his feet, I intend to move out."

"Anika, I'm so sorry to hear that."

"Yeah." Her mouth quivered and her face reddened as she pressed her lips together to stop herself from crying. "The worst part of it is, I still love him. I just can't live like this anymore."

Sophie waited while Anika pulled a tissue from her pocket and wiped her eyes.

"He's . . . so up and down. So restless. He has terrible insomnia. Sometimes, we don't talk for days. I'm not sure he even notices. And then, out of the blue, he's on a high. Feeling great. It's like living with two men. Or three . . . or four. I never know who's going to come home at night."

"Maybe he needs to see a psychotherapist."

"He's talked to several. But nothing seems to help."

Sophie had to choose her words carefully. Hearing this only made her want to confront Anika all the more. "Look, it's not my intent to upset you, but Andy said something to me this morning that kind of threw me."

Anika stared back, her expression tightening.

"He said that the night Bob and Ken Loy were murdered, he was with you all evening."

Anika closed her eyes. "Yes, I see. And you know that isn't true because you saw me at the Rookery Club."

"You were trying to find him."

Anika nodded.

"So you two couldn't have been together that whole evening."

She gave her head a tight shake, then opened her eyes wide. "You have to understand, Sophie. Andy didn't murder anyone. He couldn't."

"I don't want to hurt you or your husband in any way," said Sophie, "but this puts me in an awkward position. If the police should ask me about that night, I'd have to tell them the truth."

"But why would they ask?" said Anika, leaning toward the desk. "You weren't involved. You'd never even met Ken Loy. And as far as Bob goes, Andy loved his brother. More than that. He idolized him."

Sophie wondered if Anika wasn't protesting too much.

"Listen to me, Sophie. Please. Just let me explain."

"I'm not sure that's a good idea."

"But I need you to understand. Andy's been ill for almost a year. It's more complex than what I just told you. He's seen doctors, but they can't seem to figure out what's wrong. The night Bob died, I was supposed to meet Andy at the Lyme House in Minneapolis for dinner. When he didn't show—and when he didn't answer his cell phone—I wondered if we'd gotten our signals crossed. We eat at the Lyme House fairly often. Our other favorite spot is the Rookery Club. I called over to see if Andy was there. They said he wasn't, but I was upset. I needed to do *something* to find him, so I drove over. That's when I ran into you. By then, I was pretty angry. I thought he'd stood me up again."

"Again? He's done it before?"

"If he gets involved in his work at the paper, sometimes he loses track of time. And he's terrible about turning off his cell phone and forgetting to turn it back on. He just doesn't think."

"Did you call the paper?"

"Sure. That was the first place I called. He wasn't there. After I got done talking to you, I started to get frightened that he'd had another one of his spells. Maybe he'd been in a car accident."

"Spells?"

"He gets dizzy. Nauseated. And on top of that, he's been incredibly depressed for months."

Sophie wondered if the depression didn't have something to do with what had been happening at the paper—the Del Irazarian business. But dizziness and nausea? That sounded physical.

"About six weeks ago, Andy had this excruciating muscle and bone pain. He couldn't get out of bed. That's when he started having panic attacks. And his body would get very cold. I could see the goose bumps on his skin."

"And the doctors couldn't diagnose it?"

She shook her head. "Andy was desperate. And then, as fast as it came on, it all went away. He's been fine ever since. Oh, he was still restless and depressed, perhaps more than normal, but he wasn't in pain. And then, the night Bob died, it hit again. I drove home after I saw you at the Rookery. I found Andy on the living room couch. He'd been vomiting and his whole body was shaking. He was sweating, but he had terrible chills. He drank some brandy to warm himself up, but he couldn't keep it down. He said he'd been like that for hours."

"Did he have a fever?"

"No. That's the funny part. You'd think, with those symptoms, that it was the flu. But I took his temperature and it was normal. He was in terrible agony, Sophie. He couldn't have been out murdering two men. He could barely stand up."

Or, thought Sophie, he was having a violent physical reaction to what he'd just done.

"Why didn't he call you?"

Again, Anika looked away. "I don't know. But I thought he might die that night, Sophie. He wouldn't let me call for help. He said that doctors didn't know anything, and by then, I had to agree with him. They hadn't been able to help him before. He just wanted me to sit with him, to hold him. By midnight, he seemed a little better."

"You had no idea that Bob had been shot?"

"None. Not until the police came to our apartment early Tuesday morning. Andy was in shock. I thought the news would send him into another spell, but he got through it. The police talked to us for several hours. I told them that Andy had been with me all evening. I know it was a lie, but Andy was simply too sick to have been anywhere but our living room couch."

"What time did you get home that night?"

"Around nine. Andy said he came home straight from work. He thought it was around six."

Sophie recalled what she'd read in the paper. Ken Loy had been shot just before eight, Bob Fabian approximately half an hour later. Andy may have been lying on the couch when Anika got home, but he could easily have done the shootings and been home by nine. For obvious reasons, Sophie wasn't as certain of Andy's innocence as Anika was. Did that mean she was obligated to tell the police what she knew?

"Andy made all the arrangements for the funeral," continued Anika. "He barely survived the ordeal. When it was over, he went to bed and stayed there for several days. He's pretty upbeat right now, but that could change any second. I hate to think I'm leaving a man who has some terrible disease, but the truth is, we've had a marriage in name only for almost a year. I can't continue to live this way." She took a deep breath, then continued. "You see why I can't quit my job. I have no idea what the future holds for me. I don't give a damn about Bob Fabian's money. Andy can keep every dime of it as far as I'm concerned."

"You need to take this one step at a time," cautioned Sophie. "You may feel that way now, but in a year or two, you may change your mind. Andy would want to be fair."

"I don't care about fair, Sophie. Is it fair of me to leave a man who's in so much trouble?"

Sophie shook her head. "I can't answer that."

"The thing is, I know what Andy will do. He'll blame himself, just like he always does." She covered her face with her hands. "How can I leave a man I still love? It kills me to watch what's happening to him and not be able to help."

Sophie's heart went out to her.

Keeping her head down, Anika hugged her body and rocked slowly. Tears streamed down her cheeks. After nearly a minute, she looked up. "I shouldn't dump this on you, Sophie."

"I'm here for you anytime you need me. That's what friends are for."

Anika sniffed, wiping the tears from her face with the tissue in her hand. "We'll be all moved in by the end of the week. That will be a load off my shoulders."

"Moved in where?" asked Sophie.

"Didn't I tell you? Andy insisted we move into Bob's place. I can't imagine anything more ghoulish, but Andy doesn't see it that way. He's got an old friend coming to visit on Friday and I get the feeling he wants to impress him with his newfound wealth."

"That's not like Andy."

Anika shook her head, then shrugged. "Like I said, I don't know him anymore. The really sad thing is, Sophie, maybe I never did."

22

Bram had just finished dressing when he heard the phone ring. Picking it up in the bedroom, he heard his daughter's voice wishing him a merry Wednesday morning.

"Let's have breakfast together," she said. "Just you and me."

"What about Sophie?"

"Can't we make it just a father-daughter thing? Come on, Dad. It's not like Sophie's my mom or anything. I need time with you just by myself."

Bram and Sophie had planned to have breakfast together downstairs at the Fountain Grill. But Bram assumed Sophie wouldn't mind if he passed on it this morning. Breakfast wasn't a big deal. "Sure. You've got a date."

"I'll meet you over at the Rookery Club. I can show you where we plan to do Nathan and Elaine's wedding. It's going to be *incredibly* spectacular, especially after our lighting guy gets done with it."

"You have a lighting guy?"

"Daaaad," she brayed. "I'm a professional. I'm not playing at this."

"Sorry."

Bram wasn't the least bit interested in Nathan's wedding plans, but as a father, he needed to show his daughter that he was rooting for her new company, so he'd simply have to swallow hard when Nathan's name came up and cheer his daughter on. "What time?"

"Half an hour. I've already made reservations."

"You think you can talk your old man into anything, huh?"

"Something like that. See ya."

Bram spent a moment checking his look in the mirror. He straightened his tie, flashed himself one of his more devastating smiles, then grabbed his wallet and keys off the top of a chest and headed into the hallway. He found Sophie standing at the window in the living room, looking out at the Mississippi River. She was holding a mug of coffee and seemed to be deep in thought.

He quietly slipped up behind her.

"You smell good," she said, leaning back against him.

"You seem pensive this morning."

She sighed. "I didn't sleep well."

"Something you ate?"

"Something I learned." She turned and hugged him close.

"Anything I can help you with?"

"I didn't mention it last night, because I needed time to think. We can discuss it at breakfast."

Bram cleared his throat. "Honey?"

"Hmm?"

"Would you be terribly disappointed if we didn't have breakfast together today?"

She stood back. "You got called to the station?"

"Not exactly."

Her look grew more measuring. "Margie."

He gave her his cheeriest grin. "You read me like a book. She wants to have breakfast with me over at the Rookery Club so she can show me how the plans are going for Nathan's wedding."

Sophie winced.

"It's okay. I'm getting used to hearing his name several dozen times a day."

Sitting down on the couch, she said, "I asked him *specifically* not to get Margie and her company involved."

"Well, it's a done deal. We just have to make the best of it." He could tell Sophie was chewing on something sour. "Are you mad at me for standing you up?"

She glanced up at him. "Oh, honey. No, it's not that. It's Nathan. I simply don't want him in my life anymore, but the harder I try to get rid of him, the more ways he finds to link us together."

Bram sat down next to her. He balled up his fists and socked her gently in the arm. "Want me to punch him out? Huh? Huh?"

She laughed. "I don't think that's exactly your style."

"Maybe not now. But remember, I grew up on the South Side of Chicago. My given name was Leroy— but I changed it for aesthetic purposes. I learned a few tricks when I was a kid."

"I wish they were magic tricks and you could make Nathan disappear in a puff of smoke."

"You're really bothered by him." He didn't want

to admit it out loud, but her words made him glow inside like a seven-hundred-watt bulb. If there was such a thing. "Is that what you wanted to talk to me about at breakfast? Nathan? I'm sure I could hire one of my old Chicago pals, put a contract out on his life."

"If it were only that easy."

"Ouch," said Bram. "You're really serious."

She adjusted the silk handkerchief in his suit pocket. "Yeah, but I've got another problem, too. Except, I'm afraid, when I tell you what it is, that you'll insist I do something I don't want to do."

"And that is?"

"Talk to the police."

He unbuttoned his suit coat and pulled the ottoman over between them. Together, they put their legs up and intertwined their arms.

"Spill," said Bram.

"Well, I talked to Anika last night."

"I know that. Get to the good part. I haven't got much time."

"She admitted that she wasn't with Andy all evening the night Ken Loy and Bob Fabian were murdered."

"You already knew that."

"But what I didn't know, what I was afraid of, was that she lied to the police to give Andy an alibi. If you recall, you said that if she did that, it might make her an accessory to murder."

"If Andy was the shooter, true. And you can blow his alibi out of the water."

Sophie gave a resigned nod.

"So. The ball's in your court."

"She claims that Andy couldn't have done it, because when she got home, she found him on the couch. He was really sick. Apparently, he's been sick for months. She calls them 'spells.'"

"And he had a spell that night."

"Right."

"How convenient. Do you believe her? If she was willing to lie to the police, maybe she lied to you, too."

"I do believe her, Bram. But the problem is, she could be wrong about Andy. She didn't get home until close to nine. Who knows where he was before that?"

"Motive, Sophie. What was it?"

"What if he thought killing Loy would please his brother?"

"Kill a man to score points? That's twisted."

"Well, the whole family hated Loy for what he did to Valerie. Let's say Andy does the deed on the anniversary of Valerie's death, then makes a beeline to Bob's house to give him the good news. But Bob isn't pleased—he's horrified. He goes to the nearest phone to report the shooting. Andy walks in on him, finds that he's about to be turned into the police himself, so he shoots his brother. I know he adored him, but it could have been a simple gut reaction. Self-preservation. And then, he's so upset, he drives home. When Anika finds him, he's throwing up, sick as a dog."

"Makes sense."

"So, if I don't tell the police what I know, am I making a mistake?"

"An error of omission," said Bram, playing with

her hand. "Intriguing. But, you know, if you don't tell what you know, it's possible you could be prosecuted for obstructing justice."

"Prosecuted?"

"You thought this was just a moral issue?"

"Well . . . yeah."

"It's not. You have a legal responsibility."

"Gee, you're full of good news this morning."

"Sorry, Soph. But you're right. I think you should call Al and tell him everything."

"But Anika begged me to keep quiet. And the truth is, I really can't see Andy as a murderer."

Bram glanced at his watch. "We'll have to continue this later."

"I am *so* confused."

"Me too," said Bram, rising from the couch. "But in my case, it's a way of life."

Across town, Chris had just settled into a bubble bath when she heard the phone ring. Phil's heavy work boots hit the terrazzo tile downstairs as he rushed to answer it.

Chris leaned back, a thought striking her like a thunderbolt. What if the call was from that man? Del? She had to know what he wanted from Phil. After toweling herself off, she slipped into her robe. She picked up the extension next to the bed, careful not to make a sound. But somehow, the phone must have clicked because all she heard on the line was silence. Then:

"What was that?" asked Phil.

"What was what?" said the other man. Chris was positive it was Del.

"I heard something."

"You're awfully jumpy, pal. I wonder why."

More silence.

"When can we meet?" asked Phil.

"The sooner the better."

"Okay. Right now."

"Should I come to your place?"

"No. I'll meet you. You familiar with the university area? Prospect Park?"

"Yeah."

"In the park, next to the Witch's Hat. Half an hour."

"You better show," said Del. "Otherwise, what I've got goes straight to the cops."

Chris had no idea what the Witch's Hat was. If it was a restaurant, it wasn't one she'd heard of. She waited a few more seconds, but they'd obviously hung up.

From downstairs, she heard Phil's voice call, "Chris? I'm leaving. I'll call you later."

She tiptoed back to the bathroom. "Okay, honey."

"You take it easy today. We'll do something special tonight."

"Great."

The front door slammed.

She knew there was no use following him. By the time she got dressed, he'd be long gone.

Chris moved in front of the bathroom mirror. Her eye was almost swollen shut. It looked purple in the harsh light, and it hurt like hell. She felt guilty this morning because she'd been so stupid last night. She'd provoked her husband. It wasn't all his fault. She should have been able to tell he'd had a rough day. Dropping down on the edge of the tub, she started to cry. She couldn't help herself. Her picture-perfect life had been reduced to rubble.

An hour later, she was in the kitchen making herself a cup of coffee when the front doorbell sounded.

"Just a minute," she called, wondering who it was.

She'd spent most of the last hour going through her closet, trying to find something decent to wear tonight. Phil was totally right. Her clothes consisted of jeans, flannel shirts, T-shirts, tank tops, and one dress. She put the dress on, but she knew it wasn't good enough. She'd always felt so attractive, especially around Phil, but this morning, the weight of his words nearly crushed her. She was a grody mess. Everything was wrong. Her hair. Her clothes. Her skin. There was so much to change, it was overwhelming.

Pulling back the door, Chris found a delivery man outside. He was holding a huge bouquet of long-stemmed red roses.

"Delivery for Mrs. Philip Banks."

"That's me," said Chris.

"Sign here," he said, holding out a clipboard.

As soon as he was gone, she found the card in the mass of flowers.

"I'm sorry about last night," it said. It wasn't Phil's handwriting, but that was because he'd probably called the order in. "I love you more than life. Please forgive me and know that it will never happen again. You're my bright star, sweetheart. My only love." It was signed "Phil."

Chris hugged the flowers to her chest, smelled the sweet scent. Her mood changed instantly. She felt incredibly happy. Relieved. It was as if she'd entered a beautiful, fragrant meadow where the sun shone down on her and life was good. She and Phil would work things out. She was sure of it. She would learn how to dress, how to present the right image to the world. And whatever problem the man named Del presented, Phil would handle it. Chris relied on his strength. He was her husband, her silver fox. She would love him forever.

23

During breakfast with his daughter, Bram did a lot of teeth gritting and forced smiles. Margie talked nonstop about Nathan and Elaine's forthcoming wedding. She thought Nathan was a hunk with great taste but periodic bouts of shortsightedness. Elaine, on the other hand, was "a Prada Fascist Diva Bitch." Margie said she got along with Prada Fascists just fine, but since Elaine had all the warmth of a walk-in freezer, the Diva Bitch part was a total pisser.

"She thinks she's, like, Diane Sawyer, and, if she gets her way, this wedding is going to be in the same financial ballpark as the British Royals. I'm tap-dancing as fast as I can to offer her lots of suggestions, and Carrie's doing her Glenda the Good Witch routine. We're, like, no, we don't think muted faux Asian would be a good look for the wedding dress. Nathan, well, he'd be happy with jeans, an Izod shirt, and a sweatshirt tied around his waist. So, he's like totally in another time warp. We settled on jewel colors for the wedding. Raw silk. I mean, it's *December. Hel-lo!* And furthermore, it's hardly Elaine's first walk down the aisle, so white is totally out."

By the time Bram and Margie said their good-byes, Bram was thrilled beyond belief to think that *his* wedding was long over and that he'd never have to think about all that blather again.

As he walked back to the De Gustabus room to see what was cooking, he passed Sheldon Larr, who was tacking an announcement on the gilt-framed bulletin board just outside the Wackenhut room. Bram stopped and peered over his shoulder. "Wow, you've collected nearly fifty thousand dollars." It was the reward money for finding Bob Fabian's murderer.

"Anything we can do, we must," said Sheldon, eyeing the page to make sure it was straight. "Horrible business. The authorities don't seem interested in what I think, but if they asked me, I'd give them an earful."

"About what?" asked Bram.

Sheldon turned around. "I'd tell them"—he looked over both shoulders—"to look no farther than this club. Find the man who had, shall we say"—he lowered his voice—"a great deal to lose if Bob didn't keep his mouth shut."

"Meaning what?"

Sheldon's eyes scanned the hallway. "What *is* a Rook, my dear?"

"A rook? Well, my wife tells me it's many things."

"Name one."

"A chess piece."

Sheldon frowned. "Name another."

"A bird."

"Exactly. And what do birds do?"

Bram was at a loss. "They . . . sleep in trees?"

"They *fly*, my dear. They fly." He winked, then limped away.

Bram stood for a moment, wondering what all that had been about. Shrugging, he headed for the room off the kitchen. As he came through the door, he saw that Lyle Boerichter was sitting at the table, his head leaning against his hand, staring into a cup of coffee. With his florid face and fleshy body, he looked like a heart attack waiting to happen. Bram knew a lot about heart attacks. He'd had one a while back. Bypass surgery had saved his life, but it was no fun—and that was an understatement.

Lyle looked up from his cup. "Baldric. Morning."

"Thought I'd see if you and Vince were dining on yak knuckle sausage for breakfast."

Lyle smiled. "No, we eat pretty normally, except for our Monday night meetings. You going to join us next time?"

"Haven't decided. Mind if I sit down?"

Lyle nodded to a chair. "The coffeepot's on."

Bram had already had three cups. "Thanks, but no thanks." Since Lyle was wearing his captain's uniform, Bram assumed he was flying this morning. "You headed somewhere?"

"LaGuardia, then on to Hartsfield-Jackson. I overnight in Atlanta, then back to New York, a stop in Pittsburgh, and home."

"You like flying the big jets?"

"It's my life," said Lyle. "The only thing I'm good at." When he leaned back, he moved like a man who'd been in a fight, as if every muscle hurt.

"Hard night?" asked Bram.

"No harder than usual." He glanced at the photo of Bob Fabian. It had been moved off the end of the table and set on the buffet.

"Still miss him?"

"Like you wouldn't believe."

"The night you had that last dinner with him, Vince said he was real upbeat."

Lyle sipped his coffee. "Yeah. Well, if we're gonna be precise, he left in an upbeat mood, but he was in a lousy mood when he arrived. There'd been some big snafu at the paper. I read about it in the *Times Register* a few days ago. Guy named Del Irazarian got nailed for lying in print. Between you and me, I think Bob was real disappointed in his brother. Kid named Gladstone. Said he should have caught the problems before they ended up on the front page."

"Sounds like Gladstone or Phil Banks are at the top of the police's list of suspects in Bob's death. You know Banks?"

"I've met him a couple times. My ex was a friend of his first wife's, so we went to the wedding. Vince tells me Phil just married Chris." He shook his head.

"You don't seem thrilled."

He grunted. "That guy's bad news. His first wife used to call my ex and complain about him all the time."

Vince pushed through the swinging door and smiled when he saw Bram. "Just can't stay away from us culinary mavericks, huh, Baldric?"

"Uncle Vincent?" Chris stuck her head inside the doorway. When she saw everyone in the room, her face sobered.

"My God," said Vince. "What happened to your eye?"

Bram could tell she'd tried to cover the bruising with makeup, but she hadn't done a very good job.

She touched her face hesitantly. "Oh, you know me. Ms. Super Klutz. I was out jogging last night and

I, ah . . . I tripped. Fell flat on my face. My eye clipped a rock."

Vince stared at her. "You telling me the truth?"

Chris glanced at Bram. "Sure."

Bram didn't believe a word of it. Chris had probably gone home yesterday demanding to know why Phil had been with another woman. His answer had been the black eye.

"Did Banks hit you?" asked Vince.

"No, of course not."

"Like hell."

She stepped farther into the room. "Why do you hate him so much?"

"That bastard," sputtered Vince. He looked around. "Am I the only one here who sees what he's doing?" He turned back to Chris. "You're his alibi for Bob's murder. You told me you were with him all night."

"I was."

"If you're married to him, you can't be forced to testify against him."

"I'd never do that," she said indignantly. "Married or not."

"Don't you see? That's why he insisted on doing it right away. Tell me the truth, Chris. He hit you. Didn't he!"

"No," she said. "And I'm not going to stay here and listen to you bad-mouth him." She backed out of the doorway and took off.

Bram stood and followed her. Just as she reached the front door, he called, "Chris, wait up."

She stopped and turned around. "If you're going to bitch me out for marrying Phil—"

"I'm not," said Bram. "Come on, just talk to me for a second."

He could see that her emotions were at war. Finally relenting, they walked into the Wackenhut room and sat down at a table. The bar didn't open until eleven, so the room was empty.

"Just tell me you're really okay," said Bram.

"I'm fine." She lowered her eyes. "Did you get my note yesterday? I'm sorry I couldn't stay and meet Victoria Svensvold."

"It's okay. I talked to her about it and she's very interested. She wants to meet you."

Chris's face lit up. "Really? I talked to Phil about the idea last night and he's fine with the whole thing. Really, I'm so psyched about this."

Bram hesitated. He didn't want to push her, but he agreed with Vince's assessment of Phil Banks. The guy was a lowlife. And if Chris was hedging at all about Phil's whereabouts on the night Bob Fabian and Ken Loy were murdered, she could be in way over her head and not even know it. "Did Phil explain about the woman he was with yesterday?"

Chris nodded, chewing her lower lip. "She was an old girlfriend. He wanted to tell her in person that we'd gotten married."

The explanation sounded totally self-serving to Bram. It didn't even begin to cover what he'd seen, but he let it pass. "When can you meet with Victoria?"

She pressed a finger to the skin around her eye. "Well, I've got stuff I need to do today. Maybe I should wait a few days. Let this bruise heal up a little more."

"She's eager to get started."

"Oh. Okay. Well, how about tomorrow, then? I'll give you a call this evening. We can figure out a time."

"Sounds good." Bram could tell she was getting antsy, that she wanted to take off, but he was concerned about her. He didn't want to let her go. Not just yet. "Chris?"

"Yeah?"

"If there's anything—ever—that you need to confide in someone about, I'm your man."

She smiled. "Thanks."

"Oh, I forgot." He reached into his pocket and took out the napkin Chris had been doodling on yesterday. "You left this at the restaurant. I thought the part about Old Mill Road might be important."

She looked down at it. "Nah, that's nothing. You can throw it away. Phil rents a garage at a mini storage place over there." As an afterthought, she added, "Del was the guy who set it up for him."

Bram nodded. "Okay." She was lying and he knew it. The hard part was, Chris knew he knew, but she lied anyway. "You're going to be okay, right?"

"Fine." She touched his hand. "I'll call you tonight. Promise."

24

Anika stood inside the garage at the rear of Bob Fabian's property. She was inspecting the boxes the movers had piled under an overhanging storage ledge in the back. The move from the apartment had taken all of the morning and part of the afternoon, but the worst of it was over now, and for that, Anika was grateful. She still had to run back to the old apartment and make sure the cleaners had finished their job, but that could wait until tomorrow. Today was for digging out. Tomorrow she'd organize the new kitchen and go grocery shopping, all in preparation for Rick Lostine's arrival on Friday.

Anika intended to prepare all of Rick's favorites—standing rib roast with all the trimmings. Roasted potatoes, carrots, and Brussels sprouts. Yorkshire pudding. She was a little rusty when it came to cooking. She'd pretty much given up preparing dinner because she never knew when Andy would be home from the paper. In the early days of their marriage, they always ate dinner together, no matter what was going on. It was their time to relax, to reconnect after a hard day, and to share their small triumphs and tragedies. Their time in Marquette now felt like a lifetime ago.

Tears welled up behind Anika's eyes. After Rick left, she would finally ask Andy for a divorce. She'd come to the conclusion that there was no use waiting. Putting it off only made things harder on both of them. Andy seemed oblivious to what was happening between them, and Anika had to admit that she was curious how he'd take it. Was she hoping her decision would change him, that he'd agree to go to couples counseling, that he'd really try to work out the troubles in their marriage? Or would he crawl back into himself, as he did so often these days, blame himself for what was wrong between them, but do nothing. In the last year, Andy had truly perfected an emotional disappearing act.

Behind her, Anika heard footsteps approach. As she turned around, she expected to find a neighbor coming to check on who was moving in. She'd seen an elderly woman across the street watching from her front window. But instead of the old woman, Rick walked into the garage, a big grin on his face.

"What—" It was all she could get out before he crushed her in his arms, whirled her around.

"Surprised?" he asked. He looked wonderful. Gone were his wire-rimmed glasses. His long sandy blond hair had been cut and styled, and his beard was trimmed to a goatee. His overcoat was Gucci, and the clothes he wore under it were expensive and trendy. He looked nothing like the old, scruffy, jeans-clad Rick.

"What happened to you? I hardly recognize you!"

"If you're going to live in New York, you gotta dress the part."

"You look fabulous."

"Well, it's not just the clothes."

"Your new job?"

"Jobs come and go. I've got something better. I met a guy. Anika, I think he's the one. I've never felt this way before."

"That's wonderful! I'm so happy for you. But . . . you weren't supposed to be here until Friday."

"I found out this morning that I have an important meeting on Friday. One I can't miss. But, hell, I couldn't cancel the trip. I had John drive me out to LaGuardia and I hopped on the first plane. I can only stay tonight. My flight leaves tomorrow at noon. So, we've got to make the best of it." He looked around. "This place is incredible! God, our lives sure have changed."

She couldn't stop herself. Tears leaked out her eyes, down her cheeks.

"Oh, honey. I'm glad to see you, too." He put his arms around her, more tenderly this time. "Let's go inside and call Andy. Tell him to get his butt back here. I bought three bottles of champagne on my way in from the airport. One for each of us." He squeezed her tight. "We've got a lot to talk about."

She felt so silly, but it was great to see him. It made her think of those years in her life when she and Andy had been happy. "I've missed you." She missed so much of what she'd lost.

"I've missed you, too," said Rick. "I know this has been a hard time for you guys. But hey, you'll get through it. Come on. It's chilly out here. You got heat in that castle, don't you?"

Once back in the house, Anika led Rick into the kitchen. After a moment of dickering, they decided that he should be the one to call Andy. She sat down at a sleek glass table. Bob's kitchen was huge. All that Anika had brought from the apartment kitchen fit into three boxes, which had been pushed up next to the sink. It struck her that her world was too small for such a large house.

"Andy Gladstone, please." Rick listened. "My name? Tell him—" He cupped his hand over the mouthpiece. "What's the name of your governor?"

"Pawlenty."

He nodded. Removing his hand, he said, "Tell him it's Governor Pawlenty on the line. Make it quick. I'm an important man." He winked at Anika. "Yes that's right. The governor. Fergus Pawlenty."

Anika laughed.

Rick put his hand over the mouthpiece again. "Fergus isn't his first name?"

She shook her head.

"Too bad. It has a certain ring to it." Removing his hand, he listened a moment, then said, "Hey, you old reprobate. It's Rick." He grinned. "No, I'm here. In town. As a matter of fact, I'm standing in your new kitchen with your gorgeous wife." More grinning. "Hell, yes. I brought champagne. When can you get here?" He glanced at his watch. "Well, get out of it. Cancel the meeting. Send someone else. It's not every day a representative from a prestigious New York publishing house comes to visit you." He laughed. "Okay, Anika and I can manage for a few hours. But I gotta leave tomorrow. Change of plans. Sorry, buddy. But that means we've got to make the most of the time we have." He listened a moment more. "Okay. We'll be here waiting. The longer it takes you, the drunker we'll be, so hurry up." Another wink. "Right. See you soon. Bye."

"You really want to start drinking now?" Anika looked at the clock on the wall. It was going on two.

"Well," said Rick, hanging up the phone, "we could pop one bottle. Have a small drink, just to celebrate my arrival. What do you say?"

It sounded great to her. "Deal."

"What you got around here for munchies?"

"Not sure." She opened up a couple cupboards, finding an unopened box of Breton crackers and a jar of Kalamata olives.

Rick stood in front of the open refrigerator. "Looks like you have a great piece of cheese in here." He unwrapped it and took a sniff. "Gorgonzola, I think. You like stinky cheese?"

"Love it."

"Well then, looks like we've got ourselves a small feast."

They carried everything into the living room and set it on the stone-and-glass coffee table in front of the sectional. Anika flipped the switch on the gas fireplace, then sat down next to Rick, waiting for him to pop the cork on the champagne.

"This feels decadent," said Anika, as he poured her a glass. "What should we talk about?"

"Well," said Rick, clicking his glass to hers, then taking a sip, "we better not discuss my job or the new love of my life until Andy gets here. Why don't we talk about you. You look tired, honey. I'm sorry about what happened to Andy's brother. That must have been so hard for you two. Have they found his murderer?"

Anika shook her head. "Did you ever meet Bob?"

"Oh, sure. He was a lot older than Andy and me. He was off to West Point as soon as he graduated from high school. Andy and I were in second grade his senior year. I thought Bob was a god. Really. It must have been the strong jawline. I'm still a sucker for a great jaw. And you know how little kids look up to bigger ones. But Bob really was special. He was president of his class, class valedictorian, and he was a star on the football team. He used to throw balls to Andy and me, and he'd talk to us about West Point, about how important it was for him to serve his country. He was one of those great guys who love life, and have tons of energy and talent. He could have done anything. And then, he ends up in Viet Nam, comes home with shrapnel in his back that ends his military career. He probably would have been a general before he retired. But, hell, he landed on his feet. People say that a West Point ring can open any door. It sure did for him." Rick looked over at the fire. "The sad thing is, he grew up in such a different home from the one Andy grew up in."

"Andy never talks about his childhood."

"Doesn't surprise me. It was a bad time."

"In what way?"

Rick studied Anika over the rim of his wineglass. "You mean he's never told you anything?"

"Just that his father was an alcoholic, that Bob's father, David Fabian, died when Bob was nine. His mother remarried, and then she died when Bob was twenty; Andy was eight. So it was mostly just Andy and his dad when he was growing up."

"Yeah, that's right."

"So . . . *did* his dad drink a lot?"

"Wow, I had no idea you knew so little."

Anika felt ashamed that she'd never pushed Andy

harder to talk about his childhood. But the truth was, every time she had, he'd changed the subject so quickly that it didn't take her long to get the point. The subject was off-limits. "Tell me about it, Rick. Maybe it would help me understand him better."

He poured them more champagne.

"Well," he said, setting the bottle down, "Andy and I were buddies in grade school, but we were better friends in junior high. That was a tough time for both of us. For different reasons, we both felt like outsiders and that drew us together."

"You already knew you were gay?"

"Yeah, I did, although I was trying to hide it as hard from myself as I was from others."

"And Andy? Did you hide it from him?"

Rick shrugged. "If he knew, we never talked about it."

"What made Andy feel like an outsider?"

"God, his home life was from hell. After we moved into high school, we got pulled into different groups, so we weren't together as much. What I know is based mostly on his earlier years." He leaned forward and set his champagne glass down, then crossed his legs and leaned back against the couch cushions, ready to remember. "Once—we were in fifth grade at the time—Andy didn't show up for school. It was just before Christmas and we were all supposed to bring cookies or something for a party. It was more of a play day than a regular school day, so I couldn't understand why he wasn't there. I assumed he was sick. I decided to save some of my cookies to bring him after school. I'd never been in his house, but I knew where he lived."

"You'd never been in his house?"

"I was too young to realize the significance. We always played at my place or at one of our other friends'. Andy said his dad worked at home and that he didn't like to be disturbed."

"Was that true?"

"Hell no. That was part of the problem. Merle Gladstone had made his living as an insurance salesman. But when Andy's mother died, he fell apart. It didn't take long before he lost his job. He had lots of relatives around town who tried to help him out until he could get back on his feet. Only problem was, he never did. Eventually, all the relatives saw him for the black hole that he was. But they still felt sorry for Andy, so he was the recipient of their kids' hand-me-downs. You know how important clothes are to a kid? Andy never got to pick his. Oh, they'd slip him some spending money every now and then. It wasn't much, but it was something."

"How did they live if his dad didn't work?"

"I don't really know. I think, for a while, Merle received some sort of residuals from the insurance policies he'd sold. I do know that Andy was hungry a lot. He ate at our house a couple times a week. In junior high, I'd go over to his place sometimes and the lights would be off. The phone didn't work. His dad was usually sitting in the living room, but he never said anything to me. He gave me the creeps. Any cleaning that happened around the house was all Andy's doing. And he went to work after school as soon as someone would hire him. Grocery stores. Gas stations. Sometimes he had two or three jobs at once. He worked weekends, evenings. I suppose he paid a lot of the bills. If the heat or water was turned off, he'd take a shower at the downtown Y. He'd study at night in libraries around town. He grew up real fast."

"What about when you were in fifth grade? The time you brought Christmas cookies to his house."

"Oh, yeah. Right. So, I go over there and ring the bell. His father answers the door. I asked if I could talk to Andy. Mr. Gladstone just walked away. Or, more specifically, he stumbled off. He'd been drinking, although, at the time, I thought maybe he was sick. The house was real cold. And nothing had been done to trim the place for the holidays. I called out Andy's name a couple of times. I had no idea where his room was. Mr. Gladstone had gone back into the living room to watch TV, so I stayed out of there. It took a while, but I finally found Andy in an upstairs closet."

"Oh, my God."

"He said he'd fallen asleep, but I could tell he was lying. I think he was hiding from his dad. He had some bruises on his face, and a big swollen welt on his lower arm. I was young, but I could see he was terrified of his father. I gave him the cookies. He tried to act nonchalant about them, but even a kid knows when another kid is hungry—and hurting. He was scared to come out of that closet. I can only imagine what had gone on that morning to cause him to miss school."

Anika lowered her head and closed her eyes. "I had no idea."

"Nobody really did. Andy never had many close friends. And the people he did run with, most of them didn't know. The thing is," said Rick, crossing his arms, "the situation was bad enough all by itself. But Merle Gladstone was a bully when he was drunk, and he was drunk all the time. He took all his bitterness out on Andy. I mean, just to get through his childhood and end up with a scholarship to Marquette was an amazing feat. Andy is a super-smart guy, but his father cut him down every chance he got. Adolescence is hard enough without a parent constantly telling you you're stupid, worthless, even ugly. Andy wanted so much for his dad to love him. He tried hard to please him, to show him he was wrong. But like I said, Merle Gladstone was a black hole. The only way Andy could survive was by sucking it all inside, never admitting how bad it was. He still does that."

"Tell me about it."

Rick stopped, watching Anika for a second. "I can imagine Andy isn't always the easiest person to live with."

She gave a small nod.

"Are you two okay?"

"Not really."

"God. If there's anything you want to talk about—"

"I can't."

"I'm Andy's best friend. Maybe I'm the right person to help."

She was torn.

"How's Andy's back? That operation couldn't have been easy on either of you."

"He's much better. At least that much has gone right."

"What little back problems I've had in my life have really made me feel for the guy." He sat forward. "Listen, while you're thinking about whether you're going to confide in me or not, you wouldn't happen to have a couple of Tylenol around here, would you? Somewhere between New York and Minneapolis I seem to have developed a nasty headache."

"I've got ibuprofen in my purse."

He dropped his hand to his stomach. "I can't handle the hard stuff." He smiled.

"Andy uses Tylenol for the same reason. It doesn't do a thing for me, but he swears by it. Give me a sec." She rose from the couch and trotted up the stairs. In the bathroom, in one of the moving boxes, she found the large bottle of Tylenol Andy kept in the nightstand next to the bed. When she returned downstairs, she found Rick standing by the piano, holding a photograph of Bob.

"This guy was born with a military bearing," said Rick. "Hard, blue-eyed gaze, the kind that says, 'Hey, asshole, I'm a hell of a lot more prepared for what could happen than you are, but I'm so pumped that I don't need to make a big deal out of it.'"

"You're right. He was a lot like that. But he was also patient, and very kind. He loved his wife more than any man I've ever known. He just glowed around her."

"He must have taken her death pretty hard."

"And then some. Both Andy and I thought there was a chance he might take his own life after she died. Thank God, he didn't."

Rick looked at the photograph a moment more, then set it back down. "Ah, the Tylenol. Megasized, I see." He opened the cap and shook a few out.

Anika saw a confused look pass over his face. "What's wrong?"

"These aren't Tylenol."

"Sure they are."

"Well, they don't look like any Tylenol I've ever seen before. Do you have another bottle?"

"Andy carries one with him in his briefcase, but that's all we've got. Look, they have to be Tylenol. What else could they be? Maybe it's a generic form."

"Maybe," said Rick with a shrug. He slid them back into the bottle and replaced the cap. "I'll wait until he gets home. I'm sure he can explain it." Picking up another photo of Bob and Valerie, this one a picture of the two of them together on their boat, the one moored at a marina in Stillwater, he said, "I'm sorry Bob had to die so young. He was a good influence on Andy."

Anika agreed, but only to a point. Bob had put a lot of pressure on Andy by encouraging him to come to Minnesota and take a job at the *Times Register*. Maybe too much.

"You know," said Rick, surveying all the picture frames on the piano, "before Andy left Marquette, he told me he thought this job was his last chance to make something of himself. He said that Bob was like a father to him now, and he'd do anything in his power to please him. At the time, I realized it was a huge statement, but I understood. I had such hopes for him, and for you, too, when you left. I assumed Andy would be putting in a lot of overtime at his new job and that it might put a strain on your marriage. On the other hand, Bob was a decent human being, capable of *being* pleased—unlike Merle Gladstone. I knew Andy would work his tail off to make a success of his life here." Rick glanced around the palatial living room. "It's sad the way things had to work out, but it looks like he did just that."

25

Chris knocked on the front door of the small, one-story house. As she waited, she tried to muster her courage. This wasn't easy. She knew coming here might not exactly thrill Phil, but he'd pretty much ordered her to change the way she looked if she was going to make him happy. And this way, she could kill two birds with one stone.

When an older woman answered her knock, Chris got her first close-up look at Barbara Kerwin, Phil's ex-girlfriend. Chris's general opinion was unchanged. Barbara looked old and hard. But she did dress well, even if her makeup looked like it had been applied with a cake spatula.

"Can I help you?" asked Barbara. She had a pleasant voice. Sort of on the low side, but friendly.

"I hope so," said Chris. She pressed her hands into the pockets of her leather bomber jacket. She'd decided to play this meeting close to the chest. Chris hated herself for doubting Phil, but if he hadn't told her the truth about Barbara, she intended to find out. "My name is Chris Parillo." She watched Barbara to see if there was any recognition in her eyes, but her expression didn't change.

"Yes?"

"We have a mutual friend. Phil Banks."

Now Barbara grew wary. "Yes?"

"He told me that if I ever needed help with my makeup, my clothes—you know, developing a classy look—that I should come to you."

Now Barbara looked pleased. "Well, I'm glad to hear he has such faith in me, but—"

She was about to turn her away. Chris couldn't let that happen. "Look, I know this is an imposition, but if you could just give me a few minutes, it would be so incredible. I can see Phil was right. You have tons of personal style."

"Why . . . thank you."

"So, just a couple of minutes?"

Barbara looked Chris up and down. "You *could* use some help. I don't mean to be rude, but what happened to your eye?"

Chris touched her face. "An accident. I'm kind of a klutz. Will you help me?"

She hesitated. "Oh, I suppose it would be all right. I mean, I don't know you. But you say you're a friend of Phil's?"

Chris nodded.

"Okay. Come in. But just for a few minutes. I have to be to work in an hour, and I still have to fix my face."

My God, thought Chris. She was going to add *more* gunk?

Chris followed Barbara into her living room. It was a small room dominated by a large TV set in the corner. Except for the couch, which was retro '50s modern, the rest of the furniture was antique. She glanced into the new addition, the bedroom Phil's company had built for her. "You've got a nice house."

"A lot of that's due to Phil. We both like to antique and he loves to buy things for the house." Before she sat down on the couch, she motioned Chris to a chair.

On the end table directly next to her, Chris noticed a framed photo of Phil and Barbara. They were sitting on the hood of Phil's Corvette. That meant it had to be a fairly recent photo. He'd bought the car in June, a little more than four months ago. "There's Phil," said Chris.

Barbara beamed at the mention of his name. "We're engaged," she said, holding out her hand so Chris could see the ring.

Chris felt her stomach do a flip-flop. "You're . . . going to be married?"

"In the spring." She waited for Chris to make a suitable comment on the ring before she retracted her hand.

"It's beautiful."

"I think so, too."

Fighting back a wave of nausea, Chris smiled. "When did you and Phil first meet?"

"Oh, it must be a couple years now. It was right after Terry disappeared."

Terry was Phil's second wife. "She . . . disappeared?"

"Oh, yes. Didn't you know?"

"I never met Terry."

"No, me either, but Phil was in a terrible way when she took off. I mean, they'd been divorced for several years, but you know Phil. He never lets go of someone he loves. He still tried to take care of her. But one night, when he dropped by her house, she wasn't there. Her car was gone, and a bunch of her clothes. She must have just skipped town. Phil did his best to try to find her." Barbara lowered her voice. "She was unstable, you know. Emotionally. Phil figured she was doing drugs, that she got in trouble with her dealer and split because she owed him money. She was always hurting for money, always asking Phil for loans. If it had been me, I would have cut her off, but Phil's too kindhearted."

"Yeah, he's a peach," whispered Chris.

"I wish he didn't have to work so hard. We have so little time together."

"You planning on moving into his house when you get married?"

"His house?" Barbara gazed at Chris somewhat oddly. "Phil lives in an apartment, that beautiful old one on Spencer and Fifteenth. We'll either live here, or he's considering building a new place for us." She crossed her legs. "But if we're going to talk about a makeover for you, we better get to it."

Chris felt flattened.

"I think we should start with your clothes." When Chris didn't respond, Barbara said, "Ms. Parillo? Are you all right?"

"No," said Chris, rising from her chair. "I feel a little sick."

"I'm sorry." Barbara rose, too. "Can I get you anything? A glass of water?"

Chris shook her head. "This was a mistake. I gotta go."

"But—"

Chris made a beeline for the door. "Thanks for talking to me."

"Look, Ms. Parillo—"

"That's not my name."

Barbara stopped a few feet away. "Then, what is it?"

"Banks. Mrs. Phil Banks."

It was Barbara's turn to look shocked. "What is this? What kind of game are you playing?"

"Phil and I are married."

"That's impossible."

"If you don't believe me, ask him."

"You're lying!"

"I wish I were," said Chris, slamming the door on the way out.

For the next few minutes, Chris sat in her car crying her eyes out. How could Phil have done this to her? All his lies now seemed so blindingly obvious. She didn't even know who he was anymore. The only thing to do was to go home and end it. Phil couldn't talk himself out of his lies this time. He was in too deep.

The longer Chris sat there, the angrier she became. Maybe her uncle had been right. Maybe Phil *had* married her to keep her quiet. She hadn't been totally up front with the police about the night Bob Fabian and Ken Loy had been murdered. She'd said Phil had been with her the entire night, but that wasn't precisely true. If he'd lied to her about so much, what else had he lied about?

Fishing her cell phone and her small address book out of her purse, she scanned the names until she found Bram's number at the station. Fumbling with the phone, she made the call, waiting impatiently for him to answer. But when the line picked up, instead of Bram, she got his voice mail. Damn it, of course. He was on the air right now. All she could do was leave him a message.

"Bram, hi. It's Chris. I, ah, I need to talk to you right away." She felt tears burn her eyes. Scraping at her cheeks, she continued, "My whole life is a lie. I could kill Phil with my bare hands. I mean it, Bram. I could kill him!" She sniffed a few times before continuing, "Look, I just found out Phil's engaged to that woman we saw him with at the cafe, and that he's lied to her just like he's lied to me. God, I hate him. There's got to be some way to make him pay for what he's done." She stopped, tried to staunch her fury long enough to say what she needed to say. "Listen, there's something I need to tell you. I mean, I didn't exactly lie to the police, but then again, I kinda did. It's about the night Loy and Fabian died. Phil and me—we were at that movie together, but Phil didn't like it. He fell asleep and started snoring. He was annoying the people sitting around us so I told him to go sleep in the car. So . . . that's what he did. When the movie was over and I came out, he was in the Corvette, fast asleep. So, see, I figured he'd been there the whole time. Most likely, he was. But it's like, I can't be totally sure. I never told the police that part. Do you think I'm in trouble now because I didn't tell them everything I knew? Jeez, this is just what I need. My marriage is a sham, and now the police will throw the book at me. I'm in a really bad place here, Bram. I just don't know where to turn. So, I'll call you again. Like I said, later tonight. Maybe you can help me figure out what to do. Right now, I'm about to drive over to Spencer and Fifteenth. Apparently Phil rents an apartment over there—an old, beautiful one, according to Barbara Kerwin, his lucky fiancée. God, but I hate him. We'll talk. Bye."

26

Andy slumped into Bob's desk chair. It would always be Bob's chair, always Bob's office. No matter how hard Andy tried to pretend he could fill Bob's shoes, the truth was, it would be easier for him to grow gills and swim in the ocean.

Andy felt drained. It was bad timing that Rick had chosen tonight to be in town. Andy was planning to spend the next few nights working late, getting everything organized. If that was possible. After the direct hit the paper had taken from the Irazarian debacle, it would take months, perhaps years, to put the *Times Register* back on track. Andy was committed to that process; he just wasn't sure he was the man to do it.

Tilting his head back, he closed his eyes, wondering if Bob's sage advice, his "West Point Wisdom," would ever seem like something other than condemnation. *Isolate the lesson. Every chapter of life is also groundwork for the next chapter. Minimize regret. Grit your way through it. There's no problem that cannot be overcome through a combination of determination and positive attitude.*

Bob had been the number-three-ranked cadet in his 1968 West Point graduating class. The world was a solid place to him. He understood his role. He was a player, a strong guy who used every opportunity. He stood for things. Important, honorable values. When all was said and done, what would people say Andy had stood for?

Leaning forward, Andy ran his hand along the curved oak desk drawers. Thinking about his brother always created two reactions in him, both hard to handle. First, Bob's big, bold, successful life made Andy feel small, ineffectual, reduced. But at the same time, Bob's story inspired him, gave him something to shoot for, something to aspire to. Andy had tried as hard as he could to emulate his brother, but somehow it never worked. He could even use the same words as Bob, but coming out of Andy's mouth, they seemed comical. The fact that he was a screwup, a failure as an editor, hadn't truly penetrated Bob's consciousness—not until the last few weeks before his death. When Andy saw in his brother's eyes that he understood the depth and breadth of Andy's betrayal, it nearly killed him.

Andy was weak. He couldn't seem to get a grip on his world. He was a rotten husband, with a marriage that was on the verge of breaking up. Why couldn't he confide in Anika? He knew without a doubt that she loved him, and yet when he was with her, he froze inside.

Well, thought Andy, rising from the desk, he'd better get home and face Rick. He couldn't put it off forever. Not that Andy wasn't happy that Rick had come to town, but in his heart, Andy knew that his pleasure was for all the wrong reasons. He wanted to show Rick that he'd finally made it. He was a success story, just like he always said he'd be. But Rick was a smart guy. It wouldn't take him long to see through the facade. No matter how great Andy's world looked on the outside, it was a disaster on the inside. And unless a miracle occurred, his entire life was about to blow apart. By this time next year, he'd probably be in prison. Perhaps, in the end, that had been his destination all along.

Just as he stood up and turned out the desk light, the phone rang. Andy stared at it, wondering if he should take the call. Oh, hell, he thought. If it's more bad news, he might as well hear it now. He was so weary of hiding.

He picked up the receiver. It was probably just Rick calling to tell him to get a move on. "Gladstone," he said, his voice dull with resignation.

"Well, well, Mr. Gladstone. Hard at work?"

The voice stopped him. "Del?"

"Miss me?"

Acid welled up in his throat. "What are you doing calling me here? We had a deal."

"Didn't some old wise man once say that deals are meant to be broken?"

"Where are you?"

"At the Cross Keys Motel."

"Where's that?"

"South Minneapolis. Just off 35W. It's a dump, but it suits my purposes."

"You're still *here*? Jesus! I paid you two hundred thousand dollars to get out of town!"

"You know the drill, Andy. Once an investigative reporter, always an investigative reporter."

"What's that supposed to mean?"

"Just quiet down and listen. I need to see you."

"Are you crazy?"

"If I am, it's your funeral. You're a fluke, you know

that, Gladstone? You didn't get where you are because of talent or hard work. You got there because
of a cosmic accident."

Andy sank down in the desk chair. "What do you
want?"

"Like I said, I need to see you. I want you to come
to my motel."

"Now?"

"Yes, asshole. *Now.*"

"I can't."

"Sure you can. Just shut up and listen. I'm in room
33. I'll only be here tonight. Tomorrow I move again.
But before I do, there's something we need to discuss.
One hour, Gladstone. If you're not here by then, I call
the police. Are we clear?"

Andy took a deep breath. "We're clear."

The line went dead.

Twenty minutes later, Andy sat in his RAV4 in the
parking lot of the Cross Keys Motel, his eyes fixed on
Del's room. There was a light on inside, but the curtains were closed. Del was right about one thing. The
motel was a dump.

On the drive over from the Times Register Tower,
Andy had only one thought. Del Irazarian was a
thorn in his side, one that would never go away. Not
unless Andy did something about it. With just one
phone call, Del could single-handedly torpedo his
world. As much as Andy hated himself, he hated
Irazarian more. Del's cocky self-assurance, his sweaty,
fleshy body, and his swaggering belief that no rule
ever applied to him—all twisted something deep inside Andy. There was only one way to deal with
Irazarian. Perhaps it was a truth his unconscious had

recognized months ago, but it had taken his conscious mind longer to grasp.

Opening the glove compartment, Andy removed the .38. His hand shook as he pressed it into the pocket of his jacket. There was no other way. It was a revelation, but Andy saw now that there was something more basic to his soul than self-loathing. Survival topped everything.

Sliding out of the front seat, Andy left the mini-SUV unlocked. He approached the motel room door with caution, looking around to make sure nobody was watching. Breathing deeply, he gave a soft rap.

"Hey, man, we've been waiting for you!" Rick put his arms around Andy and slapped his back. "We've already killed one bottle of champagne. We were about to start on the second. You got here just in time."

Rick's grinning face and boisterous welcome made Andy feel like he'd walked into a carnival. Lights and sounds assaulted him. He felt that Rick and his wife were leering at him, zooming in and out, like the faces in a distorted, fun-house mirror.

"Hey, pal, you look like you could use a drink," honked Rick. Another slap on the back.

"Is something wrong?" chirped Anika.

Andy took off his coat. "A drink. Yeah. I'd like a drink."

"The champagne's right this way." Rick disappeared into the living room.

"What's that on your cuff?" chirped Anika, pulling him off balance, tugging his sleeve.

Andy looked down. "Nothing. I cut myself. It's nothing."

Jazz blared in the background.

Andy raised his hands to his ears. "Can you turn that CD down?"

"You okay?" honked Rick, adjusting the volume on the stereo. "God, it's so good to see you! You've lost weight." He cackled, his mouth opening wide like a braying mule's.

"We ordered a pizza," shouted Anika. The music swelled again.

Andy dropped into a chair. A glass appeared in his hand. He stared at it a moment before drinking it down like water.

"Slow down," shrieked Anika.

"No, let him drink," yelled Rick. "He needs to catch up."

More champagne appeared in his glass.

The doorbell chimed.

"That must be the pizza," shouted Rick. "The party has officially begun!"

27

The sound of a car door slamming propelled Chris off the couch. It was going on seven in the evening. She hadn't heard from Phil all day. She assumed that Barbara was on the horn to him as soon as Chris left her house. But Chris was past caring. She'd already packed a bag and after she had it out with Phil, she planned to split for good.

She realized, too late, that she had no job, no apartment, no money in the bank—*nothing* without Phil. But she did have the diamond ring and the gold band he'd given her, and she planned to hock them, get whatever she could for them. She still couldn't bring herself to believe that he'd had anything to do with Bob Fabian's or Ken Loy's murder, but she did see him now for the lying cheat that he was.

A key was thrust into the front lock, and a moment later, Phil's dark silhouette pushed into the foyer. "Chris, goddamn it! Are you here?"

She'd been sitting in the dark. Snapping on a lamp, she said. "Yeah. I'm here."

He stepped into the room, his face black with rage. "Who the hell do you think you are?"

"I *thought* I was your wife," she said, turning to

face him. "You lied to me, Phil. You told me Barbara was nothing to you."

"She isn't!" With his heavy work boot, he kicked a wicker chair across the room.

"That's not what she told me."

"Hell, woman, would you give me some credit? Barbara has cancer. She found out two weeks ago. I couldn't just dump her."

Chris stared at him.

"And now you nearly killed her!"

Coldly, Chris replied, "I don't believe you."

"You want the doctor's report? I can get it for you if that's what it will take."

"You've been *with* her, Phil. You aren't just 'friends.' She has your ring."

"Okay, okay. I didn't tell you everything. I wanted to let her down easy."

"You've had the entire last year to let her down easy."

"You don't understand."

"She said you live in an apartment not far from her house."

Anger rolled off him in waves.

"You go antiquing with her. Is that where you've been when you're not with me?"

He took a step toward her. "You don't want to do this, Chris."

"I don't think I've done anything—except love you. Is this how you repay me for that love? Is it!" And she had loved him, everything about him. But more than anything else, she'd loved the *idea* of him. And that's where she'd made her biggest mistake.

"Nobody pries into my life."

"You were going to keep Barbara a secret from me forever?"

"Why not? I would have taken care of the situation in time."

"She's a *situation*? Do you hear yourself?"

Phil's eyes flicked to the suitcase next to the couch. "You're leaving me?"

"I don't think I have a choice." There. She'd said the words out loud, but she felt pulverized by them.

"We all have choices, Chris."

She looked down at the pool of yellow light spilling from the lamp on the end table. "I don't want to go." Admitting weakness was probably a mistake, but she was so tired of his lies.

"Then don't." In an instant, he was by her side, holding her, stroking her back. "Don't leave me, Chris. It would kill me."

She stood woodenly in his arms. "You've lied to me so many times. How can I ever believe you again?"

"Do you believe I love you?"

She felt a tiny crack in her resolve. "Yeah. I thought you did."

He kissed her fiercely, her lips, her eyes, her neck. "Just trust me. I'd never hurt you. If you believe nothing else, believe that."

He pulled her down on the couch.

Pushing away from him, Chris said, "Will you answer one question for me? And . . . will you be absolutely truthful?"

"I promise."

"The night Loy and Fabian were murdered, you never left the parking lot, right? You were just out there sleeping in the car."

He took hold of her hand. "I swear it. I may be a

lot of things, but I'm not a killer. Look, Chris, you've got to understand something about me. I run a construction company. Construction isn't, well, it isn't a *gentleman's* profession. A lot of rough stuff happens. Sometimes I make it happen. Some people think I'm a badass. Maybe I am. But I did try to make that clear to you from the beginning. I'm a hard man. But I love you, more than anything in this world."

"Is . . . is that why Del Irazarian is calling you? It is him, right?"

He smoothed the hair back from her forehead. "Yeah."

"He's the one who got fired from the *Times Register*. Did you meet with him?"

"This morning."

"He seemed interested in what you've got locked away in a mini storage garage on Old Mill Road."

Phil smiled at her. "The guy's totally discredited. He's pissed at the world because he thought he was God's gift to the newspaper business, and it turns out he's just another media thug. Nothing he says about me would ever stick."

"What could he say about you?"

"Just his usual lies. He thinks I'm involved with drugs. Honey, I'm not. I swear it. You know how I feel about that crap. I drink, sure. Hell, sometimes I drink too much. But drugs? I'm not that stupid."

Chris hesitated. She felt more conflicted at this moment than she'd ever felt before in her life. "What *do* you have stored there?"

His smile broadened. "Oh, sweetheart. Just construction stuff. An old truck. Nothing that would interest you, or anybody else, for that matter. Now, let's stop all this arguing and fighting. You're the woman

I married. You're a tiger, and that's something I love about you." His expression turned serious. "But remember, Chris, don't ever pry into my life again. There are things about me that need to remain private. Even from you. If you can live with that, then stay. If you can't, then I guess you better leave."

He slipped his arms around her and kissed her softly.

She hated herself, but she felt so warm and safe with his strong arms around her. "I'll stay," she said.

"Good girl."

28

On Thursday morning, Sophie was in the bathroom putting on her makeup when Bram burst in.

"Listen to this!" He was still in his pajamas.

Turning to him, she saw that he had the front page of the paper in his hands. "You look like someone died."

"Someone did. Last night. That reporter from your paper. He was shot at a fleabag motel in South Minneapolis."

"Irazarian?" Sophie, like everyone else at the *Times Register*, had assumed he'd left town, possibly headed for New York to negotiate a deal. Now that he'd achieved a certain illicit fame, all the big publishers were probably beating down his door to get him to write a memoir.

"And listen to this," said Bram. "The police have examined the bullet. Looks like he was shot with the same gun that killed Loy and Fabian."

"Let me see that," said Sophie, grabbing it out of his hands. She read down the column, looking for the exact way the statement was worded. "It says—and I'm quoting a policeman now—'It was the same gun used in the shootings of Loy and Fabian.'"

Bram rolled his eyes. "Ah, yes. I forgot. Bob Fabian's still alive. Long live conspiracy theorists."

"Tell me this," said Sophie, spritzing herself with cologne, then turning and pushing Bram back into the bedroom. "Why are they always so careful to never say Bob is dead? There's a reason, Bram. The simplest explanation is, he's still alive."

Bram flopped backward onto the bed. "Ridiculous." He did a prom queen wave, looking up at the ceiling. "Hi, Bob. How's it going?" Glancing back at Sophie, he said, "Can we put that aside for a moment?"

"Gladly." She bent down and removed her red leather pumps from the closet.

"I told you about the voice message I got from Chris yesterday while I was doing my show."

Sophie could hardly forget. Chris had admitted to Bram that she'd lied to the police. She hadn't been with Phil at the theater the entire time on the night Bob and Ken Loy were shot.

"What I didn't tell you was that she promised to call me last night. She never did."

"And you think . . . what?"

"There has to be a reason why she didn't call. I'm worried about her, Soph. I mean *really* worried. That's why I phoned her house a few minutes ago."

"And?"

"Nobody answered. Remember, Phil gave her a black eye, so I have no doubt that he's capable of much worse."

Pressing her feet into her shoes, Sophie said, "Maybe you better call Al."

"What if Chris went home last night and told Phil she was leaving him? She was sure mad enough when she called me. That guy's been two-timing her since the day they first met. Suppose she said she planned to tell the police about how she'd lied to them. If he figured his alibi was about to go south, he might freak and do—God, who knows what he'd do?"

"Then, like I said, it's time to call the cops," said Sophie. She didn't say it out loud, but if Phil turned out to be the one behind the shootings, that meant Andy was off the hook. Sophie hoped that was the case, not only for Andy's sake, but for Anika's. Except, if Phil *was* the one, that could mean Chris was in terrible danger.

Following Sophie out into the dining room, Bram said, "What I don't get is Irazarian's part in all this."

"Well," said Sophie, picking up Ethel and giving her a kiss on her muzzle, "he was an investigative reporter until everything blew apart at the paper. Some of his stories had to be legit. Maybe he had something on Phil."

"Like what?"

"Whatever it was, if Phil killed him, it had to be dynamite."

"Maybe Irazarian was blackmailing him."

"Wouldn't surprise me." She set Ethel down, then slipped her arms around Bram's waist. "Wish me well?"

"Why? Hey, how come you're all dressed up and looking like a million bucks?" He nodded to her red suit.

"Dressing well makes me feel more powerful."

"And you need to feel powerful because . . . ?"

"I have a meeting with my father this morning."

"In your office?"

"Well, it used to be my office. It's just a guess, you understand, but I think he may want it back."

"Great. Let him have it."

Sophie shook her head. "I never thought I'd say this about my dad, but his instincts aren't what they used to be when it comes to the hotel business."

Bram hugged her tight. "You go fight the good fight."

"What are your plans?"

He shrugged. "Try to find Chris, I guess. If I can't, I'll take your advice and talk to Al."

"Be careful."

"Always."

On the way downstairs, Sophie stopped on the mezzanine level. She hadn't taken any time for breakfast, so a fresh blueberry muffin from the Fountain Grill called to her. As she stepped off the elevator, she noticed a familiar form leaning over the brass railing, looking down at the main floor.

Sophie's heart sank. It was Nathan.

She was about to duck into the restaurant when he turned around.

"Sophie." He grinned.

"Nathan, hi. What are you doing here?"

He didn't answer right away. Instead, he looked her up and down.

"Nathan?"

"Hmm? You look wonderful this morning, Soph. Really spectacular."

"Thanks. But you didn't answer my question. What are you doing at the hotel?" She tried to sound friendly—not like an interrogator in a prison camp—but she was totally fed up with him.

"I've got a meeting with Margie."

She should have guessed.

"Hey, what do you say we have a cup of coffee together?" He glanced at his watch. "I've got a few minutes."

"Sorry, Nathan. I don't." She started to walk away.

"Don't be like that, Soph."

She stopped. Turning back to him, she said, "Nathan, quit pushing me. If you're here to see Margie, that's fine. But I'm not part of the deal."

"You're so cold. What's wrong?" He walked up to her, sniffing the air. "You're wearing that perfume again."

She made a mental note to throw the bottle away.

"Did Elaine call you? She wanted to ask you to be her maid of honor."

"Nathan, listen to me. I won't be attending your wedding. Neither will Bram. We both wish you and Elaine the very best, but—"

"But you've got to be there. My whole family is coming. If you don't attend, they won't know what to think."

She gave a mock knock on her head. "Earth to Nathan. Are you listening? That's wonderful that your family is coming, but *I won't be there.*"

His grin returned. "You'll change your mind."

She threw up her hands. "Whatever," she said as she walked away.

Sophie could smell her father's cigar in the hallway outside her office. She'd argued with him about it, but it was one room where he insisted he be allowed to light up. As she crossed the threshold, the stink grew worse. Her father sat behind her desk, wearing a crisp white shirt and tie, red suspenders, and a golf cap. He was tapping on the computer keyboard, but acknowledged her presence by moving the cigar from one side of his mouth to the other side and nodding to a chair.

"Dad, can you put that thing out, at least while we talk?"

His eyes flicked to her. "Hell, you're as bad as your mother."

"I take that as a compliment. What are you working on?"

"The list. What else?" He finished tapping, lifted his chin to read more clearly through his bifocals, then sat back in his chair and turned to her. Taking the cigar out of his mouth, he said, "We're going to revolutionize the hotel business in this town."

"And how will we do that?"

He slapped his hands together, then rubbed them gleefully. Narrowing one eye, he said, "Like I've said a hundred times since I've been back, I learned a thing or two about hotels while Pearlie and me were on our round-the-world tour. I took lots of notes. And here's what I've come up with."

Sophie steeled herself for the reading of the list.

"We gotta think big here, Soph. Think out of the box, if you catch my drift. We've got to get beyond the whole minibar thing. There's lots more we can do for our guests than just provide them with peanuts when they're in the mood."

"Okay. Like what?"

He winked. "I am so hip sometimes, I amaze myself. What do you say if our weekend package also includes a choice of tattoo or piercing—that and a deluxe room."

Sophie wasn't shocked by much, but this shocked her. "Dad? This is Minnesota, remember? Maybe that would go over in L.A., or San Francisco—"

He held up his hand. "See, you're stuck in the mud. We gotta think *cutting edge* here, Soph." He studied her a moment, then said, "Okay, try this on for size. One hotel we stayed at had the coolest check-in policy. See, you play a hand of blackjack with the receptionist. If you win, you get your room free, or maybe we could give the guest some kind of discount at one of our restaurants. What do you think?"

She hated to put a damper on his excitement, but she was growing more nauseated with each passing second. It might be the cigar, but she feared it was the list. "Well—"

"Or, how about this? We provide a speed-dial button on our room phones that would patch guests straight to a shrink. You know, in case they get depressed while they stay here."

Sophie needed a shrink on speed dial right now. "Dad, I, ah—"

"Here's another. You know how people like to tie one on when they're on vacation. Well, what if we give them—free—some hair of the dog. On weekends only. We don't want to give away the bank."

"Hair of the dog?"

"Free cold pizza and Bloody Marys, say from ten to noon."

"Dad!"

"What?"

"Do you really think the Maxfield Plaza would benefit from any of these programs?"

"Absolutely. I know it would. You think I'm crazy, but I swear, we wouldn't be the only ones doing this. We have to stay ahead of the curve, Soph. Otherwise, we die."

She'd heard just about all the new Gen X slogans she could stand and was about to let fly with what she really thought, when Margie walked into the room.

"Hi, Henry, Sophie." As usual, her smile was amused, more of a smirk. "Gee, with a little more heat, you could smoke a ham in here."

Henry glowered. "You're interrupting. What do you want?"

"I was looking for my dad." She tucked a lock of chocolate brown hair behind her ear.

"Nathan's upstairs on the mezzanine level," said Sophie. "He's waiting for you."

"Me? Why?"

"He said you two had a meeting this morning."

Her face puckered in confusion. "Not that I know of."

Sophie turned to look at her. "You mean he's *not* here to see you?"

"Nope." The smirk returned. "Hey, great save, Sophie. You get me to think he's here to see me, so if I happen to run into him, I think there was a mixup—when in reality, it's just more of the same. You and Nathan getting together behind my dad's back."

"That's ridiculous!"

"Is it?"

Henry piped up: "Anybody ever tell you you're a real brat, Margie?"

Her smirk evaporated. "What did you say?"

"I said you're a brat. B-R-A-T. You leech off my daughter's goodwill, and at the same time, every chance you get, you stick it to her. I'm watching you, missy. You may have your dad wrapped around your little finger, but not me. Now get the hell out of here. We're working."

Margie's mouth fell open.

"Did you hear me? Leave!"

Turning on her heel, Margie stomped out.

After she was gone, Sophie reached across the table and squeezed her dad's hand.

"I know. I'm awesome. Now, let's get back to the list."

29

Bram checked the white pages and found that Phil Banks had an unlisted phone number and street address. It didn't surprise him. After thinking about the problem for a few minutes, it occurred to him that perhaps Vince Parillo might know it. He phoned right away. Vince not only had the address, but he gave Bram directions. When Vince heard about the message his niece had left on Bram's answering machine, he was furious. He muttered something about his old army buddies, two-by-fours, and paying Phil a little visit later in the day. Bram promised he'd call and let him know how Chris was doing.

Half an hour later, Bram pulled off a quiet Woodbury street and eased his new—used—silver Bentley into Phil's driveway. He cut the motor and sat for a second gazing at the stucco house. It was a modern two-story, with a lower deck that ran along one side and around the back. In Bram's opinion, it was ugly—boxlike and boring. But it was also impressive in its own overstated way. Noticing that one of the doors to Phil's three-stall garage was open, and hearing country music blaring from inside, Bram figured he'd found his man.

Slipping out of the front seat, Bram glanced at the

house again, wondering if Chris was inside. He found Phil bent over the engine of his Corvette. He was wearing jeans and a dirty sweatshirt, and appeared to be deep in thought.

When Phil looked up, he seemed confused. The confusion quickly turned to irritation. "Jeez, Baldric. For a second there I thought you were that old actor. What's his name? Cary Grant."

"We all have our doubles."

"Don't flatter yourself." Phil turned down the music. His hands were smeared with grease, so he picked up a rag and began to wipe them off. "What are you doing here? Or do I need to ask?"

"I came to see Chris."

"How did I guess?"

"She left me a message yesterday. Said she'd call me last night. She never did."

"This about that job offer?"

Bram nodded. He might as well play along.

Narrowing one eye, Phil said, "How come you're so interested in *helping* my wife, Baldric? If I didn't know better, I'd say you were hustling her."

Bram shrugged. "What can I say? I'm just a nice guy."

"Right."

"She here?"

"Nope. You drove all this way for nothing." He glanced out the garage door at Bram's car. The sight of the Bentley seemed to annoy him.

"If she's coming back soon, I'll wait."

"Sorry," said Phil, tossing the rag over his shoulder. He returned his attention to the engine. "She left town this morning. Said she needed to get her head together."

"Meaning what?"

"Hell if I know. You know women."

"Where'd she go?"

"None of your goddamn business. Now get the hell off my property."

Bram didn't believe it for a second. If Chris was gone, Phil was behind it. And that left Bram with two big questions: What had he done with her, and most important, was she still alive?

"You're lying," said Bram. "She wouldn't just leave without calling someone in her family."

Phil reared back. "Who the hell do you think you are? All of a sudden you know my wife better than I do?"

"Where is she!"

"Gone. That's all I'm gonna tell you." He picked up a wrench, hefting it in his hand like a weapon.

Bram backed up. "Your alibi for the night Fabian and Loy were murdered is bogus. Chris admitted it to me."

Phil cracked a smile. "That's hearsay, Baldric. Not admissible in a court of law."

Bram didn't mention he had it on tape, that Chris had left it on his answering machine.

"It's also not true. Maybe I'll sue your ass for slander. I got so many lawyers on my payroll, I could keep you wrapped up in litigation for years. You want to lose that Bentley, huh? That fancy diamond ring?"

"Just tell me where she is and I'll leave. Just so I know she's safe."

"You saying I'd hurt her?"

"You already did."

"The black eye?" He laughed. "That was an accident. We were sitting on the couch and I stretched my arms, caught her a good one."

Now Bram had two stories, and neither one was true.

"But if you don't get the hell out of here, the black eye I give *you* will be for real. So will the broken nose and the cracked ribs. It would be a shame to see that pretty face of yours all banged and bruised, that nice tweed suit and blue oxford shirt bloody." He brought the wrench up, tapping it in his other hand. "You either leave on your own, or I throw you off my property. Your choice."

Bram glanced at a door that opened into the house. "Chris?" he shouted, hoping she'd hear. "Chris! It's Bram Baldric. If you're in there, come out. I need to talk to you."

"You don't hear very well," said Phil, advancing another step.

"Actually, my mother agrees with you." He turned to the door. "Chris!"

"Look," said Phil, moving back behind the front end of the Corvette. "You've got me all wrong, Baldric. I'm a reasonable man. You wanna look inside? Go for it."

Bram's eyes snapped back to Phil, wondering if this was a trap. But he had to take the risk. He turned slowly and stepped through the doorway into the kitchen. "Chris?" he called again.

The house was silent.

Bounding up the stairs, Bram checked every room on the second floor. All were empty. After searching through the first floor, he located the basement stairs and started down. It didn't take him long to realize Phil wasn't lying. Chris wasn't home.

After checking the freezer just to assure himself he'd looked everywhere, Bram started back up. Phil was standing in the doorway, looking down at him.

"Find her?" he asked.

"No."

"Did you check the chimney? Maybe I stuffed her up there. Or how about the freezer? That's a perfect place to hide a body."

"Shut up."

"Oh, my my. Frustration. Like I said, Baldric, she left town. She wanted some privacy and I intend to see she gets it."

"Her car," said Bram.

"Gone," said Phil. "You wanna see? Come on back out to the garage."

Now that Bram was at the top of the stairs, he met Phil's eyes with a hard stare of his own. "You've done something with her."

"Nothing I wouldn't like to do with you, given half a chance." His breath stank of stale coffee and cigarettes.

"You married her to shut her up, but it didn't work. You killed Fabian and Loy, and now you've killed Chris."

"Prove it."

Bram was startled. He didn't even deny it. "You crazy psycho piece of crap! Tell me!"

"Get out," said Phil, his voice cold as rebar.

With his heart banging wildly in his chest, Bram said, "Gladly."

An hour later, he was standing in Al Lundquist's cubicle. "He murdered her!"

"Calm down," said Al, leaning back in his chair.

"You've got to get on this! *Now.* Banks is responsible for three deaths. I told you, Chris wasn't with him that night. He went out to his car to sleep while she watched the movie. He could have gone anywhere."

"He didn't kill Fabian and Loy."

"How can you say that?"

"Because . . . because I can. I can't say any more."

Bram glared at him. "You think Gladstone did it?"

"No comment."

"Did Sophie call you?"

Al cocked his head. "Why would your wife call me? She doesn't even like me."

Bram didn't want to get into it right now, because he didn't think it had any bearing on the murders. Still, he figured Al should know. "Anika Gladstone gave her husband an alibi for the night of the murders, right?"

"Yeah."

"Well, she was lying, too. Sophie ran into her over at the Rookery Club right about the time Ken Loy was shot. She couldn't have been with Andy unless she can be in two places at once."

Al held his eyes. "Sophie would swear to this?"

"Sure. Anika even admitted to her that she was lying. She said Andy was home sick, that he couldn't have killed his brother or Loy."

Al's eyes dropped to his desk as his fist slammed on top of a stack of papers. "Gotcha," he crowed.

"No, no. You're not listening. It's Phil! He's the one you're looking for."

Al thought for a moment, squeezing the back of his neck, then picked up his phone and punched in a bunch of numbers. "It's Lundquist. Yeah. Where's

Molly?" He listened. "Well, when she reports in, tell her to call me ASAP. Got that? *ASAP*."

"You're targeting the wrong guy," said Bram, even before Al hung up the phone.

Al shook his head. "Okay, I hear you. Phil's an asshole. He's also a rough character. You should be glad he didn't clock you right there in the garage. You could be climbing out of a drainage ditch right now instead of talking to me."

"But you're not listening."

"I am. Any guy who would hit a woman is a total sleaze. But he was ringing your chimes today, pal, and probably enjoying the hell out of it. The fact that Chris wasn't there doesn't mean a thing. If, in twenty-four hours, she still doesn't turn up, file a missing person's report."

"*This* is what I pay taxes for?"

"What do you want me to do? Go out there and arrest him? For what? On what evidence?"

The phone on Al's desk gave a jarring ring. Al picked it up. "Lundquist." He listened a moment, then cracked a smile. "We got him. Yeah. I'll explain when I see you. Stay there, okay. I'll be right over."

Bram flung his arms in the air. "You're just going to blow this off? I know in my gut that Phil's done something with her. All right, so maybe he *was* playing with me, maybe he didn't kill her, but he's got her locked up somewhere so she can't hurt him. Who knows how long it will be before he does decide to get rid of her?"

Al stood and shrugged into his Twins baseball jacket. "You've got a lethal imagination. You're also assuming he's our perp. If he isn't—and I know for a fact that he isn't—he's got no reason to hurt her. Unless it's a domestic, in which case somebody else will have to cover it." He put his hand on Bram's shoulder. "You're a great guy. You care about people. But you're off base on this one. Okay? Trust me. I've been doing this a long time. Now, I gotta go." Pushing Bram out of his office, he added, "Do yourself a favor. Go home, take two aspirin, and take a nap."

Bram couldn't let it go. Chris was either dead or in danger. Either way, somebody had to find her. He remembered that her mother's first name was Nora. Sitting in his car, he used his cell phone to call directory assistance. A few minutes later, Nora Parillo was on the line:

"Hello?"

"Is this Nora?"

"Speaking."

"My name's Baldric. Bram Baldric."

"Oh, sure. I recognize your voice from the radio. You're a friend of my daughter."

She sounded a lot like Chris, except that her voice was deeper. "I am. I was wondering if you'd heard from Chris today? I'm trying to reach her." Bram didn't want to alarm her.

"Well, yes, I did. But I didn't actually talk to her. I was out walking the dog when she called. She left me a message."

Bram's heart skipped a beat. Maybe Chris *was* okay. "Can I ask what she said?"

"Just that her car was on the fritz. She planned to drive it over to Phil's mechanic's place and leave it there for him to look at. Phil said he'd follow in his car so he could drive her back home. She said she wanted to talk to me today, but not to call her at the house. She said she'd get back to me."

"That's all she said?"

"Well, yes. And that she loved me."

"What time was the call?"

"About eight fifteen."

So that meant if Phil had done something to Chris, it had to have happened between eight fifteen and ten thirty—when Bram arrived at Phil's house. Not much time.

"Why are you so interested?" asked Nora.

"Like I said, I'd like to get in touch with her today."

"Is this about that job offer? She told me all about it. I think it would be a godsend for her to do something with her life other than wait hand and foot on that horrible man."

"I couldn't agree more. You don't by any chance know who Phil's mechanic is, do you?"

"No idea. Sorry. Listen, Mr. Baldric, if you find her, will you tell her to call me right away? She sounded kind of nervous in that message she left me. Maybe nobody else would have noticed, but I'm her mother. I worry about her."

"I understand. And I promise. As soon as I find her, I'll make sure she calls."

30

When Anika was thirteen, she saw a man being pulled from Chatham Lake. It was an image she would never forget. It was wintertime, and the lake was a favorite spot for skaters in her small Michigan hometown. That December day, Anika had been walking home from school when a squad car, lights flashing, whizzed past her and made a hard right on Tarnauer Road, heading for the lake. By the time she reached the warming house, she saw that a paramedic truck had already arrived and that men in wet suits were attempting to walk out onto the lake.

People were scattered around in small groups, muttering softly. Anika stood close to one of them and learned that a man had fallen through just a few minutes before and had disappeared under the ice. Anika watched as one of the men in wet suits jumped into a gaping hole.

Ten minutes later, rescuers tossed ropes to the diver as paramedics helped drag the man from the water. Anika inched closer to the warming house as the man was carried past her on a stretcher. What seemed so astonishing to her then—and ever after—was how he was encased from head to toe in a thin, glistening sheet of ice. It looked like shiny plastic, perfectly molded to his clothes and skin. She could see the horror on his face as he must have struggled to find a way out.

The man's eyes were open, but he was dead inside an ice cocoon.

As Anika looked over at her husband now, watching him behind the wheel of their car driving back to Bob's house, just minutes after dropping Rick off at the airport, she was certain she saw that same ice cocoon forming around him. She shivered as she turned her eyes away.

After arriving home last night, Andy had drunk one glass of champagne after another. When the bubbly was gone, he started in on the Scotch, refusing to eat any of the pizza. Anika couldn't pinpoint just what was wrong, but she knew that whatever it was, it was huge. She'd never seen Andy so fractured—laughing gaily, almost desperately one minute, zoned out the next. The booze was obviously a way to anesthetize his pain, though it eventually cut him off entirely. Shortly after nine, he'd excused himself and lurched his way upstairs to bed.

After he was gone, Anika and Rick talked for a while. Rick was devastated by the change in his old friend. Together, they tried to analyze Andy, using every pop psychological theory they could come up with to explain his behavior, but by eleven they both realized neither one of them knew how to help.

After getting Rick settled in one of the guest bedrooms, Anika entered the room she shared with Andy. It was only their second night in the house and everything still felt foreign. She found him asleep on top of the velvet spread. He'd fallen face-first onto the pillows and looked as if he hadn't moved since he hit them. She took off his shoes and covered him with a quilt. Sitting next to him for a few minutes, she caressed his hair, weeping for the two people who had once been so in love. She slept in the next room, aware for the first time of how dank and gloomy the house felt—how it seemed to be filled with moving, angry shadows, and secrets that held her husband in a hard grip and wouldn't let go.

Andy had awakened with a hangover. He'd come down to breakfast looking scrubbed and pink from a hot shower, but no less troubled. Once again, he wouldn't eat a thing. He tried to make conversation with Rick, tried to be the old Andy, but the detachment Anika had seen glimpses of in the last few months now consumed him completely. Andy had looked forward to Rick's trip to Minnesota, but for whatever reason, his disconnection with the world around him now seemed total. He was like the man in the ice cocoon. He wasn't dead, but what was vital and human inside him was surely dying.

Both Anika and Andy were silent on the way home from the airport. After parking in the driveway, Andy shut off the motor.

"We've got to talk," said Anika, turning to look at him.

He closed his eyes and leaned his head back. "I know."

He seemed so vulnerable, so utterly defenseless. But if he couldn't or wouldn't share his problems with her, what chance did they have? It was intolerable to think that she was about to add to his defeat, but if she didn't make a stand, he'd take them both down. "Andy . . . I'm leaving you."

His body jerked, but he kept his eyes closed.

She waited, but when he didn't respond, she said, "Did you hear me?" That's when she noticed the tears on his cheeks. Her heart twisted inside her. "Andy? Say something."

He opened his eyes and placed both hands on the top of the steering wheel, as if to anchor himself to the earth. "I don't blame you."

"That's it? That's all you've got to say?"

"You wouldn't believe me if I told you I loved you." He leaned forward and rested his forehead against his hands. "God," he whispered, sucking in his breath.

If she left him now, it was like she accepted that he was doomed. She wanted desperately for him to pull her back from the brink, but at the same time she knew he couldn't.

"I've already packed a bag."

He swallowed a couple of times. "Where will you go?"

"I'll take a room at the Maxfield for now. We can . . . figure the rest out later. When you're feeling better."

He nodded.

There was nothing else to do but get out of the car. She stared at him a moment more, feeling the finality of her words, but not quite believing that she'd actually said them. And then she opened the door and got out.

As she was coming down the stairs a few minutes later, carrying her suitcase and an overnight bag, she heard the doorbell chime. Andy walked into the foyer, glanced at her for a second, then stepped over to the door and opened it.

Anika set her bags on the floor as a tall, lanky man in a baseball jacket introduced himself as Detective Al Lundquist. He was accompanied by two burly uniformed police officers. "Mr. Gladstone?" he asked.

"Yes?" said Andy.

The detective motioned to the uniforms.

Before Anika could absorb what was happening, they'd handcuffed Andy and the detective was reading him his rights.

"He's being arrested?" she said.

"Yes," said the detective. "Like I said, for the murder of Del Irazarian."

Anika gasped. "He's dead?"

"He was shot last night in his motel room."

Anika and Andy locked eyes.

"We have a search warrant for your home, Mr. Gladstone." He removed a sheet of paper from his pocket and held it up for Andy to read. When Andy looked away, he handed it across to Anika.

She took it, but she couldn't focus. Everything inside her screamed that this couldn't be happening.

The detective nodded and more officers, this time a crew of eight, entered the house. Anika remembered the shirt Andy had thrown into the hamper this morning, the one with blood on the cuff. Her mind slid sideways.

As they led Andy away, he shouted over his shoulder, "Anika, call my lawyer. Ray Lawless. The number's in my address book in my briefcase. Tell him to meet me at the police station."

"Right away," she called after him. Stepping up to the door, she stood behind the screen and watched as her husband was helped into the backseat of a waiting squad car.

So this was it, thought Anika. The storm she'd been expecting. There was a certain relief in finally seeing it descend. But never in her wildest nightmares had she imagined that her husband could be a murderer.

Sophie was working the reservation desk on the Maxfield's main level when she noticed Anika come through the front double doors. She was surprised to see her again so soon, and even more surprised to find her carrying a suitcase. In Sophie's mind, it was an ominous sign.

Anika approached the desk. "Ah, hi," she said, setting the suitcase down. "I, ah . . . I need a room."

"Are you okay?" asked Sophie. She could see how unsteady Anika was.

"No."

Sophie tapped a couple numbers into the computer terminal while sneaking peeks at Anika. She came up with a suite on the ninth floor. After making a couple of key cards, she grabbed the minibar key and came around the front of the reception desk, picking up the suitcase. "I'll take you upstairs."

"Thanks, Sophie. I could use a friend right about now."

They got on the elevator along with several other people and rode in silence up to nine.

Once in the suite, Anika removed her coat, tossing it over the desk chair. She looked as if every muscle in her body hurt. She sank down on the couch with a dazed expression on her face.

Sophie turned on the lights, then opened the curtains. Remembering the minibar key, she opened up the bar and removed a tiny bottle of brandy. Cracking the top, she poured the golden liquid into a glass, handing it to Anika. "Drink some of this. You'll feel better."

Anika stared at it a moment as if she wasn't sure what it was. "Oh. Yeah. Good idea." She drank it down in two neat swallows.

Sophie removed the glass from her shaking hand, then perched on the edge of one of the club chairs. "Do you want to talk about it?"

"I . . . I . . ." She lowered her head, closed her eyes. "It's a nightmare. Andy was arrested a couple hours ago."

"Oh, no." Sophie was afraid it had been something like that.

"They put him in a lineup and a witness picked him out." She rubbed the back of her neck.

"I didn't think there were witnesses to either of the murders."

Anika's head popped up. "He was arrested for shooting Del Irazarian."

"But . . . I thought—"

"They're all connected. Apparently, the same gun was used in all three murders. Andy has a gun. He kept it in the glove compartment of his car. But it's not a match. Since they don't have the murder weapon, Andy's lawyer thought the case for Bob's death and Ken Loy's would be hard to prove. But once they find the blood on Andy's cuff—"

"What blood?" asked Sophie.

Anika took a deep breath and exhaled slowly. "When Andy came home last night, he had blood on his cuff. The police think it will prove to be Irazarian's. They've got an eyewitness that puts him at the motel, so more than likely, it will be a match. Andy didn't even deny that he'd been there. But he insists he didn't do it. That when he got to the motel, Irazarian was already dead."

"Wow."

"Yeah. I know." Anika nodded to the minibar. "I think I'd like another."

Sophie got up and found another brandy. She handed the bottle and the glass to Anika and then sat back down. "Who's his lawyer?"

"Raymond Lawless."

"Ray Lawless is the best."

"So I've heard. But, see, Andy has a motive for Irazarian's murder. I mean, Irazarian lied to him again and again about those bogus stories. It made Andy look like a fool at the paper. And it got him in terrible hot water with Bob. Andy hated Irazarian. I mean, *really* hated him."

"But just because he hated him, it doesn't mean he'd murder him."

Anika cracked the top of the brandy and drank straight from the bottle. "No, but before I left the police station, Mr. Lawless told me that the police found a briefcase with almost one hundred and ninety thousand dollars in Irazarian's motel room. In one of the pockets they found Andy's card. They fingerprinted Andy when he got there. From what Mr. Lawless said, Andy's fingerprints are all over the briefcase. They think he gave the money to Irazarian."

"Why?"

"Andy refuses to say."

"Do you think Irazarian was blackmailing him?"

"That's what Mr. Lawless thinks. But if Andy doesn't open up to him, tell him the whole truth, I don't know how Mr. Lawless is going to defend him." She folded her arms protectively over her chest. "He'll spend tonight in jail. In the morning, there will be an arraignment. He has no criminal record, so there's a chance he could be let out on bail."

"Then why are you—" Sophie stopped, thinking that perhaps she'd entered a territory that was too personal.

"Just before the police arrived at the house, I told Andy I was leaving him." She started to cry.

"Anika, I'm so incredibly sorry."

"He's a good man, you know, but he's not strong. This could crush him."

"Will you go to the arraignment?"

She lifted a tissue from her purse and wiped her eyes. "I don't know. Probably not. The fact that he was arrested doesn't change anything between us. Our marriage is a sham. I'll be there for him if it comes to a trial, but I can't live with him. Not anymore. He won't let me in, Sophie, so what would be the point of going back to him?"

"Is there anything I can do?" asked Sophie.

Anika laughed, but then grimaced. "Find the real murderer. Short of that, I don't think there's anything anybody can do."

31

After Bram's radio show was done for the day, he drove across town, sailed over the Roberts Street Bridge, and eventually located Old Mill Road Mini Storage. Chris had doodled the name "Del" the day he'd taken her to lunch. She'd also written down the name "Old Mill Road." If the Del was Del Irazarian—and Bram had a hunch they were one and the same—there had to be a connection. Bram recalled that when he asked Chris about it yesterday, she'd said that Phil rented a storage garage "over there." It seemed a good bet to Bram that if Del Irazarian was mixed up in it somehow, that the mini storage place might be an important spot to check out.

Sitting in the parking lot, he removed his cell phone from his vest pocket and punched in the office number. He disguised his voice because he was, after all, a well-known radio personality in the Twin Cities. Perhaps he flattered himself, but he didn't want anything to prevent him from getting the information he needed.

A male voice answered: "Old Mill Mini Storage. This is Mike."

"Mike, Phil Banks. Hey, I'm leaving for Brazil tomorrow, going to be out of the country for the next couple of months. I was just writing you guys a check so you don't toss my shit out on the street." He smiled, thinking he'd nailed Phil's limited vocabulary. "But I don't have a bill in front of me, so I need the monthly amount. Oh, and your mailing address."

"Okay. Let's see," said Mike.

Bram silently sent up a prayer of thanks. His ruse had worked. He could hear the guy tap his computer keyboard.

"You've got a double. That's one-thirty-seven a month. Two months would be two-seventy-four."

"Maybe I should be on the safe side. Do it for three. That would be four-eleven, right?"

"Exactly."

"Hey, give me the number of the unit. I always put that on my check, but I don't have it in front of me."

"It's 2298. And our address is Box 481, St. Paul, 55103."

"Thanks. I'll drop the check in the mail on my way home from work. Later, man."

Bram cut the connection.

Now that he had the number, he could begin phase two. On the way across the lot to the office, he decided he'd missed his calling. With his looks and charm, and his obvious ability to ferret out information, he should have been an international spy. But that would actually mean he had to work. Nah, on second thought, he liked his radio gig much better.

Stepping up to the counter, Bram waited for Mike to take a drag from his cigarette and then stand up.

"Help you?" he asked. It was more of a grunt.

"I'd like to rent one of your storage units." He waited to see if the guy recognized his voice. When there was no look of recognition, he figured Mike either didn't have a radio in the office, or he had no taste.

"We got two sizes. Single and double."

"Single would be fine."

"Fill this out." He pushed a form across the counter.

It took Bram only a couple of minutes to complete it. As he wrote in his name and address, he asked the man about security.

"We got good security. You gotta have the correct numbers to get in and out of the gates. And nobody gets over that fence, believe me, not unless they want their legs sliced up."

"What about at night?"

"What about it?"

"Do you have a security guard on duty?"

"If you want that kind of protection, you better hire yourself a private company. But don't worry. We haven't had a theft in all the time I've been working here."

"And how long is that?"

"Going on eight years."

"You like the job?" Bram looked around the dingy office.

"It's a living."

He finished the form and handed it across the counter.

"Now, you gotta pick a personal password—a four-digit number—to get you into the lot. Just write it at the bottom there." He pointed. "There's only one way in and one way out. It's well marked. When you get up to the gate, tap in the number of your unit and then your password. It's gotta be in that order or the gate won't open."

"What's the number of my unit?"

"3412."

Bram scratched "0007" at the bottom. The extra zero didn't bother him, and it seemed to fit the occasion.

The guy looked at it. "You know how many 0007's we got here?"

"You mean I'm not the only one?"

"World's filled with wise guys."

"Maybe I better change it."

"Up to you."

Bram thought about it for a second. "No, it's okay." What did it matter? He'd only use it twice.

Mike circled the number and said, "That'll be eighty-seven dollars even."

Bram wrote a check. "What are your hours?"

"The office is open from eight to six. But you can get into the storage lot 24-7. Just use your unit number and your password. We'll bill you by the month." He handed Bram the paperwork.

"Thanks."

"No problem."

On the way back to his car, Bram surveyed the lot, locating the entrance gate about twenty yards to the right of the office. The entire property was surrounded by a high fence topped with wicked-looking razor wire. Mike had been right. Nobody but an idiot would try to climb over it.

After tapping in his unit number and his humiliatingly trite password, the gate swung open and Bram drove in. Instead of looking for 3412, he eased slowly

down the lanes searching for 2298. He found it at
the end of a long row of doubles. Slipping out of the
Bentley, Bram quickly checked the padlock. It was a
standard issue steel-and-chrome variety. A heavy bolt
cutter would slice through it like butter. The fact
that he didn't have a bolt cutter was a minor issue.
By tonight, when he came back, he'd own the very
best.

After hunting down a hardware store, Bram drove
to Lyle Boerichter's downtown St. Paul condo. He'd
been thinking about Lyle all afternoon, recalling the
comment that his ex-wife had known Phil's second
wife. Bram was trying to get a bead on Phil, figure out
whether he really was capable of giving Chris more
than a black eye.

Bram had called Chris several times on her cell
phone, but with no luck. Maybe Al Lundquist was
right. Maybe he was worried about her for no good
reason, but after talking to Phil this morning, the bad
feeling in his gut wouldn't go away. If anything, it
was getting worse.

Bram tried calling Lyle from the station during one
of his breaks. His voice mail had picked up, but Bram
hadn't left a message. The condo wasn't far from the
Maxfield, so he decided to give it another try, this
time in person.

After driving around forever looking for a parking spot, Bram finally entered the building, quickly
locating Lyle's name on the list of residents posted
in the central hall. He used the security phone and
punched in the numbers. After the third ring, Lyle answered.

"Hello?" He sounded like he'd been sleeping, his voice low and groggy.

"Lyle? It's Bram Baldric."

No response. Then, "Ah . . . hi. What's up?"

"I need to talk to you. It won't take long."

"This is kind of a bad time. I'm flying out this evening, and I've got a bunch of stuff I need to do."

"Headed someplace glamorous? Hawaii? Tokyo?"

"Just L.A. and back."

"Look, it would only take a second."

More silence. "Well, okay. I guess."

When Bram heard the buzzer, he pulled back the door and entered the lobby. The cavernous old building had once been a furniture manufacturer's salesroom and warehouse. A few years back it had been renovated and turned into condos.

Bram took the elevator up to four. Lyle was standing out in the hallway, waiting for him. Even at a distance, Bram could see how disheveled he looked. His stomach hung over his sweatpants, his white T-shirt was a stained mess, and his hair looked like a whirlwind had combed it.

"Thanks for letting me come up."

Lyle nodded to his door. "Like I said, I don't have much time."

As he passed into the condo, Bram couldn't help but notice that Lyle reeked of liquor. He turned around and stared at him. Lyle's eyes were bloodshot and his face was an unhealthy splotchy red. *This* was a man who was about to fly a plane? "Are you feeling okay?"

"No. I've got a rotten cold. Took some Nyquil and been sleeping most of the day."

That might account for the alcohol smell, thought Bram, but it was so strong that he doubted it.

Lyle dropped unsteadily into a chair and immediately fired up a cigarette. "What do you want?" he asked, tossing the Bic lighter next to an ashtray on the coffee table. "I gotta shower and shave. So make it quick."

Bram sat down opposite him. He wondered if he should say something. Lyle was in no shape to get into a cockpit. "Maybe you should call in sick."

"I'll be fine. I just need to wake up." He took a long drag, then blew smoke out of his nose.

"Okay. You mentioned the other day that your ex was a friend of Phil Banks's second wife."

"Good friend."

"And that Phil's second wife used to call your wife and complain about him."

"God, yes. Terry called all the time."

"What did he do to her?"

"Beat her up. Accused her of cheating on him."

"Did she?"

"Hell no. She was terrified of him. When they got divorced, she dropped off the face of the earth. Left the state and never called my wife again. You know, Sonny came by once."

"Sonny?"

"Oh, sorry. Sonny was what Terry used to call him. It was apparently a family nickname. His dad's name was Phil, too, so when he was a kid, they called him Sonny to differentiate. Anyway, Phil came by once when my wife was out. He told me he was trying to locate Terry because he owed her money." Lyle grunted. "Like I should believe that. My wife figured she was hiding from him. All I can say is, I hope to God he never found her."

"You think, even after they were divorced, that he might have tried to hurt her?"

"Phil doesn't get married, he takes prisoners. Same with his first wife. Her name was Candy. I never knew her personally, but I'd see him with her every now and then. We used to frequent the same bars. I'll tell you this much, she was one frightened woman. I saw him slap her around more than once. That guy's a mean son of a bitch."

"What happened to his first wife after their divorce?"

Lyle shrugged. "No idea." He tapped ash into the ashtray, then took another long drag. "How come you're so interested?"

"Chris. I stopped by their house this morning and Phil said she'd left town, gone on a trip. It sounded fishy to me. I talked to her mom later. She said Chris had left her a message around eight fifteen, said her car wasn't working right and that she was going to drop it off at Phil's mechanic's place. Phil was going to give her a ride back home."

Smoke drifted out of Lyle's nose. "You think he did something to her?"

"I think somebody's lying and I don't think it's Chris."

"Jesus." Lyle stubbed out his cigarette. "Call the police."

"I did. But they can't do anything until she's gone for twenty-four hours."

Lyle shook his head. "Figures."

As Bram's gaze traveled over the living room, he

noticed an open bottle of Johnny Walker Red sitting on top of the TV set.

Lyle turned around to see what Bram was looking at.

"Listen, Lyle, are you sure you should be flying tonight?"

"None of your goddamn business," said Lyle, jerking to a standing position. "It's nobody's goddamn business. Not yours. Not Vince's. Not Bob's. I know what my limits are."

"Bob's?"

"You're all the same. You think because a guy takes a little drink every now and then, his judgment goes AWOL. I drank when I was in Nam, and I drink now. So what? Doesn't make me an alcoholic. You ask me, people use that term pretty damn freely."

He seemed so instantly belligerent, Bram assumed he'd had the conversation before. "Did Bob think you had a problem with alcohol?"

"So what if he did? He didn't know everything. He wasn't *God*."

"Did he threaten to talk to Sunrise Airlines if you didn't get help?"

"Get out," said Lyle, lurching past him and disappearing into the kitchen.

Bram got up and followed. He found Lyle standing at the kitchen sink with his back to the door. Next to the sink was another bottle of Johnny Walker Red. This one was empty. "Answer me. Did Bob threaten to talk to your employer?"

"Yes!"

"Did you fight about it? Did you—"

He whirled around. "What are you saying?"

"Were you the one at his house that night?"

In one lightning-quick movement, Lyle was at his throat, pressing him backward, knocking over a chair and toppling the kitchen table. "You think I hurt Bob? Do you?" He grabbed Bram's lapels and slammed him into the wall. "He fucking saved my life! I owe him everything. Do you get that? I loved him. Guys like you . . . you can't begin to understand the bond we had. War is like fire, Baldric, fire that melted our souls together. We're *brothers*! You think I shot him? I would have done anything for him. *Anything*." His eyes were wild.

"I believe you," said Bram. "I do. Honestly."

Lyle glared at him a moment, his eyes boring into Bram's; then, as suddenly as the attack had begun, it ended. Moving back over to the sink, Lyle said, "Get out."

Bram eased around the table. "I believe you. But I agree with Bob. I think you need help."

Lyle bowed his head. "Just leave."

Bram felt that a hasty exit was, for now, the better part of valor.

On the way down in the elevator, his thoughts turned to the conversation he'd had several days ago with Sheldon Larr. At the time, Bram had shrugged it off, thinking Sheldon was just being his usual eccentric self. But Sheldon missed very little that happened around the Rookery Club. Perhaps he overheard a conversation between Lyle and Bob. Whatever the case, his words now took on an ominous meaning. They'd been talking about Bob Fabian, about who might have murdered him. Sheldon said he knew. But he'd been typically cryptic. He'd asked

Bram to define the word "rook." Bram said it was a bird.

"And what do birds do?"

Bram could hear Sheldon's response even now.

"They fly, my dear. They *fly*."

32

"I was about to send out the Marines," said Sophie, glancing up from her computer keyboard. She was sitting behind her desk in her office at the Maxfield.

Bram had just come in. He poured himself a cup of coffee and then sank down on the couch. "You didn't get my message?"

"The one about Chris being missing?"

"The one telling you I'd be late."

"Nope." She tapped in one last word, then turned her full attention on him. "Want the latest news flash?"

"Let me guess. There's been an arrest."

"Andy Gladstone. It happened this afternoon."

Bram shook his head. "I told Al they had the wrong guy."

"But here's the curveball. It wasn't for Bob Fabian's murder, or Loy's."

Bram was just about to take a sip of his java. He blinked his surprise at her over the top of the cup. "Whose, then?"

"Del Irazarian. They put Andy in a lineup and somebody identified him. That plus a bunch of damaging evidence found inside the room makes Andy their man."

"Evidence?"

"Money. Almost two hundred thousand in a briefcase that belonged to Andy. The police think Irazarian was blackmailing him. By the way, Anika moved into a suite upstairs. Apparently, she'd just told Andy she was leaving him when the cops arrived with the handcuffs."

Bram groaned. "Poor bastard."

"Phil may have murdered Bob and Ken Loy, but it looks like a good bet that Andy's responsible for Irazarian's death."

"I wish I knew what the hell was going on." Whatever the truth turned out to be, Irazarian was connected to Phil as well as Andy. Bram's mind was awash in disconnected facts and suspicions.

After the conversation he'd just had with Lyle, it looked as if *he* had a motive for Bob Fabian's murder, too. Here was another man who would have done anything for Bob. Ken Loy's death could easily have been part of a revenge plot—making Loy pay for the death of Valerie Fabian. But when it came to Bob himself, motives turned murkier. If Lyle thought Bob was about to tell Sunrise Airlines that he wasn't fit to fly—that he was a drunk who refused to get help—who was to say what he might do to protect himself? Bram recalled Lyle once saying that flying was all he knew, the only thing he was ever any good at. If his livelihood was suddenly threatened, at his age, his financial prospects were bleak at best. At worst, he could lose everything. A man might behave totally out of character to protect the life he'd always known.

He might even go so far as to kill someone he claimed to love.

"What are you thinking?" asked Sophie.

"Are you up for a little adventure tonight?"

"Are you kidding? After sitting in this office most of the day? Just name it."

"I need a partner in crime."

"Crime, huh? Sounds interesting."

"A little breaking and entering."

Her expression brightened. "I love it when you talk sexy."

"We could get in trouble."

"I'll take my chances."

On the way to the mini storage garage later that night, the image of Chris, hurt, trapped, perhaps unconscious, drilled its way into Bram's consciousness. He had no idea where she was, but if he just kept picking at the edges of Phil's life, maybe he'd get lucky. If he couldn't find her, maybe he'd find a clue, something that would lead him to her before it was too late. It was that dread that he pushed away from him as he and Sophie cruised across the Roberts Street Bridge.

It was after midnight when they finally pulled up to the gate.

"You're pretty clever," said Sophie. "Renting that unit just to get inside."

Bram tapped in the code, then glanced into the backseat. "Let's hope that bolt cutter lives up to its hype."

Wind blew dry leaves across the lot as the Bentley eased through the entrance. High-beam lights sliced across the long rows of garages, casting most of their illumination along the edges of the property. They drove up and down the quiet lanes for a few minutes, seeing if anyone else was around.

"This place is like a graveyard," said Sophie, tucking her leather coat more tightly around her neck.

Making one last pass down the central track, Bram pulled the car up to Phil's double garage. "This is it."

Sophie squinted into the darkness. "Doesn't look like much of a lock."

"I talked to a guy while I was inspecting the garage I rented. He rents the one on the other side. He gave me some advice, told me to buy myself a standard lock. Seems that if you put some super-heavy-duty thing on it, it's like advertising you've got something expensive to steal. He said there isn't a lock that can't be broken anyway, so just go with the standard."

Bram eased out of the front seat. After grabbing the bolt cutter, he approached the door.

Sophie followed.

Before he could clamp it on, she put a hand on his arm. "Wait. I thought I heard something."

Bram turned around. "A car?" he asked in a whisper.

She nodded, pressing a finger to her lips.

They waited for a few seconds.

"What if it's Phil?" whispered Sophie.

Bram didn't have an answer. Stepping to the end of the garage, he scanned the lot for signs of life. After nearly a minute, he tiptoed back to Sophie. "Maybe you heard a car out on Old Mill Road."

"Maybe," said Sophie. As Bram lifted the bolt cutter, she added, "but it sounded closer."

Bram glared at her. "Come on. Let's get this open."

Just as the snipped lock dropped to the asphalt, headlights hit Bram square in the eyes. He whirled away, stuffing the bolt cutter under his coat. The light was so bright he couldn't see the car behind it, but whatever the make and model, it was heading straight for them.

Instinctively, Bram moved in front of Sophie, blocking her from view. "Pick up the lock," he whispered, barely moving his mouth.

Sophie eased down behind her husband's back and slipped the lock into her purse.

A moment later, the car turned off the lane, heading for another section of the lot.

"Boy, that was a close one," said Sophie, leaning back against the double garage door.

Bram wasn't convinced they were off the hook. What if the guy in the car was playing with them? Since he never got a good look at the driver's face, for all he knew, it could have been Phil. "We need to get this door open fast. I want to see what's inside and then get the hell out of here."

"I'm with you," said Sophie. She stood back as Bram bent down and heaved the heavy door upward.

Removing the flashlight from his side pocket, Bram pointed the beam inside, letting it wash over the interior. Two vehicles were parked inside. The rest of the space was filled with construction materials. Insulation. Boxes of nails, tools, paintbrushes, masking tape. Several air compressors. Various-sized windows.

"That's Chris's Escort," said Bram, stepping into the darkness.

"Are you sure?"

"Positive. But what's it doing here?" The answer to that question might be one he didn't want to hear. He tried the door, but found that it was locked. Shining the light inside, he breathed a sigh of relief when he saw that it was empty. At least the car wasn't Chris's coffin.

Sophie had her own flashlight. She was moving around the other vehicle—a large truck. "This thing must belong to Phil's construction company. It says 'Banks Construction' on the side. And there's a number twelve."

"He's probably got a fleet of trucks. He numbers them so that he knows who's got what at any given time."

"Why's this one parked here?"

"Good question," said Bram.

Sophie pointed the beam of her flashlight into the front seat. "Honey—"

"What?"

"I think you'll want to see this."

"What is it?" He scrambled around the back of Chris's car.

"A gun," she said, holding her light steady on it. "You see? There on the front seat next to that Coke bottle."

Bram tried the door. "Locked. Figures."

"Are you thinking what I'm thinking?"

"That we just found the murder weapon?"

"Last I heard, the police didn't have it."

"Nah. Couldn't be."

"You saying we suck as detectives?"

"The police have been searching for it for weeks, Sophie."

"Yes, but they didn't know about this storage unit. *You* did."

"Do you have your cell phone with you?"

"Am I ever without my cell phone?"

"Now might be a good time to call the cops."

"Sure, now that *we've* solved the case."

As Sophie found the phone in her purse, Bram grabbed the top of the garage door and started to bring it back down.

Sophie shushed him. "I heard something."

"Oh, *come on*, Sophie. Don't do that to me again. We need to get out of here." He stuck his head out of the garage and surveyed the lane in front of the unit.

"No. In here—in the garage. I heard something."

"It's probably a rat."

"Rats don't moan."

Bram listened. After a few seconds, he heard it, too. "It sounds like it's coming from the trunk of Chris's car." He thought a moment, then pocketed his flashlight and pulled the garage door closed.

"Why'd you do that?"

"So nobody will hear me when I do this." He slammed the bolt cutter into the driver's-side window, breaking the glass all over the front seat. Pulling up the door lock, he grabbed Sophie's flashlight and trained it on the dash. It only took a second to find the trunk button.

"That opened it," whispered Sophie. She was back by the trunk. Lifting the lid upward, she gasped.

Instantly, Bram was by her side. His heart nearly stopped when he saw Chris lying in a fetal position inside, her hands and feet bound with duct tape, a cloth bag pulled over her head. There was a small gash on her upper leg and her bare arms looked deeply bruised and battered. "Dear God," he said, leaning down close to her ear. "Chris, it's Bram and Sophie. You're safe now. Don't be frightened. I'm going to remove the cover from your head." He did so as gently as possible, hoping that the sound she'd made meant that she was still alive.

When the bag came off, Chris's eyes were wide-open and wild with terror. She shivered as she sat up. Bram removed the duct tape from her mouth. "Are you okay?"

Her voice was low and raspy, but still strong. "Get me out of here!"

Sophie took off her coat and put it around Chris's shoulders while Bram continued to work on the tape.

"Is anything broken?" asked Bram.

"I don't think so," responded Chris. "But hurry. Please! He could come back any minute." She was terrified, shaking uncontrollably, barely holding it together.

Once she was free, Bram pulled up the garage door, then stepped outside to look around. Everything seemed quiet. Moving back inside, he lifted Chris and carried her out to the backseat of his Bentley. While Sophie got her settled, he eased the garage door back down and then replaced the mangled padlock, making it look as if it was still functional. It might buy them some time.

Jumping into the front seat of his car, Bram hit the ignition, then the gas, and took off.

"She's like a block of ice, honey. Put on the heater."

As he glanced into the backseat, he caught sight of a car swinging onto the road behind him. The headlights in the rearview mirror momentarily blinded him.

Chris turned to look. "It's Phil!"

"We don't know that," said Sophie.

"And we're not about find out," said Bram, hanging a quick left and making straight for the exit. For a few seconds, he thought he might be able to outrun the other car, but then he remembered that to get out of the lot, he had to go through another gate, and to get it to open, he had to punch in the code. That meant he had to stop—all the time he'd gained was moot. As he saw it, he had two choices. Gun the motor and hope the car was heavy enough to break through the gate, or play it safe and stop to enter the exit code.

Seeing the heavy gate loom suddenly up in front of him, he was afraid that if he ran into it at full throttle, Sophie and Chris would rocket into the front seat and probably out through the windshield. None of them had taken time to put on their seat belts. Feeling that he had no choice, he stomped on the brakes.

"He's coming," gasped Sophie, her voice squeezed tight with fear.

Bram concentrated on the task at hand. He lowered the window and tapped in the code. As the gate swung open, he floored the gas pedal and roared off.

"The gate's closing," called Sophie. "The other car's still inside."

Bram breathed a sigh of relief as he sped out onto the frontage road and headed back toward the bridge.

"Better go straight to a hospital," said Sophie.

"No!" cried Chris. She lurched forward, grabbing Bram by his shoulder. "I'm fine. You have to hide me. If he finds me, he'll kill me."

"You're safe, Chris. Trust me. I won't let anything happen to you." He turned right on Blackman and pulled into the lot of a 7-Eleven, parking in back next to a Dumpster. "Maybe we can wait on the hospital, but we need to call the police."

"Yes. Okay," said Chris. "But can we stay here for

a while? Just a few minutes? I feel safe here. I just need to feel safe!"

Bram cracked the car door, looked back at Chris. "Sophie give me your cell phone. I have to call the cops. And then I'll get Chris something hot to drink. Something to eat. You must be starving."

Chris shook her head. "God, how did you ever find me?"

"Long story," said Bram. "Sophie, you fill her in and I'll be back in a flash."

Standing next to the front door, Bram tapped in Al's home number. It was going on one in the morning. Bram figured he'd find his buddy in bed.

"Lundquist," came a sleepy voice. "This better be good."

"Al, it's Bram."

"Christ, Baldric. It's the middle of the night."

Bram quickly filled him in on what had happened.

"Let me get this straight," said Al, clearing his throat. "You broke into a mini storage lot?"

"No, no. You're not listening. I *rented* a garage. Totally legal. But, well, yes, once I was inside, I did break into a unit that belonged to Phil Banks. But that's beside the point now. If I hadn't, Chris would be dead."

"Why didn't you call me? I could have sent a squad car."

Now Bram was outraged. "I told you about Chris this morning. You said I had to wait twenty-four hours before it became a police matter."

"Baldric, you are a true work of art, you know that? Tell me what the gun looked like."

"It looked like a gun. It was metal. Ugly. Like I said, it was lying on the front seat next to a plastic

Coke bottle. There were a couple of other Coke bottles scattered on the floor. The guy's a pig. What can I say. Maybe he used them for target practice."

"Why do you say that?"

"Because the bottoms were blown out."

Al exploded. "Jesus, Baldric. Why didn't you say that right away?"

"Say what?"

"Hang up the damn phone and bring the woman in."

"Are you going to take care of the storage garage?"

"I will as soon as you hang up!"

Bram cut the line. He returned to the car a few minutes later with a cup of hot coffee and a couple of candy bars. "Sustenance," he said, handing it all to Chris.

"You've got to hear this," said Sophie.

"Hear what?" said Bram, climbing back in the front seat.

Chris began slowly. She seemed calmer now, but dazed. "He only married me so I would give him an alibi."

"Chris—" said Bram.

"It's okay. I know I'm a fool. I guess I've known it all along."

"Don't blame yourself," said Sophie.

"No?" She looked out the window. "Then who should I blame? I was making us some breakfast this morning when Phil must have knocked me out. Next thing I remember, we were in my car and I was all tied up. God, I was so scared. Phil was silent all the way to the mini storage place, but once we got inside the garage and he'd closed the door, he slipped back into the front seat and started talking.

"He told me he'd killed Ken Loy because Loy killed his sister, Valerie. The lawsuit he'd filed against him wasn't going anywhere, and besides, he said, it was too slow. He'd been watching Loy for months. He knew all his habits. He was just biding his time, waiting for the right moment. And then we went to that movie. I chased Phil out, told him to go sleep in the car. But when he got outside, he took off. He drove to the mini storage lot. He keeps one of his construction company trucks there. It's fairly close to where Loy lived. Maybe he planned that, too. I don't know. Anyway, he found Loy riding down Shepard Road, so he pulled up next to him and shot him. He was feeling really pumped about what he'd done, so he cruised over to Bob Fabian's place to tell him the good news. Apparently Bob didn't feel the same way Phil did. He tried to call the paramedics, but Phil shot him before he could finish the call. Then he drove back to the storage garage, exchanged the truck for his car, and headed back to the theater."

"So it *was* Phil," said Bram, feeling vindicated. "I knew the police had arrested the wrong guy."

"But see, there was a problem."

"Irazarian?" asked Bram.

"Right. Seems he'd just learned that day that he was about to be fired. So he went to Bob's house that night to talk to him. But as he was about to ring the doorbell, he heard a muffled gunshot. Next thing he knew, Phil was charging out the back door. Irazarian followed him all the way back to the storage unit. It didn't take him long to put it all together. That's when he called Phil, tried to blackmail him with what he knew. That was a big mistake. Phil said he met Irazarian yesterday morning and agreed to pay him a bunch of money to keep his mouth shut. He was supposed to deliver it last night around nine. But he got to the motel early."

"Phil murdered Irazarian?" asked Bram.

Chris nodded. "He told me he hadn't decided what to do with me yet. That he'd be back. I knew he couldn't keep me around, not after telling me everything he'd done. But it was like . . . like he was proud of it. Like he needed to crow about it. And the only person he could safely tell was somebody who wasn't going to be around long."

Sophie put her arm around Chris's shoulder. "It's over now."

"Is it?" asked Chris. She shook her head. "I wish that were true. But until they find Phil and put him behind bars, my life isn't worth two cents. And even then, I have a feeling Phil's reach is a long one."

33

On Friday morning, Andy was informed he was no longer under arrest. As he was being processed out, he noticed that there were a number of reporters milling around outside in the hallway. Some he recognized. Others just had that lean and hungry look. The clerk on the other side of the counter shoved a bag of Andy's belongings across to him and asked him to check to make sure everything was there. Cell phone. Car keys. Wallet. Watch. Wedding ring. He signed the receipt.

Nobody was waiting for him and that was probably for the best. Ray Lawless had left a message saying that he'd be in touch later in the day to discuss Andy's questions. Andy didn't have any questions—at least, none that a lawyer could answer.

Once out on the street, he hoofed it to the Times Register Tower. It was only a short walk, a matter of a few minutes. It felt good to breathe fresh air after being locked in a cell all night. The secretary in his office looked surprised to see him when he sailed through the door. He nodded to her, but didn't stop to talk. He had business to take care of and didn't have a lot of time.

For the next few hours, a steady stream of staff entered and left his office. Everyone congratulated him, insisting they knew all along that his arrest had been a mistake. The men slapped him on the back; the women smiled. A few wanted to shake his hand. Andy was an officially innocent man. And with that innocence came the realization that he was now the true owner of the paper. All power resided in him. Under other circumstances, Andy might have enjoyed the chorus of cleverly camouflaged sucking sounds that emanated from his staff. Everyone wanted to have a drink with him, or coffee—or invite him to dinner. By noon, he'd seen everyone he needed to see. Arrangements had been made.

On the way out the door, he told his secretary to take the rest of the day off. Next week would be exceptionally busy and he needed her to be well rested.

Hailing a taxi out on the street, he headed home. Thankfully, the driver wasn't the talkative type. Andy leaned his head back and closed his eyes, but after only a few seconds, he opened them again and looked down at the wedding ring on his hand. When the clerk had given him his belongings, he'd wondered if he should just put it in his pocket. But that had seemed so wrong. His hand felt naked without it.

After paying the cabdriver, Andy stood for a moment in front of Bob's house. He'd realized now that he'd been wrong to insist on moving here. The place was too big, too Bob in every sense. The furnishings were sleek and modern, and looked as if they had been selected by an interior designer for a power life. The house was in perfect shape. Every window opened with ease. All the caulking was exact, every room clean and tidy. Andy was more comfortable with flaws and human disorder.

Once the front door was closed and locked behind him, the silence in the house pressed hard against him, making him almost gasp for air. He tossed his suit coat over a chair, loosened his tie, and proceeded into the living room. Snapping on the radio, he listened for a moment as some government official talked about the war in Iraq. But it was too far away from what was going on here and now. Andy turned up the sound, but zoned out the words. He had his own war to fight, and to win it, he needed total concentration.

On his way out of the living room, he paused next to Bob's graduation photo from West Point. He looked young and strong, clear-eyed and ready for whatever life threw at him. "I'm sorry," whispered Andy, setting the picture back down on the piano. "I tried, but I could never measure up." He grabbed a bottle of vodka from the bar, then bounded up the stairs to the bedroom.

Opening the double doors onto the upper balcony, Andy stepped outside. The smell of dying vegetation filled his nostrils with a kind of instant nostalgia. Autumn always made him feel gloomy, made him ache for something he'd never had. It was a beautiful late October day, sun filtering through the nearly leafless trees, the damp, decaying leaves forming a kind of pentimento on the back lawn.

Andy stood there with the sunshine warming his face, feeling naked under the limitless sky. The earth was off its axis today. Somewhere out there Andy believed that pigs were probably flying and that hell had suffered a hard freeze. All his life, he felt as if he'd been involved in a fruitless battle. Had he wanted too much? Hadn't he tried hard enough? Was he simply weak? Worthless? *Had* has father been right all along?

Remembering the bottle of vodka in his hand, he unscrewed the cap and took several swallows. The liquid burned as it went down. He hated liquor, hated anything and everything that reminded him of his father. But after what he'd done, a little booze seemed like a minor infraction. He leaned against the rail and downed half the bottle before finally returning inside.

Once back in the bedroom, he bent down and slipped a briefcase out from under the bed. He manipulated the rings on each side of the handle until the proper numbers popped up, then opened the case and dumped dozens of plastic prescription bottles on top of the bedspread.

The room seemed cold after the warmth of the afternoon sunlight. But it didn't matter. Cold was better than fear. He couldn't remember a time when he hadn't been afraid.

Removing a pen and a piece of paper from the briefcase, he sat down on the bed and wrote:

I love you with all my heart, Anika. Even before I met you, I warmed myself with the hope of you. Forgive me. Andy.

He cracked open the bottles and downed the pills with the rest of the bottle of vodka. He didn't know how many there were, but it was enough.

34

Bram breezed into the kitchen and kissed Sophie on the top of her head. "They released Andy and they've got Chris in protective custody. Oh, and the cops have impounded everything in Phil's mini storage garage."

"How'd you find all that out?" asked Sophie. She was cleaning up their lunch dishes. Bram had prepared one of his famous omelets.

"I just got a call from Al on my cell."

"Did he say anything else?" She was worried that they might be charged with burglary—or breaking and entering at the very least.

"You mean about us? We're off the hook, Soph. Al released a story to the papers that said we were at the mini storage place last night because we have a storage unit there. And that while we were driving by one of the double units, we heard a woman cry out for help. Not only are we free and clear, but we're heroes. I intend to talk about the whole thing on my radio show this afternoon."

Sophie turned around, slipping her arms around his waist. "My husband, the hero."

Bram flashed his eyes and adjusted his tie. "If the shoe fits."

"What about Phil?"

"They're looking for him. Ballistics matched the gun in his truck to all three homicides."

"Did Al say that *precisely*?"

Bram narrowed an eye. "He said the gun that was used in Bob's shooting was the same one used to murder Loy and Irazarian."

"See. He said 'shooting.'"

Bram sighed. "Yes. Shooting. As in *murder*."

"But he didn't say that. Not exactly."

"You're splitting unbelievably tiny hairs."

"But I'm not wrong."

"Look, you add a charge of felony kidnapping to the murders and Phil won't see the light of day for the rest of his natural life. *That's* the bottom line. Oh, and get this. In all three murders, he used a plastic Coke bottle as a silencer. They found two of them— one at Bob's place, and another at Irazarian's motel room, but they never gave that bit of info to the newspapers. That's why Al went nuts last night when I told him what I saw in the front seat of Phil's trunk. It must have been the one he used when he shot Loy."

"What an evil man," said Sophie, leaning back against the counter.

"He's a classic sociopath, sweetheart. Sociopaths don't grow up; they metastasize. But he'll be in custody soon."

"What if they can't find him?"

"They will. Every policeman in the state is on alert."

"He could run to Canada."

"I suppose it's possible, but for Chris's sake, I hope they nail him soon."

Sophie couldn't begin to imagine what that poor

young woman had gone through, and now here she was, scared for her life, waiting for Phil to be caught. There was one bright spot. With all the forensics the police were probably developing, the case wouldn't rest solely on her shoulders.

"What are you up to today?" asked Bram. "Fomenting more conspiracy theories with Mother?"

Sophie folded her arms across her stomach. "I thought I'd stop down to see Anika on my way to my office. Oh, and I have to run over to the Times Register Tower for a meeting late in the day."

Sophie assumed Margie hadn't spoken to Bram yet about the verbal assault she'd received from Sophie's dad yesterday morning. Just thinking about the conversation warmed Sophie's heart. But while her dad probably figured the tongue-lashing was the end of the story, Sophie knew better. Margie never took criticism in stride, probably because, in her own mind, she was never wrong. She was undoubtedly on the warpath, just waiting to explode all over a cozy evening, or a romantic breakfast. "Did you talk to your daughter yesterday?"

"No. Well, she did leave me a voice-mail message. She sounded sort of sniffy, like she'd been crying. I didn't have time to deal with it. I'm sure we'll talk today." He tipped Sophie's chin up. "Do you know what it was about?"

She shrugged, wiping any trace of amusement off her face. "You know Margie. Could be anything."

Sophie listened outside Anika's door for a few seconds. When she heard the TV switch off, she gave a soft knock.

Anika appeared a few moments later, still wearing her bathrobe.

"I assume you heard what happened," said Sophie. It had been all over the morning news.

Anika brushed a shock of blond hair off her forehead. "Come in."

Sophie entered hesitantly, judging by the grim look on Anika's face that the news hadn't changed anything. Sitting down on a chair next to the couch, she said, "Andy's been released."

Anika perched on a chair next to the desk. "You know that for a fact?"

"Bram talked to the detective in charge of the case."

She nodded. "Of course, I'm incredibly relieved. I never believed Andy could murder someone in cold blood. I suppose he went back to Bob's place."

"I would think so," said Sophie.

Anika seemed to ponder the situation. "He hates being alone. Even on a good day, that house feels like a tomb."

"It's certainly big."

Anika thought a few more seconds, then turned a hard gaze on Sophie. "You know the situation. If I go back there, he'll get the wrong idea. He'll think I've changed my mind, that I'm coming back to him."

"Possibly."

"But that's not going to happen. I mean, how can I do that to him, get his hopes up just to crush them? I can't stand much more of this myself."

Sophie could tell she was in pain.

Looking away, Anika said, "You think I should go see him, don't you."

"It doesn't matter what I think."

"Yes," she said softly. "It does."

"Well then," said Sophie, choosing her words carefully, "yes, I think you might want go see him. He's been terribly wounded by the arrest. You can explain that you're not staying, but that you just wanted to be with him for an hour or two, just to make sure he's okay. I'm sure he'd understand, and that he'd appreciate it."

"If I didn't still love him . . ." Her voice trailed off. "I am *such* a mess. I don't know how I could help anyone."

"It's up to you," said Sophie. "Just . . . don't completely rule it out until you give it a little more thought."

An hour later, Anika hurried up the walk to Bob's front door. Pressing the key in the lock, she entered to find the local MPR station blaring from the living room. Feeling relieved that her husband must be home, she took off her coat and walked into the living room.

"Andy?" she called, snapping off the radio. "Where are you? Andy?"

He didn't answer. She wondered if he'd gone outside. Stepping over to a long row of windows overlooking the backyard, she did a quick search. When she didn't see him, she decided to check upstairs. Maybe he was taking a nap. He was no doubt tired from spending the night in a jail cell.

Up on the second floor, she saw that the door to the bedroom was open. She couldn't exactly call it their bedroom because they'd only spent two nights in the house, and one of those nights she'd slept alone in a guest bedroom.

As she entered, she saw that he was asleep. His head was at an odd angle on the pillow, but he was a restless sleeper. Thinking that he must be cold, she grabbed a quilt off the top shelf of the closet. As she draped it over him, she noticed the empty pill bottles. Dropping the quilt, she started to count them. Eight. Ten. Fourteen.

"My God, Andy! What have you done?" When she bent over him to check his pulse, she kicked something with her foot. Looking down, she saw an empty bottle of vodka lying on the floor. "Damn you!" she screamed, backing up. She stared at him a moment, then leaned her ear close to his nose. He was breathing, but just barely.

Grabbing the phone off the nightstand, she punched in 911.

One ring, two—"911 emergency."

"This is Anika Gladstone—my husband's just taken a bunch of pills! He's breathing, but it's shallow! You've got to help us! Please! Right away!"

35

Bram returned to his cubbyhole office after his radio show. As soon as he sat down behind his desk, the phone rang. "Baldric," he said absently. He was still thinking about his last caller. Or, more precisely, he was smoldering.

"Hey, buddy. It's Al."

"Hi. Any news?" He leaned back and put his feet up on the desk.

"I caught the last hour of your program."

Bram grinned. "What'd you think?"

"You're not gonna want to hear this."

"Why? What?"

After the first hour, Bram had opened up the program to callers. The topics: three recent homicides in the Twin Cities; the scandal at the *Minneapolis Times Register*; had the *Twin Cities* turned into the *Evil Twins* of big-city crime? Since the news stations had already picked up what had happened last night, Bram couldn't exactly deny that he'd been instrumental in bringing new information to light on the Loy, Fabian, and Irazarian homicides. The lines lit up as he described the evening's events in vivid—perhaps even a tad melodramatic—detail. He carefully left out certain facts that he'd been asked to keep quiet.

But there was still plenty of fodder for his talk-radio audience. Phil Banks had made a lot of enemies in his years as the owner of Banks Construction. The dirt flew hot and heavy, mainly during the last hour. "Something you didn't like?" Bram asked Al.

"Not me, pal. *Banks*. If he was listening, you're probably number one on his list of guys he'd like to see splattered across a concrete wall."

"Meaning what?"

"That you should stick a sock in your mouth, go home, and keep a low profile until we find him. Jesus, Baldric. What were you thinking? Do you have some sort of death wish? Were you trying to wave a red flag in front of an angry bull?"

"If my program dislocates him from wherever he's crawled to hide, then fine. I'm happy to oblige."

"You're an idiot."

"I beg your pardon?"

"Look, just take my advice. Now, I also called to tell you that we've got his house staked out, his construction company, and the restaurants where he's part owner. We also linked the gun found last night to a murder that happened up in Duluth in '95. Believe me when I tell you, you don't want to mess with this guy."

The message was beginning to penetrate. "Okay, okay."

"Keep your nose clean. I gotta run."

"One question first."

"Make it quick."

"Bob Fabian, he's dead, right?"

"Of course he's dead."

"Banks shot him."

"Yes."

"The bullet *killed* him."

Silence. "Like I said, I gotta run."

"The gunshot didn't kill him? So if he's dead, something else must have. What?"

"Go find yourself a nice cozy rock and crawl under it, okay? I'll tell you when it's safe to come out."

"Gee, that's just wonderful, Al. Just peachy keen. More evidence of my tax dollars at work."

"Later, pal."

Bram sat for a few moments, mulling it all over. Al hadn't answered him, not directly, but in a way he had. Phil may have shot Bob, but Bob had actually died from something other than a gunshot wound. That's what all the hedging had been about. When it came to Bob Fabian, the police were looking for two murderers: Phil, who made an attempt, and someone else, who succeeded.

Tucking his jacket under his arm, Bram was out of the office in twenty seconds flat. He wanted to get home and talk it over with Sophie. Maybe she could help him make sense of it. Glancing at his watch, he saw that it was just after four. Sophie had that late meeting over at the *Times Register*, so it seemed a good bet she wouldn't be home. That's when a thought struck him. He wondered if Chris had told the police about the apartment Phil had in St. Paul. It seemed a good bet that she had, but just in case, Bram decided to swing by and see what he could see.

In the phone message Chris had left him, she'd said that the building was on Spencer and Fifteenth, and that it was old.

Fifteen minutes later, Bram drove along Spencer past a sixplex, circa 1930s. It was the only apartment building anywhere around, so it had to be the right one.

Cruising past in his very obvious Bentley, Bram felt as if he were behind the wheel of a neon exclamation point. He sped by quickly. Glancing in his rearview mirror, he saw a woman come out of a back door carrying a load of boxes. He was already too far away to see her face, so pulled a U-turn at the corner and came back for a second look.

A Ford Explorer was parked in the rear lot. As he edged in behind a delivery truck, the woman disappeared inside the building. It seemed apparent that she was packing to leave. He watched the rear door and waited. A few minutes later, the woman reappeared. She set the boxes she was carrying on the ground next to the rear hatch of the SUV. This time, Bram got a good look at her face. "Damn," he whispered. He might be wrong, but he was almost positive it was the same blonde he'd seen with Phil Banks at the Speakeasy Cafe.

Looking around, Bram didn't see all that many cars, certainly none that looked like part of a stakeout. He had a sick feeling that the cops didn't know about this place. Pulling his cell out of his pocket, he tapped the 5 key. He had Al on speed-dial now. He wasn't sure if that was a good sign or a bad one.

"Lundquist," said a gruff voice.

"Al, it's Baldric."

"I don't have time for this."

"You arrogant son of a bitch, just listen to me! Did Chris tell you about Phil's girlfriend—and that he had an apartment in St. Paul?"

"Yes to the girlfriend, no to the apartment. Where is it?"

Bram gave him the address. "You better get here fast. The girlfriend is packing up a car."

"I'm on it," said Lundquist. "Don't be a hero, Baldric. You see Phil Banks, you run."

"Bye, Al." Bram had no intention of getting involved, but he couldn't just let Phil get away. No, he'd sit and wait—until the cops arrived.

36

Anika sat in the hospital room, her eyes rarely straying from her husband's face. Just minutes after she'd made the 911 call, paramedics arrived at the house and whisked Andy away in an ambulance. By the time Anika got to the hospital, he was in the ER. With nothing else to do, she sat in the waiting room and catastrophized. What if he died? Was it her fault? Had leaving him pushed him over the edge?

Anika wasn't sure what the doctors had done to him, but before they took him up to a room, a burly man in blue scrubs had come out to talk to her. He said that the drugs and the alcohol hadn't been in Andy's system very long. Most of the pills were still fully formed in his stomach. He felt they'd been able to remove most of it. He also informed her that Andy would probably sleep for a while, and he might have a whopper of a hangover when he woke up, but that he should be fine. As a grim addenda, he said that another half hour and the prognosis would have been vastly different. He asked if Andy had ever attempted suicide before.

Anika had a hard time getting her mind around the word. She told him that her husband had been depressed for quite some time, but that he'd never tried to hurt himself before. She insisted it was a one-time event, an aberration, maybe even some sort of bizarre accident. They'd been having marital problems. The doctor encouraged her to talk to a staff psychologist. He also suggested that anyone who had attempted suicide was deeply troubled. They might both benefit from talking to a therapist.

Sending up a silent prayer of thanks, Anika glanced at the clock on the wall. It was going on four thirty. She'd been at the hospital just under four hours. She desperately wanted Andy to wake up, but had no idea what she'd say to him when he did. Maybe she should start with the basics.

She whispered, "I still love you, Andy Gladstone."

As if he'd heard her words, his eyes fluttered and then opened. He groaned as he turned to look at her. "God, I feel awful." His gaze swept the room. "Where am I?"

"St. Joseph's Hospital."

"How—"

"I found you at the house and called 911."

"Oh, God," he said, closing his eyes. "I never meant for you to walk in on that."

She took hold of his hand. "Why, Andy? Was it me? Was it the separation? Is that why you took all those pills?"

"No," he whispered. His voice was raw. He'd had a tube down his throat, so it wasn't surprising. "It wasn't you. It had nothing to do with you."

"The police let you go. You're exonerated. An innocent man."

"Innocence," he repeated, clearing his throat, "is a pain in the ass." He concentrated on her face. "God but you're beautiful."

She didn't know what to say.

"I'm a coward," he said finally.

"No, you're not. You're always so hard on yourself."

"Irazarian was blackmailing me."

"Yes, I know. Because you were his editor."

He closed his eyes again. "No. Because I'm an addict. He was my supplier."

Anika felt her heart skip a beat. "I don't believe you," she said finally, but the catch in her voice said otherwise.

"It was the back surgery that started it. The doctors took me off the painkillers too early—I still needed them. So I went doctor shopping, looking for a way to get more meds. But I got scared because it's illegal. When Del did that story on drug addiction in the Minneapolis Police Department, he met a lot of unsavory people. I confided in him one night, told him that if he ever came across any Vicodin, or Percocet, to hang on to it. I acted like I was joking, but he got the message. He started selling them to me. When I realized that he was making stuff up for his articles, that his unnamed sources didn't exist, he threatened to tell Bob about my pill habit."

"But if he was selling them to you, he could've gone to jail."

"Oh, yeah. Nobody's hands were clean. But I had more to lose than he did, and we both knew it."

"That's why you let him get away with those false stories?"

"I had to. I didn't have a choice. And I needed the drugs, except I knew they were wrecking my life. That's why I tried to quit."

Anika felt as if a light had gone on inside her mind. "The time you got so sick?"

"And the day Bob died. I tried to go cold turkey both times, and both times I couldn't stand it. I thought I was going to die. The only reason I got better was because I started using again." He squeezed Anika's hand. "Don't you see? I'm just like my father. I'm no good. I need drugs to live my life, I can't do it straight. But the drugs are killing me. They ruined our marriage. They would have eventually ruined my relationship with Bob."

It was all becoming clear. "Why didn't you tell me?"

"I couldn't. You, Bob, and Rick are the only people I ever really cared about, and I knew what you'd think if you found out."

"Oh, Andy. You're so wrong." She got up and bent over him, kissing him lightly on the lips. Sitting down on the bed, she held him in her arms. "You're not your father. You're not." She could feel him shaking.

"I love you so much," he said, his words choked with sobs.

"It's okay, sweetheart. We'll find you the help you need."

"I don't know if I can do it. Not alone. I've felt so alone all my life. I'm always so afraid someone will see through me, see the real me, and then they'll leave."

The guilt she felt was crushing.

"If you could just . . . stay. For a little while longer. God, I just need someone to believe in me and not leave when it gets rough. Do you understand?"

"I've always wanted to be that person, Andy." And she had. But she didn't believe in soap opera endings—

that mushy desire for everything to turn out for the best. In real life, it rarely did.

"Then, you could still love me? Even knowing what you know?"

She smoothed back the tousled strands of hair from his forehead. "I never stopped. We'll get through this. We have to." She held him close, willing it to happen.

37

Sophie stood outside the Maxfield, waiting to ask a bellman to get her car. But late on a Friday afternoon, the hotel was a madhouse. The circular drive was packed with cabs and airport vans. Not only was it a football weekend, but Elton John was scheduled to appear at the Target Center. The Minnesota Symphony was hosting an internationally known choral group from South Africa. The latest Broadway version of *Cabaret* was playing at the Ordway, and Peter, Paul and Mary were scheduled to appear Sunday afternoon at Northrup Auditorium. And that was just a few of the attractions that might bring visitors to town.

Sophie checked her watch. If she didn't get a move on, she'd be late for her meeting at the paper. Deciding to let the bellman take care of guests instead of her, she trotted across the street to the parking garage. The Maxfield rented several of the bottom floors for guests and employees. Sophie kept her Lexus on level DD.

As she descended the metal stairway into the dimly lit, dank subbasement, she thought she heard footsteps above her. When she stopped, they stopped. It was probably just her imagination. She'd been imagining all sorts of things lately. She hadn't told Bram, but she was growing more and more paranoid about Nathan, feeling his eyes watching her as she walked through the hotel or worked at the reservation desk. It was impossible for him to spend that much time away from his restaurant, and yet she had the sense that he was there. She couldn't believe he'd want to hurt her, but if he didn't quit popping up out of the blue, it wouldn't be long before she'd feel like she was being stalked. She even thought she saw him earlier in the afternoon—jeans, white chef's coat, dark hair and beard—but when she looked more closely, she realized that it was one of her sous chefs from the Zephyr Club.

By the time Sophie reached level DD, she was completely spooked. She headed straight for her car. A few feet away from it, she pushed UNLOCK on her remote. She glanced in the backseat before opening the driver's door, just to make sure. As she tossed her purse into the passenger's seat, the dark tinted window in the van directly next to her suddenly rolled down. An arm thrust outward. Attached to the arm was a gun.

Sophie froze.

"I've been waiting for you," said Phil Banks. He cocked the hammer and grinned.

Sophie looked around wildly, but there was no place to run. "What . . . what do you want?"

"You," he said, his expression hardening. "And then your husband. Or maybe I'll just do you. That way he can suffer for the rest of his miserable life because of his stupidity." He eased out of the van.

"Look . . . I mean . . . let's talk about this."

"You and me, we're about to take a little drive."

"Where?"

"None of your damn business." He caressed her face with the barrel of the revolver. "You're an attractive woman, Sophie. Maybe we'll have a little fun first. What do you say?"

He stank of sweat and alcohol. The idea of being touched by him repulsed and terrified her to her very core. "I can get you money, help you get out of the state. Whatever you need. Really. I can help!"

"Oh, you're going to help me, all right. But money?" He laughed. "Maybe while we're driving, you can think of other, more intimate ways to help." He grabbed her arm and shoved her around the back of the car to the passenger's door. "Get in," he ordered. "And move over to the driver's seat. You're gonna drive. Oh, and don't try anything funny or I'll blow you away right here. Now make it quick."

As he released the hammer, Sophie climbed in, but before she'd moved more than a few inches, she heard him cry out. She whirled around just as a man in a leather jacket yanked him backward and slammed his hand into the rear fender. The gun was dislodged, skittering across the floor and landing against a concrete column.

Sophie's eyes opened wide when she saw that her savior was Nathan.

In an instant, Nathan had Phil down on the ground. They were rolling together, wresting each other for control.

Sophie didn't wait to see who the winner would be. She rushed past them, headed for the gun. But before she reached it, Phil had managed to get away from Nathan and beat her to it. He shoved her aside and grabbed for it, falling as he did.

"No," screamed Sophie.

Nathan was on him again, trying to pry the gun out of his hand. Sophie turned away, looking for something she could use as a weapon. Anything heavy and hard. And that's when she heard the gunshot. At the same moment, she felt her arm sting and go limp. Looking down, she saw blood dripping from her sleeve and spreading across her raincoat.

"Are you all right?" called Nathan.

She sank down on the back bumper of a Chevrolet.

"You freaking asshole!" exploded Nathan. He sank his teeth into Phil's hand and didn't let go.

Phil howled in pain. The gun dropped as he fell to his knees. Nathan kicked him hard in the stomach. Phil doubled over. Nathan kicked him again and again, until he seemed beyond putting up any more of a fight. Then Nathan scooped up the gun, pocketed it, and raced over to Sophie.

"Let me see," he said.

She felt dazed. The stain on her raincoat had grown larger.

"Press your hand over it," he ordered. "Hard. I know it hurts, but it will help stop the bleeding."

She looked up. Horrified, she cried, "Nathan, watch out!"

Phil slammed into him. They both hit the concrete with a deep grunt. But the older man was no match for the younger. Nathan pinned him in a matter of seconds and then just kept slugging him. Phil could only try to fend off the blows.

"Stop," said Sophie. She looked away.

But Nathan kept it up. It was like some genie of rage inside him had been released. He gripped Phil by his coat, heaved him up, and hurled him into one of the concrete columns.

Phil sank to the ground, his greasy gray pompadour wilted over his forehead.

Nathan heaved him up and did it again. He seemed to be enjoying himself.

"Nathan, you've got to stop."

"Shut up," he yelled. Brushing himself off, he sat Phil against the pillar. Phil was out cold now and past caring.

"Nathan?" she called cautiously. "What are you doing?"

"Watch." He crouched down close to Phil and removed the gun from his coat pocket.

"Nathan!"

He aimed, cocked the hammer, and fired.

She screamed. She couldn't believe her eyes. Nathan had just shot a man in cold blood. She watched in stunned silence as he dropped the gun next to Phil.

A moment later, he was by her side, flipping open his cell phone and tapping in 911. "It was him or me, Sophie. You saw it. We fought. I got the gun away from him and fired. It all happened in a matter of seconds."

She stared at him. That wasn't the way it happened at all. But she got the message. It was what she was supposed to say when the police questioned her.

"I saved your life, Sophie. I don't want gratitude. I just want you to finally realize how much I love you, that I'd do anything for you." He listened to the phone. "Yes. My name is Nathan Buckridge. Send a squad and an ambulance to the Northland parking garage in downtown St. Paul, level DD. Hurry. A woman was just shot in the arm."

38

The following Monday, Sophie woke to the sound of singing. When she opened her eyes, she felt as if she were floating in a beautiful garden. But then she remembered that her arm was in a splint, and the beautiful garden was a bunch of unwanted bouquets provided by one man.

Nathan entered, his tenor voice crooning out Sarah McLachlan's "Angel." He knew it was one of her favorites, but coming out of his mouth—with the spin he put on it—the song didn't have the desired effect. She wasn't happy to see him, nor was she thrilled with his effort to turn her hospital room into a floral exhibit. As far as she was concerned, it was just one more example of his obsessive, excessive nature. If he hadn't just saved her life, she would have insisted he be barred from the hospital.

Sophie had seen a part of Nathan that not only terrified, but sickened her. Since she was admitted to the hospital three days ago, he would pop in whenever he felt like it. She asked him to call first, but there was a new wariness in her requests, one that he seemed to relish. Perhaps he read it as acquiescence, that he'd proved his point: not only did he have a right to be part of her life, but she *needed* him. He hadn't said it out loud, but they both knew he'd been following her the day she'd been attacked. Okay, so if he hadn't been there, she might be dead now. It was that inescapable fact that had caused her to go along with his fiction about how Phil died. In some deeply twisted way, she knew it bound them together.

Sophie had wanted to tell Bram the truth, but she was afraid that if she did, he wouldn't be able to keep quiet about it. Either he'd go off half-cocked and beat Nathan to a bloody pulp, or be beaten himself, or he'd insist they tell the police what really happened. It wasn't that he was a stickler for total honesty, but Sophie was sure he'd think that Al could help her beat any charges stemming from lying to the police, and Bram would salivate at the chance of putting Nathan away for good. Her decision to allow Nathan to suck her into his lie hadn't been a smart one, but for good or ill, it was a done deal. As it stood right now, the police were calling Phil's death a justifiable homicide. Everything would blow over in time. She simply had to make Nathan understand that they weren't fated to be together.

But the worst part was how the entire situation had affected Bram. The poor man had to be grateful now to Nathan for saving her life. Bram felt he owed him—big-time—and yet he still hated the sight of him. Nathan had committed the perfect crime. He'd wormed his way into Sophie and Bram's life in a way that couldn't be easily dismissed.

"How's the patient this morning?" asked Nathan, pulling another bouquet of roses from behind his back. This time, they were peach. Sophie hated peach-colored roses. "Here, smell?" He brought them close to her nose.

"Thanks," she said.

"I know. I don't like the color either, but the fragrance reminded me of all the nights you and I spent in the Rose Garden by Lake Harriet. Remember?" He moved over to the window and made room on the ledge for his newest gift. "So? How's the arm?"

"It hurts." The bullet had fractured her left humerus, then lodged next to it. Sophie had undergone surgery a few hours after being brought to the hospital. The prognosis was good, but the recovery would be lengthy and painful.

"I thought the flowers would help." He smiled down at her. "Guess it will be a while before we can go dancing."

"Nathan—"

Out in the hall, Sophie could hear Bram's laugh. Her blood pressure zoomed. She hated it anytime Bram and Nathan collided. As her husband pushed through the door, she saw that Al Lundquist was with him.

"Well, Mr. Buckridge," said Al, extending his hand. "Good to see you again."

"Hi," said Bram. The smile on his face had already faded.

Nathan grinned. "Just brought Soph some flowers to cheer her up." Glancing at his watch, he added, "But I've got to dash. I have a restaurant to run."

"So I hear," said Al. "I'll have to get over there one of these days."

"Just let me know," said Nathan. "Dinner's on me."

"Hey, thanks."

"See you around," said Bram.

Nathan took one last look at Sophie, and then left. "So," said Al, pulling up an orange plastic chair, "how's that nasty break doing?" He seemed totally unaware of the currents of emotion surging through the air.

"I think I'll live," said Sophie.

"She'll live, all right," said Bram, sitting down on the bed next to her and giving her a kiss. "I'll make sure of that." Folding his hand around hers, he said, "Al has news."

"About Phil?" asked Sophie.

"About Chris. Get this. Since she was married to the bastard before he died, she's now a relatively wealthy woman. He apparently had a lot of debts, but after she sells the house and the construction company, she figures she'll still have enough money to take care of her for a long long time. And she's going to keep the interests he had in various restaurants. Who knows? She may turn out to be a real restaurateur one day."

"I'm so glad," said Sophie. She'd been worried about Chris. The fact that there wouldn't need to be a trial now was undoubtedly a big load off her shoulders—and Sophie's.

"Okay, Al," said Bram. "Now that the case is closed, can you please tell us what the deal was with Bob Fabian? If he didn't die because of the gunshot, what did he die of?"

Al scratched the back of his neck. "Well, I suppose I can talk about it. We're nowhere on the case, and if my gut tells me right, it's probably headed for the cold case file. It seems he was poisoned."

"Poisoned?" repeated Sophie. "How? By who?"

"Like I said, we don't know. We don't even know what the poison was. But you're right. The bullet didn't kill him. We rushed him to the emergency room.

The doctors were sure they could save him, but he died on the operating table. His body just flat-out shut down. They did some tox screens, and they're positive he ingested something lethal, but as far as what it was, who did it, and why, we've got nothing but a big goose egg."

"So two attempts were made on his life that night," said Sophie softly. "He was dying even before Phil shot him."

"Appears so."

"I guess when your number comes up, it really comes up," said Bram.

"At this point, the case remains open," said Al. "But it will probably be ruled a suicide. A sad end to an amazing life." He stood. "Well, duty calls. I'll leave you two lovebirds alone and get back to the grind."

"Thanks for coming, Al," said Sophie.

"You get better now." He cracked a knuckle.

She winced. "I will."

As soon as he was gone, Bram asked Sophie to scoot over so he could lie down on the bed next to her.

"Don't get any frisky ideas."

"Of course not," he said, turning on his side and putting his arm around her waist. Very gently, he pulled her close. "How long was Prince Charming here?"

"Only a few minutes."

He was silent a moment. "Soph?"

"Hmm?"

"I've been thinking."

"Uh-oh. You must be exhausted."

"Cute." More silence. "Nathan said he was in the

parking lot Friday afternoon because he'd come by to see Margie. Except, she wasn't around."

"Right."

"The police bought it, Sophie, but I didn't."

She'd been expecting this conversation. She was surprised it hadn't happened earlier.

"He was following you, wasn't he."

She looked up at the ceiling. "Yes. I think so. I can't prove it."

"He's clever."

"I never know for sure. I think he's been . . ." Her voice trailed off.

"Stalking?"

She hadn't wanted to say that word out loud, but yes. That's exactly what it felt like. "I don't know what to think. Believe me, I've been doing my best to eject him from my life, but he never seems to get it."

"Oh, he gets it, all right. But he's got a different agenda in mind. Do you think . . . I mean, is it possible he's dangerous?"

Sophie looked down at her wedding ring. "I think he could be."

"I don't care if the pope makes him a saint. If he causes us any more problems, I'm getting a restraining order against him."

All she could think to say was, "Okay."

"God, I wish he hadn't just saved your life. I was the one who should have been there. Instead, I was sitting outside Phil's apartment, watching his girlfriend pack."

"You didn't know."

"But I should have. Al warned me to go home and keep a low profile. What I said on my radio show might have pushed him over the edge."

She turned and kissed him softly. "No more of this. What's done is done. We're both alive, and that's what's important."

He stared at her a moment, then smiled. "If my wife says it, it must be true."

She couldn't help but grimace.

Glancing around the room, he continued, "I would have brought you flowers, but they're so impersonal. Know what I mean?"

She laughed. "Absolutely."

"So," he said, dipping his hand into his jacket pocket, "I brought you this instead."

Her eyes lit up. "Kransakaka! From my favorite bakery?"

"Nothing else would do."

"Oh, honey, you know the way to a woman's heart—at least, this woman's."

"True."

This time when he kissed her, he didn't stop.

39

"I have *never ever in my whole life* had someone talk to me like that," blurted Margie. "You *have* to *do* something about him, Dad. I think, at the very least, Henry owes me an apology."

Bram had taken his daughter to the Rookery Club for dinner. Sophie would be released from the hospital tomorrow, and he wanted to spend a little time with Margie before he brought his wife home.

"Look, honey—"

"That man *hates* me. Me! I'm one of the nicest people I know! Besides, what have I ever done that was so bad? He thinks I'm leeching off you and Sophie just because you're helping me out! I mean, that's what parents are *for*. They're supposed to help their kids. Like, I didn't *ask* to be brought into this world."

"Calm down, sweetheart." People in the restaurant were starting to stare.

"He called me a *brat*, Dad. He even spelled it, like I was some sort of moronic dweeb."

"Well, yes, dear, that was totally beyond the pale." Bram sipped his Manhattan and tried to look concerned.

"Damn straight it was. In my opinion, he's drawn

a line in the sand. *Our* family against his. That's the way I see it. And if he wants war, he's got one."

"Margie, Sophie's father is used to giving orders. You interrupted him while they were working. It's really not that big a deal."

"Not a big deal? Not . . . a . . . big . . . deal! Dad, he sat there and accused me—*me*, the last word in diplomacy and tact—of sticking it to Sophie every chance I got."

"Well, actually—"

She turned her outraged eyes on him. "I try *so hard* with that woman. She is *not* my idea of a mother figure. Even my business partner, Carrie, agrees she's way too snooty, too self-centered, too . . . too judgmental and uptight to ever give me the kind of love and attention I deserve."

"Are we talking about *my Sophie*? That small blond woman I live with? Because, if we are—"

She cut him off again. "Oh, I knew you'd take her side, try to make light of it. But Henry wounded me, Dad. *Deeply.*"

"Margie, there are no sides. We're a family. And believe me, Sophie doesn't think you're a leech. She loves you. She just isn't always sure you like her very much."

"Well, she's right about that." Margie took a sip of her wine.

"I'll talk to Henry, I promise. See what's up."

She turned her attention to the menu. "Fine."

Bram watched her. "Are we still pals?"

"I think I'll have the salmon."

"Margie?"

"Hmm?"

"Are you angry at me?"

She didn't respond.

"Because, if you are, you have to understand, you've put me in the middle here."

"Right, Dad. I get it."

"Do you?"

"I have to fight my own battles. Don't worry, I'm up to it."

"I don't want you to fight anyone, honey, especially Sophie or her father."

"Let's change the subject, okay?" Her eyes brightened. "Hey, look. There's Mrs. Josefowicz again. I should go over and say hi. Did I tell you? She's thinking of using Carrie and me to do her niece's wedding next spring."

"That's great," said Bram, watching her get up and walk over to the table. Mrs. Josefowicz and her companion seemed delighted to see her. Margie sat down, and immediately the threesome were deep in conversation.

Picking up his drink as he rose from the table, Bram passed by his daughter, whispering into her ear. "I'm going back to the De Gustabus room. I won't be long."

Margie gave him one of her dazzling smiles and waved over her shoulder.

So much for her lousy mood.

The other reason Bram had for coming to the club tonight centered around Al Lundquist's comments about how Bob Fabian had died. Bram had the beginnings of a theory, and he wanted to poke around and see if he could firm up something.

Flicking his eyes to the NO RESERVATIONS REQUIRED sign above the door, he squared his shoulders and entered. It was Monday night. He assumed Vince and

Lyle would be dining on stir-fried bat wings—or whatever. He wasn't disappointed.

"Baldric," said Vince, looking up from his plate. "Join us."

Lyle nodded hello.

"What's on the menu?"

"Stuffed goose neck with a red ant chutney," said Vince. "And crisp roasted termites over polenta."

"Oh, yummy," said Bram, feeling his stomach lurch.

"You missed the dried fly larvae on toast points," said Lyle. "That was our appetizer."

Bram thought he detected a smirk. "Well, I guess I'll just have to drown my sorrows for my bad timing." He lifted his glass, saluted them, then took a hefty swallow. "I want to talk to you boys."

"Yeah?" said Vince. "About what?"

"Bob Fabian." Bob's photo was still sitting on the buffet, but the crepe paper had been removed. He'd been dead almost three weeks now.

"Shoot," said Vince, taking a sip of wine.

Bram pulled out a chair and sat down. "My connections in the St. Paul Police Department tell me Bob didn't die of a gunshot wound."

"No?" said Lyle, wiping his mouth with a napkin.

"Nope," said Bram. "Seems he was poisoned. It will likely be ruled a suicide."

Both men continued eating. Neither looked surprised.

"Know anything about it?" asked Bram.

"Why would you think we'd know anything?" asked Vince.

"Well, actually—"

"You still think I did it?" asked Lyle. Glancing at

Vince, he added, "Baldric here came to my condo the other day. Accused me of shooting Bob in cold blood. Now it appears he thinks I poisoned him. You got a one-track mind, Baldric. Like I told you then, Bob was my best friend. I owe him my life. You think I'd hurt him, you're crazy."

Bram scratched his head. He knew he was missing something. "But you guys . . . you were the last people to see him that night."

"So?" said Vince.

"Then again, you loved him."

"Right," said Lyle. "And FYI, Bob would never have committed suicide. He was very religious. Thought Valerie was in heaven. If he took his own life, he figured heaven would be banned from him forever."

"Kind of an innocent way to view life," added Vince. "Especially for a West Point grad, and a Viet Nam vet. But that's what he thought."

"If it wasn't suicide," said Bram, "then it must have been murder." Lyle glared at him. "Try thinking outside the box for once, Baldric."

"Meaning what?" said Bram.

"Meaning," said Lyle, "that there's more than two options."

"For instance," said Bram.

"Well," said Lyle, "if you were to join our little culinary club, attend our Monday night dinners regularly, we might, say, over a bottle of root beer, let the truth slip. But we'd have to trust you first. And the only way we'd ever trust you is if you became a member. Blood brothers. That sort of thing."

Bram sat up straight. "You're kidding, right? You'd tell me what really happened if I joined your group?"

"Well, you'd have to swear you'd never pass it on to your 'connection' in the department. There are rules to secret societies," said Vince.

"You're not a secret society."

"Yeah," said Vince. "True. We're just two silly old guys with lots of survivalist literature in the trunks of our cars."

"You are?"

Vince knocked him on the shoulder. "Kidding again."

Bram stared at the crispy little bodies covering the polenta.

" 'Course, you never know what secrets lurk in the hearts of men." Lyle stifled a burp. "But join our group and you can find out."

Bram didn't know what to believe. One thing was for sure. They were certainly enjoying themselves at his expense. If they really had murdered Bob, why all the good humor? The whole thing seemed way the hell too bizarre. But, it appeared the only way he would ever get the answer he wanted was to join their group. Unless that was another joke.

"Okay," he said. "I'm in."

"We have to vote," said Lyle.

"And then drink a cup of fresh horse blood," said Vince.

"Horse blood!"

Lyle laughed. "It's just so fun to watch your reactions, Baldric."

"Raise your left hand," said Vince.

"My *left* hand?"

"We don't do things in here like regular folks," said Vince. "But you already know that."

"We're adventurers," said Lyle. "By the way, Baldric,

I took a leave of absence from my job. I'm entering rehab on Wednesday."

"Good man," muttered Vince.

"The hand," said Lyle. "Raise it."

Bram raised his hand.

"Repeat after me," said Vince. "I, Bram Baldric, do solemnly swear that I will live life to the fullest, not be afraid of new ideas—or foods—and that I will keep my trap shut about whatever is said in this room."

Bram repeated it, word for word.

"Welcome to the De Gustabus Club," said Lyle.

Vince slapped him on the back, then got up to shut the door.

"You guys are total *madmen*."

"Yup, very likely," said Vince. "Here. Try some of the termites."

"No, you first," said Bram, eyeing the tiny fried varmints warily.

"Well," said Vince. "It's all pretty simple. After Valerie died, Bob went on and on about how much he missed her. Like Lyle said, he believed in heaven. He thought that when he died, he'd be reunited with her. So, ergo, he wanted to die to go be with her, but he couldn't kill himself."

"So we told him," said Lyle, tucking into a thick slice of the goose neck, "hell, we didn't have any problem with killing. We'd both killed lots of people in Nam. 'Course, this was a little different."

"A lot harder,' said Vince. "Harder than we ever imagined."

"See, Vince and me, we think heaven is a crock, but hell, every man to his own beliefs, right?"

"Right," said Vince firmly. "So here's the deal. We

thought that maybe, in time, Bob would change his mind. We told him we'd give him one year. If, during that period he had a change of heart, he'd let us know. But, if he didn't tell us, he could expect that on the anniversary of Valerie's death, we'd take care of it for him."

"Send him to his heavenly reward," said Lyle. This time, he'd stopped eating. His voice was thick. "He was never the same after Valerie died. We could tell he was just biding his time. The old zest for living had already gone out of him. We just helped the rest of him go."

"I mean, we didn't want him to die," said Vince, putting his fork down, his expression sobering. "But we made a pact. We loved him enough to do what he wanted done. We miss him like hell. And we figure he's in his grave, but maybe, just maybe, he was right. Heaven does exist. Maybe he's up there right now looking down on us, smiling, his arms around Val, right where they belong. God, I hope he got his wish."

Bram just sat there. He wasn't sure if he should be appalled or moved—or if he should believe it at all. "What did you use to poison him?"

"None of your business," said Lyle, sniffing into a handkerchief.

"We may want to use it again," said Vince, winking at Lyle.

"You're kidding, right?" said Bram.

Lyle grinned. "Yes, we're kidding."

"But not about Bob."

"Well, maybe we are," said Vince. "Then again, maybe we aren't."

"Your problem, Baldric," said Lyle, "is that you

think we sit around here every week playing Russian roulette with poisonous blowfish."

"Yeah, that about covers it," said Bram.

"Well, we don't," said Vince firmly.

"What about the police?" asked Bram. "Aren't you afraid they'll eventually figure it out and put you in jail?"

Both men shook their heads.

"Not unless you tell them," said Lyle.

"We'd deny it, of course," said Vince.

"So," said Lyle, shrugging, "life goes on. Such as it is."

Bram's head was spinning.

"Now that we're done with the initiation," said Vince, dishing Bram up a plate, "let's eat."

"Vince has outdone himself tonight," said Lyle, wiping at his eyes with the handkerchief.

"Remember our motto," said Vince, pushing the plate across the table.

"No reservations required?" repeated Bram.

"Amen," both men replied.

Vince grinned. "Come on, Baldric. Dig in."

Sophie's Favorite Kransakaka Cookie

Kransakaka is generally made as a wedding cake in Scandinavia, so it's a big hit (ya, sure!) in Minnesota, too (land of ten thousand Nelsons, Johnsons, Petersons, and Olsons). Give it a try. Oh, and trust me. You'll like it a whole lot better than you will mealworm dip or deep fried crickets.

2 cups almond paste
1 cup granulated sugar
2 egg whites, beaten slightly (may need slightly more if the batter is too thick)

Preheat the oven to 325 degrees Fahrenheit.

Cover a baking sheet with parchment paper.

Crumble the almond paste into small chunks; then add the sugar and the egg whites. Using an electric mixer, beat the mixture together until well combined. Fill a pastry bag with the batter and squeeze out long (approximately 1 inch wide by 4 inches long) cookies onto the parchment paper. Bake for 15 minutes, or until the surface is golden brown. Handle with care when they are hot because these cookies are fragile. Cool. Frost with melted chocolate, powdered sugar icing, or just serve plain. Be sure to put the coffeepot on. Scandinavians always have coffee with their sweets!

MYSTERY

ON THE INTERNET

Subscribe to the
Mystery on the Internet
e-newsletter—and receive all these
fabulous online features directly
in your e-mail inbox:

- Previews of upcoming books
- In-depth interviews with mystery authors
  and publishing insiders
- Calendars of signings and readings for
  Ballantine mystery authors
- Profiles of mystery authors
- Mystery quizzes and contests

Two easy ways to subscribe:
Go to **www.ballantinebooks.com/mystery**
or send a blank e-mail to
join-mystery@list.randomhouse.com.

Mystery on the Internet—the mystery e-newsletter
brought to you by Ballantine Books